A *Juneteenth* KIND OF LOVE

NIKKI-MICHELLE & KAI LEAKES

ISBN: 978-1-955916-00-4

Chapter 1: Kamal

Moving to Sojourner Falls hadn't been a part of my plans. During the winter snowstorm last year, their town's doctor, Hunter Martyn, was badly injured by the town's ex-mayor. I still wasn't clear on all the details, but they needed my services. After stitching Hunter up and getting him back to health, I returned home to Helen, Georgia and thought no more about. My nurse practitioner, Mrs. Olivia Howard-Pegee, stayed behind to assist with Doctor Martyn's patients until he was in tiptop shape again.

Around February, the now mayor, Blade Martyn, reached out to me in hopes he could convince me to take on the position of doctor in the town next to his brother, Hunter, and Doctor Kenya Jones who was a pediatrician. He said with the town growing and more young folk moving back, he would need another doctor on payroll. I told him I would think about it and get back to him. I still hadn't given him an answer by the first of spring.

Blade and Hunter tried to warn me about the power those old folks possessed, but I thought nothing of it. The way they spoke of their elders was as if they had some kind of all-knowing eye or magical powers that somehow got the younger folk to do what they wanted, even if we didn't want to. Much to their chagrin, I laughed it off.

Next thing I knew, Easter rolled around, and I got caught in a rainstorm that stranded me on the side of the road in Sojourner Falls. I had smelled the rain coming but paid it no mind because I had all intentions of passing by Sojourner Falls and heading home before the rain caught up to me.

It was just my luck, my old clunker of a truck blew a tire and the engine sputtered out as I tried to battle the sheets of rain falling that night. My truck was passed down to me from my father, by way of my aunt, who got it from his grandfather. For twenty years that truck had been good to me. I suppose I shouldn't have been surprised it died on the side of the road. Luckily, Doctor Martyn and Marcus Legend came to rescue me … so to speak.

Once the city council, better known as the elders, got me cornered at the Bellamy Inn, I had no choice in the matter. It was hard to say no to a room full of elders who had determination in their hearts and the wisdom of all their ancestors in their eyes.

I grew up in a small town—knew a lot about small town living—but to say Sojourner Falls was just an average small town wouldn't do it any justice. It was a majority Black town just outside of Helen, Georgia. For a long time, it was Northeast Georgia's best kept secret. At least, I learned it had been for all the Black townsfolk who lived there. Not to sound too cliché, but there was something magical about the place that no one could explain.

As I drove down the long stretch of the only main highway in the area, I took in the smells of spring on the cusp of summer. From the horse and cow dung renting the air to the hint of the berries wafting from the Jameson Farm—which was a berry farm— the smell of the season was all in the air. That included the faint scent of incoming rain.

I chuckled as I pressed pause on my dash panel. I'd been listening to a book on Audible but decided to just enjoy the sound of the breeze whipping by. I let my windows down some more, then looked over at the Legend Barn. Construction was still being done on the place after a fire almost burned it to the ground a little over a year ago. I'd learned that the town relied on the farm for all their meat and dairy needs, which made me wonder how they had been affected by the fire.

I glanced in my rearview mirror to see gray storm clouds forming. Sojourner Falls' weather could be prickly this time of year. One minute it would be bright and sunny, and in the blink of an eye, it would look like a tornado was about to roll through. It was rare that we got tornados in this part of Georgia. Still, I was happy to be driving my brand-new Sierra Denali, especially since the winters were nothing to sneeze at. After my old, 1975 Ford truck died, I knew there was no use in trying to fix it.

I was deep into thoughts of my living arrangements when something, or someone, along the side of the road caught my attention. A golden PT Cruiser was idle off the side of the road. The driver side door was open, a woman sat sideways on the seat, both feet on the ground, and her head was in her right hand while her left held a cell phone to her ear. She was shaking her head and she looked distressed as she glanced toward my truck. Slapping her cell in her hand, she stood up, threw her hands in the air, then hit the top of the vehicle.

"Good Lord," I mumbled when I took in the sight of her.

Sitting in the car, I hadn't been able to get a good look at her, but when she stood, in her fit of rage, it reminded me that I was all man. Her skin was walnut brown, and she had long, sandy-colored, kinky hair that the wind tossed every which way. The khaki-colored pant suit with the wide pant legs amplified every curve her plus-sized body owned.

I put my blinker on to pull over behind her vehicle. She turned a stern gaze in my direction. It wasn't lost on me that she had slyly moved her hand inside of her vehicle, grabbed something, and then moved it behind her back as if she was adjusting it on her belt.

I stuck my head out the window. "Good afternoon! Do you need some help?"

"No. I'm fine. Thank you," she said, then turned around to look at her phone again. Her response had been clipped and curt.

"Ah, rain is on the way and it's going to be dark soon. You sure you want to be out here alone?"

She looked at me, and I saw the nerves in her jaw tick. "I called my dad," she said. "He should be here soon. I'm fine."

"Is there somewhere I can drop you off?"

"No! What are you? Hard of hearing? I said I'm fine."

I chuckled, not at all offended by her rude demeanor. She was smart not to accept a ride from a stranger, but I didn't think she understood what a rainstorm in this neck of the woods was like. Judging by her attire, and the red stiletto heels on her feet, she was a city girl.

"Tell you what," I said as I moved my locs back, "I'm going to just wait here for your father to arrive. It would be against my Southern, gentlemanly manners to see a woman stranded and just leave her on the side of the road."

I parked my truck, then reached over to pull out a bag of boiled peanuts I bought from a fruit stand a few miles back. Reclining my seat, I kept my gaze on the beautiful woman as I snacked.

She groaned and then rolled her eyes before scowling at me. "I-I don't need you to do that, okay?"

I was about to reply when her phone rang.

She answered quickly. "Yes, Dad! Yeah … no, I can't hear you … what?" Frowning, she moved farther away from her car, held the phone up in the air, then put it back to her ear. "Dad! No, I can't. … Listen, if you can hear me, I'm on the main highway about ten miles past the Jameson Farm. … Dad! Hello! Dad!" Pulling the phone away from her ear, she screeched with anger.

I guess I'd been kind of wrong about her being a city girl. She knew the Jameson Farm so she must have been familiar with the area in some way. Suddenly, the woman threw the phone so hard, it bounced off the ground, onto the pavement, then bounced back into the grass, half of the pieces shattered on the road.

"Oh no, oh no," she cried as she rushed to pick up the pieces of the phone.

"Yeah … that was real smart," I mumbled, then tossed some peanuts in my mouth.

In the distance, I heard the big rig before I saw it. I sat up and tried to call out to the woman. She wasn't paying attention as she fussed and ranted about "small towns having crappy cell service." The truck was barreling down the road. I hopped from my truck, then jogged to where she was. It was the first time I felt as if my cowboy boots weighed my feet down. Still, I made haste. My locs beat around my shoulders as the wind rushed through them.

Just as she went to grab the battery to her phone from the road, the driver of the big rig blew his horn. She looked up, terror in her eyes, and froze. Fear had stolen her ability to save herself. I rushed behind her, grabbed her in my arms, and made a mad dash to get us out of the road. It all happened so fast, I tripped over a hidden rock in the grass, and we went tumbling down the small ditch.

I landed on my back with her using my body as a landing pad. The fall knocked the wind out of me. So much so, I heard myself groan. Opening my eyes, I saw the sky spinning and felt a bit silly at the thought. When my eyesight adjusted, I peered into the wild, black eyes of a woman who had sprigs of grass about her mouth, cheeks, and in her hair. I couldn't help but laugh. Her hair was all over the place and she looked fit to be tied. Those black eyes of hers told me she didn't know whether to thank me or cuss me.

"You know, if you wanted to get to know me better, you could have just told me that," I joked.

She used her tongue to push grass out of her mouth before shoving off my chest. She gazed down at me, and then her breath hitched. She studied me as if she just realized that I was actually there.

I smirked.

Scoffing, she continued to try to get off me. "I would say thank you, but that would probably inflate your ego which is already the size of Texas it seems."

"Right now, to my groin, it feels like your knee is the size of Texas," I said, then grunted.

Panic clouded her eyes before she realized just where her knee was. "Oh my gosh," she said on a gasp.

After awkwardly rolling off me, the woman hopped up quickly. Once standing, I turned to discreetly adjust myself before turning back around. The woman, whose name I still didn't know, was grabbing her purse, along with file folders out of her car. I assumed she was going to finally take me up on my offer to give her a ride. However, when she started angrily—but oh so sexily—stalking down the road, I sighed and shook my head.

I heard the distant rumble of thunder and yelled, "Miss, you're going to be soaking wet by the time you get to wherever you're going. I don't mind giving you a ride. Besides, I don't think those stiletto heels are going to get you far."

She stopped her stride and whipped around, her hair being tossed by the wind. "I am not getting in that truck with you. You could be a murderer or something. What kind of man won't take no for an answer?"

I looked up when I felt a drop of rain on my head before sending my gaze back to her. "The kind of man who was raised right, who is a gentleman, and one who knows a woman in distress when he sees one. I'm also the kind of man who can smell rain coming."

Shaking her head, she switched her folders from one arm to the other with a sardonic chuckle. "You people out here are so old fashioned. No one can *smell* the rain coming," she said skeptically.

"I can."

"Let me guess, do your knees or back start to hurt when a cold front is coming, too?"

I chuckled, folding my arms across my chest. "That has been known to happen a time or two."

"I'm not—"

"You're worried about getting in my truck, but you are willing to trek this long stretch of road with nightfall afoot. Don't you think that's more dangerous? Also, I don't think I'm going to be foolish enough to mess with an angry woman carrying a small handgun."

Frowning, she switched her weight from one foot to the other. "What? How do you know that?"

"I saw your sleight of hand earlier."

She cast distrusting eyes at me, and her eyes were beautiful. It was like staring in an inky abyss. "Whatever. No rain is coming, and yes, I'll take my chances on the dark, desolate road."

I glanced back at my truck, then up at the sky. "All right. Suit yourself, but I hope you at least have an umbrella in that bag."

She muttered something under her breath that I was sure I didn't want to hear, then turned and kept walking. My gut told me she had to be heading to Sojourner Falls. To be sure, I phoned into the inn.

"Thank you for calling Bellamy Inn. How may I assist you today?" Grace Bellamy answered in a singsong voice that I was sure appealed to all of her customers.

She and her grandparents, an eccentric throuple to say the least, ran the Bellamy Inn. It had been in her family for generations.

I smiled. "Hello there, Grace. How are you?" I asked.

"I'm well, Doctor Brookhaven. Are you calling to make your normal reservation for dinner to be delivered to your room?"

"Not really, but first, are you feeling okay? You sound a little winded."

"I'm fine … I think. I've just been more tired than normal, which is odd since these older women won't even let me get water for myself." She chuckled.

Grace Bellamy discovered she was pregnant during the Christmas celebration last year. By the King holiday she'd discovered she was eight weeks along. So far, her pregnancy had been smooth sailing, but my nurse practitioner, who also happened to be a women's health nurse practitioner, was concerned about her blood pressure.

Keeping my eyes on the walking woman, I said to Grace, "Ms. Olivia tells me she's worried about your blood pressure. She said it's been up and down, but she doesn't like the way it seems to spike out the blue. We want to see you in the office tomorrow so we can monitor it for an hour or so."

"Oh … okay," Grace said, sounding a little hesitant. Or it could have been fear. No expecting mother, especially those first-time mothers, wanted to hear that something could be remotely wrong. "It's probably just the excitement of all the new things happening in and around town. Also, with getting the funding to add new rooms to the inn, and with more tourists coming in, we're so much busier. You know Blade is finally moving back. He's looking for a place to refurbish or some land to build from the ground up. We have a farmer's market coming. Hunter is finally able to add on to the medical center. But the big attraction is the Juneteenth celebration in four weeks—"

"Whoa, slow down," I said, chuckling.

"See what I mean? It's a lot, right?" Grace laughed, then exhaled. "However, I promise I'm not overdoing it. Not only will Blade bust a gasket, but the elders would fuss up a storm, and the whole family would chime in. Then I would have to deal with you and Ms. Olivia. I don't need that kind of trouble in my life."

I chuckled. Nurse Olivia was known to lay into her patients who didn't do as she suggested in order to get better, so I understood Grace not wanting to tick her off. She and I discussed her and the baby a little more. I reminded her of her appointment time, then I got to what I really called her for.

"Hey, Grace, do we have any new people coming to town?" I asked.

If anyone knew, she would. Her family owned the Bellamy Inn. All the town's gossip came through there.

"Well, yeah! Sheriff Tucker's daughter, Willow, was due a couple hours ago. He stopped by about thirty minutes ago saying her phone didn't have good signal. He was wondering if he should go out and look for her just in case something's wrong. Why? Everything okay?"

"Yeah. Tell the sheriff I think I've found his daughter. Looks as if she had car trouble and is stranded on the side of the highway."

"Oh no, is she okay?"

I decided against telling Grace the woman had almost been run down by a big rig. "Other than being as mean as a pit viper, she's fine, and as soon as I convince her to get in my truck and allow me to drive her to town, she *and I* will be even better."

I told Grace about all that had happened so far, minus the truck incident, then asked her to let the sheriff know I'd get his daughter to town safely.

As soon as I hung up the phone, a boom of thunder shook the sky. A split second later, rain started to beat down on the road. I jogged to my truck and hopped in. Down the road, I heard Little Miss Hurricane squeal as she tried to stuff her file folders in her purse. I chuckled to myself as I watched her from behind the wheel of my truck. After wrestling them into her bag, she held the bag over her head, glanced around as if she was looking for shelter to magically appear, then ran toward my truck.

Chapter 2: Willow

By the Loa! Was this my welcome back to Sojourner Falls?

"Geez," I shouted.

There was an earthy-charged smell of rain in the air, and any other day, it would have been wonderful. I had goosebumps from the light chill. The country humidity accented with the deep aroma of grass, grain, ozone, and animals reminded me that I was home. I could not believe that I was running in my Louie's, dodging rain with my purse filled with wet folders while dragging my lilac, hardcase carry-on behind me. This was not how this trip was supposed to go. I wanted to scream.

"Can you feel the heat?" the stranger asked when I hopped into his truck after he helped me and my bags inside.

A deep frown marred my face in annoyance at my current situation. Moments ago, I had been on my happy, but anxious, little way before disaster struck. Thanks to two phone calls and an obnoxiously rude cow, I sat shivering in a stranger's truck, smelling like outside, nearby farm ozone, and rain. My cute, red bottom stiletto heels were scuffed, and I was wet with kinky, fuzzy hair from the surprise spring storm and humidity that wanted to greet us.

Lost in my thoughts and missing the innuendo that might have been there, I angrily put my seatbelt on, then grumbled, "Yes. Thank you. We can go now."

"As you wish, Miss Pitman. I placed your extra bag in the back."

Warmth encapsulated me, drying me off. I reached up to smooth out my shrinking, coiled hair, knotting it into a large, fluffy top bun when I realized what I thought mister man had said.

"Excuse me?" I turned toward the man behind the wheel.

I know he didn't call me Miss Pitman! I cut my eyes at the stranger who smelled like eucalyptus, amber, and a fragrant cigar without the harsh smoke or potency. His scent was gentle, light, and comforting. It would have been alluring if I weren't still in a funky mood with a wet purse on my lap.

A deep chuckle came from my knight, the comedian. He gave me an innocent smirk, then carefully pulled onto the road. "I said, welcome to my roadside assistance services." A pleased and teasing smile spread across his face. "My name is Kamal Brookhaven, ma'am, and my cellphone is right by your hip. If you wish to make a call, go ahead and use it. I'm here to help, as is the right thing to do."

His baritone with the subtle Georgia low country lilt to it was akin to eating a comforting plate of sweet, buttery cornbread, greens and ham hocks, gooey mac and cheese with candied yams touching the sides. I was tongue tied by the ease of what he said. I didn't like that.

I also didn't enjoy the sudden hit of attraction I felt rising in my blood for him. It was too much for me. I didn't know this man. But my Lord! His voice, mannerisms, and sharp jawline with his clear complexed, rich amber brown skin …

One would have to be blind not to see how striking he was. His African ancestors were etched in his face for sure, and represented in his thin, shoulder-length locs. But that wasn't what solely drew me in. It was his energy and more. How he walked away when he hopped out of his truck to get my bags?

Whew! He had a slight bow-leggedness and confidence in his stride. The brotha was soul food with a glass of sweet tea. Or Hibiscus sorrel in June. And here I sat, a prickly pear full of 'ready to get the heck out of dodge.'

"No thank you. I can make my calls when we get into town." I was doing my best not to drink up his visage any more than I already had. "You can you take me to Bellamy Inn. I'll direct you there so that you don't have to use your GPS."

The truck drove effortlessly over the country road. The heavy fall of rain against the truck blended with the soft R&B playing. I almost smiled at hearing Maxwell's "Urban Hang Suite". I glanced at Kamal, then out the passenger side window. I noticed a brief frown on his face as he turned off the heat.

He shook his head, and finally said, "It's been a long day for you. I'll get you to the inn as soon as possible. I happen to be staying there, too, so I know the way, little hurricane."

I opened my mouth to say something curt but decided not to go there. "You're right. Today was not a good day. My day was not supposed to be this caustic. I apologize for my tone with you and am grateful that you're not some highway serial killer."

"Gotta let go of that Investigation Discovery channel, Miss Hurricane."

The mood in the truck seemed to lighten on his end. I tried to distract myself from his pull by watching the rolling farmland with its pepper of buildings, and familiar grass field Indian mounds. My anxiety and worry over what could have possibly made my father ask for me to come home made my leg shake and I didn't know why.

"I hope that you trust me enough to tell me your name, or is that not something done in kind in the city?"

I shifted in my seat, then remembered that Kamal had said he's also staying at the inn. There would be no ducking or hiding from him after this. So, he was right. Giving him my name shouldn't be a problem. But I was in a mood, and I didn't want to.

"Willow Tucker," I heard myself say much to my own chagrin.

"Beautiful name, Ms. Tucker. I'm familiar with another Tucker in town. I'm glad that I was able to help you on your caustic day." Kamal drove his truck without issue on the rainy, wet road. "If you don't mind, I'm a curious spirit who enjoys a good story, tell me what happened. We have a little time before we hit the town."

My lips pressed together in a tight line before I realized that I was betraying my own lack of trust in others by talking to this man. "If you know another Tucker in town, then that would be my father, the sheriff."

"I figured." Kamal shifted gears to adjust for the wet road. "Though …"

"Though we look nothing alike?" I interjected to test his respond.

"Hmm. That's not true," he casually said. "You both have the same smile and shape of eyes." He paused to look at me with a gentle smile, then continued. "So, you grew up in Sojourner and are not the city girl you look to be? Interesting. The prodigal child of the area returning to see her father?"

I blinked a few times at his insight and shifted in my seat. I wasn't sure how I felt about partially being correctly read in that way. "Something like that."

"And that's what caused your day to go bad, outside of the accident?"

The witty shift in his tone made me scowl. It sounded as if he wanted to laugh.

"Look, no … there's more to the story, and it was the cow's fault along with my rental's battery overheating and dying. That and …"

"And what? And a cow?" Laughing, Kamal turned off the music. "A cow tripped you up?"

Shame shone on my face. I looked to see the township of Sojourner Falls welcome sign framed by ivy, flowers, and artistic work rising proudly in greeting. Farmland turned into lush greenery with a scattering of creeks, streams, and rows of forests. The acreage was still beautiful and vibrant. Long gone were the patches of overworked land and dying plots. My heart felt proud in the development going on.

"You okay, Miss Tucker?" Kamal asked with concern.

"Oh, yeah. It's … um, been a long time," I whispered, then cleared my throat. "So, yes to answer you, a cow took me by surprise. The fat thing was crossing the road when I ran up on it. When my car spun out and I was able to pull over, that thing looked at me while chewing whatever grass it was eating, as if I was in the wrong!"

Rich, deep laughter came from Kamal.

I bit my lower lip, wondering why it felt good to talk to him with such ease now. "It's not funny. That silly cow waved me off with a swish of its tail, too. The cow was rude."

"And that made you real mad, yes?" Kamal's copper eyes twinkled.

A sweet heat fluttered in my stomach, and I waved a hand to brush off the feeling. Before me, red brownstone shops appeared, and the black pavement turned into smooth asphalt mixed with red bricks. What used to be rough, patchy, and dilapidated buildings were now fresh and restored with new life. We turned away from Main Street and I pointed out the window.

"Yes, yes it did. That and the fact that on my way here, my job decided to tell me I was fired and that a clerical error caused my 401k to be no more. Meanwhile, my fiancé just ended our engagement and relationship because he was embarrassed about my work and activism, which didn't fit into his plans. He's classist and a colorist. So, you see, I had reason to say my day was a mess. Anyway, that's my childhood home on the corner there. Do you see the large, Creole-style, white, two-story cottage with the haint blue wooden door and wraparound porch?"

Kamal slowed down and pulled near a stop sign so he could take a look. "Your fiancé sounds bougie and foolish. Your job, on the other hand, sounds idiotic as well."

A smile played at the corner of my lips at his words. "Thank you, I feel the same way."

"Not a problem. Should I pull up to the house? The yard is immaculate," Kamal said. "I drove by it before, and it drew my attention. It was the tall wisteria tree that I can see peeking from behind the house that got me."

"I loved that tree, too. My twin sister and our brother built a treehouse beside it,, and we'd sit in the tree, eating plums while I'd paint and sculpt. Or practice for the Juneteenth parade. My elder brother was a drum major while my twin and I were majorettes in the 'So Truth' marching band." I smiled at the sweet memories. "My father's great-great-grandmother planted the plum and wisteria trees. Legend has it that she ran from Texas to hide in Sojourner due to disguising herself as a white, male marshal and collecting bounties to send the money to our enslaved and freed family in Louisiana."

I stared with light tears rimming my eyes, sharing with this stranger instead of keeping my mouth shut. "There's an indigo, and flower garden with various herbs and vegetables. Mama planted the flowers; Daddy did the vegetables and herbs. There was a small pond for fish and lily pads with a tiny rock waterfall in the corner of the backyard. Foolishly, I guess in a bit of dismissiveness of the town, my siblings and I told my father to give the old house away. I assumed Daddy was going to rent it out, but that wasn't the case. Our beautiful home, built by craftsman and masonry O'ziah Martyn is now owned by the owner of Jameson Bakery, Tammy Jameson-Legend, and her husband, Marcus Legend."

"I'm sorry to hear that. You had a beautiful home with a precious history and connection." Kamal's warm gaze studied me.

Pulling myself together, I sighed. "I don't know why I just shared all of that with you. We can go, and I can tell you about O'ziah Martyn if you'd like."

"I don't mind you sharing about yourself and the town. It's helping me learn you, Miss Hurricane. Besides, this is polite talk between two individuals put together in a wild situation. So, talk. I'm enjoying the sound of your voice and your fresh view of the town's history."

"Oh ..." I felt embarrassed but I pushed through it. "Well, O'ziah Martyn and his family escaped slavery, traveling from Helen, Georgia. As they traveled their own Underground Railroad, they were allowed to hide in Indian burial mounds by the local Nacoochee tribe—a few of those protective mounds still plank Sojourner, resembling a guarding wall. O'ziah Martyn landed in Sojourner Falls, where he became part of the founding families. He practically built the town and most of the houses with his own hands, using techniques he learned from his travels to London with his former master."

Kamal gave a nod of his head while turning his truck into Bellamy Inn's curved driveway and grand house.

I figured I might have been sharing too much, so I added, "I know all of this due to my daddy's love of us telling the story about the founding of the town, our elders, and our founder parades."

"That's a good thing. We've lost so much of our cultural history in this nation and globally. The fact that you have that gift of knowledge makes me envious. That and you like to paint. Next time, I hope to find out what type of work you did to anger your ex and your job, and I'd love to see your art."

Eyes focused on his parking, Kamal smiled, then added, "Looks as if we're here and I'm honestly disappointed about that. I was stalling."

This man was an anomaly of Southern hospitality and gentleman ways.

"You were?" I quirked an eyebrow, waiting.

"Yes. As I said, you have a beautiful voice, and I was enjoying learning about the town." He parked his truck and smoothly opened his door to climb out with a glance over his shoulder. "I also gained insight into who you are, which I was enjoying more."

Surprised, I sat gathering my purse while he walked around the truck to come to my side, which I wasn't expecting. Again, his stride distracted me, along with his words. I swear this man had a little cowboy in him, geez. When my passenger side door opened and his large palm extended to me, all I could do was take it and quiet my thoughts.

"Thank you, Kamal," I gently said, covering my head from the rain.

"Glad to be of assistance," he replied.

I stared up at the man before me. Earlier, I had been too frustrated to gather his whole appearance. This man had to be all of six-four in height and built like a horse rider. Muscled but lean in a "might have been a warrior in the past" kind of way. If I hadn't glanced past him to see my father, I knew that I would have stood there stuck staring all day. I didn't know what was wrong with me, but it needed to stop, so I was thankful for another save, this time by my father.

"Willowshine!" My father's warm, booming voice washed over me in a fatherly embrace and my heart swelled.

"Daddy!"

Towering at a respectable six-four as well, Sheriff Trent Tucker swooped me into his arms and held on to me as if he had won the lottery. His black Stetson hat sat low, shielding his eyes until he shifted it up. The muddled sky broke to let sunlight shine over my adoring father. I smiled in pride to see how great he looked.

Back in the day when I was just a child, my father was the town's gatekeeper in the sense that he used his privilege to keep it safe. Sojourner Falls was once rich with life, but by the time me and my twin sister, Sage, were born it was already struggling on a last heartbeat. Due to that, Daddy— the town's young, handsome, white appearing deputy with the mega-watt movie star smile— developed a plan for the town and the kids of the town. He used his proximity to whiteness to get investments for our advancement.

He began networking to pool money together under his family's old trust company founded by his great-grandmother, the cowgirl marshal. His willingness to allow people to think he was white helped him create a fund for us kids at the time. All money helped us town kids go to college or was reallocated as investment money for those of us who didn't go to college. My father's heart and business brilliance were incredible.

We knew he wasn't a big fan of passing for white, but the town understood that he felt that he had to do what he had to do. My big brother, TJ, my twin sister, Sage, and I left a year early before college to spend some time in Highland Park, Chicago, Illinois to live with my mother's wealthy parents. We missed our parents dearly. We even missed our Sojourner Falls elders. I'd never forget the well of emotions etched in my father's cerulean gray eyes while we drove away to start our new lives.

Daddy was an ox of a man, now with a portly stomach. Though many would assume that my father was white, I knew otherwise. The salt and gold goatee added to his ambiguity, marking him as possibly Appalachian or Bayou Texan. But again, I knew different, as did the town. The man before me was my world and I was glad that I had listened to him to make the trip home. Regardless of the negative baggage that came with it.

My father let me go, kissed my cheek, then looked at my bags. He grabbed a few, but Kamal respectfully stopped him. "I'm glad Doctor Brookhaven was able you help you," he said, still eying Kamal. "But now I might have'ta shake him up a bit for acting like I can't gather my daughter's personals."

Surprise made me quirk a brow. Doctor? This lean linebacker with the cowboy boots was a doctor? Oh, Loa! Now it made sense why he was so easy to talk to. I looked back at the man my father was currently shaking hands and laughing with.

"No, sir. You have every right to. However, I wasn't raised to let an esteemed gentleman like yourself carry all the weight. Besides, I don't mind helping when I can be of service, as you know." Kamal glanced my way. "Helping is the right thing to do when you are able and willing. Especially during a storm like today. Or what felt like a little hurricane."

I heard my father chuckle, then say, "Spring is sumptin' else," but my attention was not on the man who helped create me.

There was a subtle kiss of interest in Kamal's chestnut eyes, while holding my bags. When a sultry smile spread across his handsome face, revealing a dimple in his right and left cheek, I turned on my heels and hurried my humming body inside of the inn.

Not today, Satan!

Today had not turned out how it was supposed to and wasn't about to stick around to find out how it might turn out later in the day. Thanks to my doctor knight in shining armor, I now was worried about how my day would turn out tomorrow. The last thing I needed was the town elders sniffing anything possible between us. I was freshly single and worrying about other things in my life, like what was I going to do about being without a job? But being the honest woman that I was, I had to admit, Doctor Kamal Brookhaven was a problem.

I needed to not find out how tomorrow would fair knowing that he was somewhere in the inn or Sojourner Falls. My father and figuring out my life were my priority. Getting my rental off the side of the road, a pastry at Jameson Bakery, and a new cellphone, were my other priorities. Not mister man in the truck with a medical degree.

My life was a little hurricane, indeed.

Chapter 3: Kamal

"Can we all come to order?"

I took a seat with a steaming mug of coffee in my hand then looked ahead. It was six in the evening, and I had been seeing patients most of the day. If I wasn't seeing patients, I was walking around the newly renovated medical center, making sure everything was working properly.

Mayor Blade Martyn had flown to Los Angeles to make the final arrangements for the sale of his condo there. Doctor Martyn was in Detroit with his son, Hawk, and his son's mother, Caridade. They had gone to check on an old friend of Hawk's with his uncle, Vincent, and his fiancée, Doctor Kenya Jones, in tow. I had the honor of making sure all of his patients—those home and in the center—were taking all their medicines and doing as he suggested. That was on top of making my rounds to assure that the people, especially the elders, continued to get acclimated to me and my way of doctoring.

Sojourner Falls was different from Helen even though both were small towns. Helen bustled with life like that of a city. Sojourner Falls was the proverbial small town in every sense of the word. Everyone knew everybody else's business. Everyone knew other people on a personal level. The people came together when the times got tough and even when the time were goods. There was the proverbial Main Street, rolling acres of farmland, shady groves, and the like. I was still getting used to it.

I looked to the front to see Grace Bellamy was round and plump with life. She also glowed as only a beautiful, pregnant woman could. Just moments before, some of the women had gathered around her to fawn over the big rock decorating her ring finger. Now she stood on the small, raised platform with several sheets of paper in her hand while she looked out over the room.

I sat on the very back row of the room where townhall meetings were held. Since I was one of the doctors in the town now, I was considered a prominent member by default, which meant I needed to attend all meetings. This would be the second one I'd attended. The first had been to announce my acceptance of the position of the town's third doctor and the first surgeon. The feast afterwards still made my mouth water.

The meeting was held in the main room where the town normally held holiday dinners. Seven rows of chairs sat on each side of the room with a long table for refreshments in the back. The chocolate brown carpet had been freshly vacuumed. The big, bay windows on either side of the room were open to let in fresh air. The walls had a new coat of ecru paint on them. I knew that because I'd been one of the people to help Blade, Hunter, and Marcus Legend repaint the room.

I saw the sheriff and wondered if his daughter would be in attendance. Thinking back to our brief time together the day before, I chuckled inwardly. I didn't know what to make of the fact that I was disappointed she hadn't come down for breakfast at the inn this morning. I'd been looking forward to seeing her again. Something about the woman pulled at everything primal in me. I liked the feeling of adulation she left me with. It wasn't new, but it was intense in a way I'd never experienced before. Her voice tugged at my gut and made me want to listen to her talk even if it was about nothing.

"Doctor Brookhaven, good to see you, son."

I looked up into the wise eyes of Mr. Walt. I stood and took his hand to shake. "Mr. Walt, good to see you, too. How'd the day treat you?"

The man was dressed in a red, polo-style shirt, khakis, and black loafers. His eyes shone with mischief as always and his smile was bright.

"I can't complain, young man. Can't complain at all. Look, is it possible I can speak with ya after this here meeting?"

I studied the old man I'd come to respect, trying to see if something was wrong. However, his poker face was strong. "Everything okay?" I asked.

"Everythang's fine. Just need to speak with ya …"

I nodded, not sure I believed him. "Sure thing, Mr. Walt. Meet me at the clinic—"

"No, no. I'd rather meet you at the inn. That way my loved ones won't get suspicious."

My brows furrowed as I moved my coffee mug from one hand to the other. "You sure everything is okay?"

"I said it was, didn't I?" he snapped.

His tone didn't offend me. He was one of those types of old people who said what he said just how he'd said it.

"I'm worried. You don't want me to meet you at the clinic but want to talk in private at the inn. I need to be sure one of the town's most beloved people is in good health."

The old man frowned, then shifted his weight from one foot to the other. "Just meet me in the dining room of the inn at about nine this evening."

Mr. Walt gave me that order, then walked off to sit on the other side of the room with his loves. I watched the old man as he retreated, trying to determine if he was limping or if I could note anything painful in his demeanor. I saw nothing. I chalked it up to him wanting to ask me something non-medical related.

"We have a lot to discuss tonight, so let's come to order please," Grace said again.

"And hopefully one of those things will be that big rock on ya finger, young lady," Ms. Wilma, one of the town's elders, said.

Hoots and catcalls went up in the room. Grace blushed.

"Tell us, Grace, did Blade pop the question?" Tammy Jameson asked.

Grace held up her hand, palm facing her, then wiggled her fingers. "He did!"

A raucous round of applause thundered in the building.

"And he did it the right way. Came asking me and Walt for her hand in marriage. A baby and a wedding," Mr. Clark said with a prideful smile on his face.

"With some of the young folks returning and the town getting tourists again, feels like Sojourner Falls is coming back," Ms. Nita said. "I get a bit teary-eyed thanking 'bout it."

I looked around the room to see a lot of the elders nodding in agreement.

"I know," Grace said. "This has been a long time coming. The ancestors have heard all our prayers and accepted our offerings. There is no place like home, and Sojourner Falls has a magic that's its own. It's been two years since we almost lost this haven, our birthright. The ancestors who came before us and the elders who're still here have been great gatekeepers. However, like my fiancé, Blade, said two years ago, it's time for us young folk to take the mantel and keep this town alive and well." Grace looked around the room. "We have had some new faces join us." She nodded my way with a smile, and I tipped my hat in her direction. "And we've had some old faces return home."

Just as she said that, the double doors swung open and in walked Willow Turner. I took a sip of the hot coffee, then smiled when the elders let out applause.

"Another one," yelled Mr. Percy.

He was a hefty man of butterscotch complexion. He was Grace's uncle and her cousin, Caridade's, father.

"They all comin' back, praise be the ancestors," Ms. Wilma said.

"Not quite *all* yet, but give it some time," Ms. Nita chimed in. "Give it some time."

Willow's brown face turned ruddy. It was clear by the way she ducked her head into her shoulders and gave a timid wave that she didn't really cotton to being in the spotlight.

Sheriff Tucker walked to where his daughter stood, then glanced around to see if there was a place for her to sit. I removed the Stetson from my head, stood, and pointed to my chair. Since the sheriff was a fellow Stetson wearer, he knew that gesture meant I was doing the gentlemanly thing. He tipped his hat with a nod to me, then ushered his daughter over.

Catching my eye, Willow smiled coyly. She looked vastly different than the city girl she presented the day before. She had on jeans that hugged her voluptuous hips and backside so well, I didn't even realize I was staring. The plaid shirt she wore tapered to her waist and brought attention to the buxom bosom she possessed. Her wild mane was pulled back into a bushy ponytail. She only wore pearl earrings that gave her face an innocence I didn't take note of before.

I put my eyes back in my head when I heard the sheriff clear his throat. When I met his eyes, they were deadpan. He tilted his head to the right, a signal he wanted to talk to me out of earshot of Willow.

"I would threaten to shoot you, but seeing as there are about ten other men in here, including one of my deputies, who are giving you the stare of death, I don't think I have to worry about my daughter's virtue around you, eh?" he said as soon as I followed him to the corner.

I gave a quick glance around the room to see he was correct. There were several men who had all stood, and I assumed, had wanted to offer Willow their seats. They were also glaring at me as if they wanted to challenge me to a duel at high noon.

I chuckled. "Sheriff Tucker, I mean your daughter no harm and her virtue is hers to keep. However, you can't blame a man for admiring beauty when he sees it, and Willow is indeed as beautiful as her name."

"Yeah, well, you just remember I'm the sheriff around these parts in case you get any ideas, young fella."

With that, he tipped his hat and walked to the other side of the room. Just so I wouldn't have to watch my back when I returned to the inn, I stayed standing in the corner.

Once the room had quieted down, Grace said, "I was trying to wait for Hunter and Blade to get back, but we need to go ahead and get started since both their flights have been delayed. We have a lot to discuss tonight. One being, we still have Stacy Davenport in the town's jail. It's going on six months now, and it's time we decide his fate."

From the little I'd heard, the ex-mayor, Stacy Davenport, shot Doctor Martyn, injured his son, Hawk, stabbed the mayor and his uncle, Vincent … and that was on top of being accused of stealing a majority of the town's wealth.

Sheriff Tucker took his Stetson off and gave it a small wave. "I know a lot of you youngins think we should have him shipped to the county jail, but … something I wanna run past y'all first. Some of you may not know this, but in Sojourner Falls we tend to take care of our own, even our criminals. That means we jail them and mete out their punishments, too."

"I think that man should be handed over to federal agents immediately," Marcus Legend stated.

"I think the same," said his wife, Tammy. "He harmed a child, shot Hunter, and cut Blade and Mr. Vincent. Why shouldn't we turn him over?"

I noticed that a lot of the younger people were nodding and verbally agreeing.

"As much as I hate to say this, he one'na ours. Turning him over to *them* … just don't sit right with my spirit," Ms. Nita said.

"Though it's tempting," Mr. Clark mumbled as he played chess with Mr. Walt.

"I got a good mind to agree with the young folk," Mr. Walt chimed in.

Ms. Nita got up and swatted at both her husbands who jumped back and mumbled under their breaths but didn't say anything else.

"I get it. I understand, trust me, but it's the principal. We take care of own, even those we have to handle with the law. We got a perfectly good jail right here. My two deputies are military trained and fully capable of keeping him locked away through shifts. A part of being a community is taking care of our own. Davenport ain't been the first yellow-bellied scoundrel we had to deal with from within the community. Sure, he's a criminal, but what law says he can't serve out that time here? What law here says we gotta turn him over to folk who gonna treat him like a slave rather than a prisoner?"

"No disrespect, Sheriff Tucker, to you or the other elders, but Davenport tried to kill Hunter. He *shot* him," Grace said emphatically. "Do we really want that kind in Sojourner Falls?"

A round of applause went up from the younger adults.

"No, we don't," Mr. Percy said once it quieted down. "Still … we can better keep'a eye on him here. It don't feel right letting the laws out there handle him and lock him away in a place worse than hell."

"He hurt a child," Mrs. Legend repeated.

She was the first elder I'd seen completely side with the younger adults.

"Pamela, you wanna let them heathens out there have one of our own?" Mr. Clark asked.

Mrs. Legend's first name was Meredith, but Mr. Clark called her by her middle name. I learned that when he had too much trouble pronouncing a name, he took to calling the person another of their names he could pronounce better.

She stood. The dark-skinned, older woman had long, silver hair that cascaded down her back. She was plus sized, but wore her jeans, boots, and a button-down well. She didn't look a day over forty although I knew she was closer to sixty.

"That man has done so much, to keep him here would be like blithe over this town. He behaved just as those heathens, as you called them, would have. He forgot what this town meant, was willing to help *others* take it from us as opposed to helping. He's greedy, untrustworthy, and a crook. Why shouldn't we want him gone? He was willing to use violence to further his agenda. I gotta say, I'm with the young folk on this one. He needs to go."

For the next ten minutes, I listened and watched as the elders argued their case for letting Davenport serve his time in the town's jail.

"This is intense," I heard to the left of me.

I was so focused on the happenings that I didn't see Willow walk over to where I was. She had a green mug filled with tea in her hand, and she smelled divine. Much better than she had yesterday.

"Tell me about it." I set my empty coffee mug down, then slid my hands in my pockets. "I feel like an outsider. Like I shouldn't even be hearing this."

"Me too. And I'm from here," she said, then chuckled before taking a sip of her tea. "Can you believe all they say that man did? Wow! I can see why some want him gone. He was always a sneaky, underhanded something or the other, but seems as if he's gotten worse since I've been gone."

I nodded. "I can see why they want him gone, too. However, I also understand what the elders are saying as well."

She quirked a brow. "You do?"

"Yeah. I mean, think about it. The police were created to be slave catchers, and given the sordid history this country has with over policing us and our communities, the harsh sentencings and all, I think the elders are thinking along the lines of history with this while the younger people just want off with his head."

Willow grunted. "I hadn't thought about it that way, and the elders make a valid argument. However, as Mrs. Legend said, he was willing to use violence to further his agenda. Do we really want or need that kind of person anywhere in our town?"

"Okay! Okay," Grace yelled over the melee.

The room quieted. Willow and I turned our attention back to the meeting.

Grace took a deep breath, then said. "We're not going to settle this tonight, and we can't anyway as Hunter and Blade aren't here. Mr. Vincent isn't either, and they're the ones he caused the most bodily harm. They're also beneficiaries of some of the monies and jewels Davenport squirreled away. We will wait for them to revisit this topic. Until then … let's move on."

"Just one more thing, Grace, if you don't mind," Sheriff Tucker said.

Grace nodded. "Of course, Sheriff. Go ahead."

The sheriff walked to the front of the room this time. With his hat in his hand, he said, "I want you young folk to know that we elders hear you. We do. We don't want y'all to ever think you don't have a voice. So even if we disagree on some thangs, this here place will be left to y'all and y'all will have to run it the way y'all see fit. However, we also hope y'all take our wisdom and advice into consideration as well. We all want what's best for Sojourner Falls, and we ain't got this old or this far by being stupid." His eyes roamed over the room as he spoke, lingering on the younger crowd. He then nodded. "That's all I want to say."

Grace smiled. "Thank you, Sheriff Tucker. And just so you and all the other elders know, we young folk never once want any of you to think we'll throw you or your voices away. We need you just like you need us."

A few minutes later, Grace opened the floor to the Juneteenth celebration. I listened on as Grace excitedly read off events for the celebration.

"Now, tonight, we're just discussing the basics," Grace said. "We have four weeks to get this thing together …"

"It's been years since we've had one," Willow said to me out the blue.

"Why is that?" I asked.

I noticed she said we as if she hadn't been gone for x-number of years.

She shook her head as she turned to refill her mug with green tea. "Finances, taxes, folk leaving, and more. I have to say, it feels good to see it bustling again." She took a cautious sip of her tea. "Feels good to see this town coming back to life."

Whatever else she was about to say was cut off when Grace said, "I know it's dinnertime and we all want to eat, but I'd like us to officially welcome Willow Trent back home to Sojourner Falls."

The room erupted in applause once again. Willow's eyes widened and she turned beet red under her brown skin. She looked horrified then looked back at me as if she expected me to hide her. I almost outright laughed when her father came to get her and usher her to front.

Passing me her mug, she mouthed, 'Help me,' as he did so.

I took her mug and mouthed, 'Sorry …' then chuckled.

Chapter 4: Willow

He led me to the wolves!

Here we go with the great, loving intentions. Panic roiled in my spirit due to having all eyes on me. I'd known somehow and some way, I would be put on the spot. That was why I had been so late.

I meant to sneak in quietly, but those old doors were louder than Heaven's gates letting in ol' Briar Rabbit, as Old 'Pastor' Pathwalker would say back in the day when he was alive and teaching us children the spiritual practices of our African and American Indigenous ancestors. A smile spread across my face at the old memory. Thanking my father for this shameless mess, I exhaled to address the darling faces in front of me.

I heard, "Just breathe, sis. You got this," by my ear. I took the mic from my old friend, Grace, admiring her calm, pregnant glow, then spoke into it.

"By the Loa, I'm glad to be home," I said softly with genuine pride in my heart. "I missed everyone here and didn't expect my visit to have taken this long. I'm truly sorry for that."

"Aw, bless her heart, she's still a shy one," I heard one of the elders say.

"Visit?" Another elder sucked their teeth with disapproval. "We not about to have no visit, we gotta change that. We missed'cha too much to see ya go too quickly now, baybee."

The room burst in loud agreement, and I laughed with them. My gaze focused on the owner of that sweet, loving voice—Ama Nita, as we kids called her. I waved her way. She was right. With the changes that just happened, I might have to extend my stay, thanks to having lost my job. I glanced around at the people who felt like family and realized that they might need my services.

"Yes, ma'am," I said. "I may change my mind if the bakery still makes those glazed beignets and iced chai chicory lattes? But that's another conversation for later."

Everyone laughed with me, and Ama Nita chimed in, "If that's all it takes, then we'll get you a dozen set up with a large tumbler of chai for ya. Ain't that right, Tammy?"

Tammy's iridescent smile made me wave her way. She was also my old best friend. She winked my way. "If people would stop buying them the moment the come out of the oil, then I could have some saved for you, sis ..."

I playfully pouted, and the audience laughed. "Again, I'm glad to be home," I said. "Daddy … Sheriff Tucker made sure that I came home promptly, and from what I'm hearing, it was in good timing. I remember being part of the Juneteenth celebrations and parade. Whatever the town needs of me, on top of helping with Juneteenth, I'll be of service."

"My Willowshine used'ta be one of the lead majorettes, mmhmm," my father chimed in. "And her work as a forensic social worker in Chicago with kids and families is partially why I asked her ta' return home. I think she'd make a great asset in helping with the celebration and expanding the Kwanza Kids program."

Blindsided, I gawked at my father's bold declaration. "Ah, D-Daddy, maybe we can talk about that in private later?"

"Maybe so, baby girl, but ain't no time like the present ta put that out there on the roster fa'ya. Besides, ya mama, Monica, bless her soul, would be so disheartened if ya couldn't help. That's all I'll say on it at the present." My father crossed his arms over his chest while standing near the front of the room. He watched me with a wise and mischievous twinkle in his eyes.

"Welcome back home, sis. You know they already have a hidden agenda for you," Grace lovingly said with a hint of humor. She mouthed,

'But, I got you,' then took the mic to close out the meeting, because the whiff of fried chicken was making the stomachs of everyone in the room growl.

It was a relief and saving grace. I hated being the center of attention. I never understood why I stayed a majorette as a kid or why I continued it in college until I was an adult. I enjoyed the happiness I helped put in everyone's spirit, and being home, knowing I had helpful skillsets uplifted me and gave me that same elation. Even though I was tense from all the attention and plans my father had. Making it toward the back while smiling and waving at everyone who nodded my way, I settled my eyes on the tall glass of iced tea in the Stetson hat.

I felt Kamal watching me the whole time with a light smirk on his face. He held it even now, and it made me shake my head. Our discussion about how the town should handle old scammer Stacy popped back in my head. I had vast experience in dealing with people who claimed that they had the best interests for others in the community, but truly were shady vipers. I knew through grassroots activism and community planning that there was a way to handle 'our own' as the elders said, regarding safe policing.

However, with former Mayor Davenport, there was no fence for me to straddle. There also was no loving history with his ties to this town to embrace in protecting him. He was a blight on his family legacy and a thief. He was desperate, greedy, and selfish, which ended in a dangerous, almost devastating, and deathly situation for everyone in the town. From what Daddy told me, I knew in this case, that man needed to spend some time in a real jail.

"So. A forensic social worker and hurricane. I'm surprised. It's fitting," Doctor Knight in the Stetson Hat stated as he handed me mug back, filled with fresh tea. I gladly took it. "The town loves you," he added.

"I love the town." I smiled in thought.

I couldn't recall if I had told him that I lost my job when we first met or that I was a doctor as well considering I had a Ph.D. I had been so tired and rattled that day that being near him made me dump all my business onto his lap.

Copper, black-rimmed eyes lit up with subtle humor and Kamal said over his cup, "Then it's a good thing that fate shook up things in your life. The elders have a footing in convincing you to stay."

Inwardly groaning, I blinked. I *had* told him that I lost my job. "My shaken life is between us, sir."

"Uh huh. My name is Bennett, and I ain't in it, or however that saying goes." Kamal gave a light chuckle, then turned away from me. "Though, I am curious about—" He stopped midsentence and swiftly said, "The marshal is approaching with two elders."

"I smell the chicken calling my name. I think I might seek that out."

He tilted his head and moved toward the door leading to the back. "I'm glad you're doing well, and it was nice to see you here. *Have a good day, Ms. Tucker.*"

The last of what he said was uttered loud for the elders to hear, mainly the man he referred to as 'the marshal.'

"You too, Doctor Brookhaven." I chuckled, then greeted my father, who held the town's treasure, Ms. Sara Lee Williams, on his arm. The second and closest elder to have lived when a few of the founders were still alive. It made my heart warm in wonder at her tenacity and loveliness in her all-white outfit. By her side was Ama Nita.

"Well, Miss beautiful Doctor Willow Emory-Tucker." Ms. Williams' soft, wrinkled hand reached up to caress my cheek, then settled back on her cane. "I heard you had car trouble on ya way here? And you battled some rain and mud that had cha smelling like an ol' goat?"

This town held no real secrets unless it was deep and buried, I swore. I'd called the rental company and they told me they'd take care of the car after issuing me a full refund. I chuckled at her remark and held her soft hand when she offered it to me. We all walked toward the eating area; cozy chairs near long, wooden tables and ceiling-tall windows that let us see the beauty of the center of the town. Near the tables was the main buffet of food: fried and baked chicken, fried green tomatoes, mac-n-cheese, bowls of leafy salad, roasted vegetables, and drinks.

"Nana Sara! Smelling like an old goat? No, ma'am, never! Old Chester if he's still around—"

"He is," Nana William's fondly chimed in. "Old thang wanna be around a long as I am. I use'ta ride him as a toddler, so I can't tell ya why that 'billy is still around. Speakin' of, Prissy Bessie was who had cha sliding in a ditch?"

"That heifer had the nerve to give me the stank eye, as if I was the one in the wrong!" I laughed while shaking my head. "Now, how did you know all of that?"

"Yo' Daddy likes ta get to talking when he sits with me for our breakfast at Tammy's. Keeps me abreast of thangs since I'm the head of the Elder Council. It's how thangs been done since you were a twinkle in ya daddy's lothario eyes."

My mouth dropped and I looked at my father who was now a pretty shade of red. "Daddy! You were a lothario?"

"Baby girl, only for ya mother, I promise." Grinning, he looked off to the distance with warmth in his eyes. "Had an adventure making her fall in love with me and believe me about our family background, we do fall in love quick."

I smiled and reached out to wrap my arm around his solid but soft bicep. I missed mama in this moment but loved hearing him talk about her.

"What he said is true. Was something else. You know? He met cha mama on that same road in the same typa situation? Ya mama the city college gal got lost headin' to Helen and hit a pothole. Back then we were hand patchin' the roads ourselves."

"Hold on, she hit a pothole? It wasn't Bessie again because she shouldn't have been alive then," I teased. My heart swelled in hearing everyone's laughter.

"No," Ama Nita chuckled. "It was Ol' Chester. Your mama said that old hustler was planted right in the middle of the road just sitting, as if waiting on her, eating some'thang."

I shook my head at the sensationalism in this town. It was full of magic indeed.

"Uh huh," Ama Nita continued. "Monica told me that she honked her horn, and the old goat just belted back at her every time she hit the horn."

"That's when your pappy came riding up on his stallion, like the spirit of Bass Reeves, but lookin' like that young, handsome thang … that a, um, Theo James in that Jane Austin masterpiece theatre movie my grandbaby had me watch, *Sanditon*. Young man got that Creole look ta him. Mmhmm, ya mama was not pleased, so I heard," Nana Williams explained with mischief in her voice. "What were you doin' out there then, son?"

By this time, we all sat surrounding Nana Williams. Even the good doc had found his way back to the table to set a plate and drink in front of Nana Williams and listen to how my parents met. I felt embarrassed only because he was new to this community, but I enjoyed the moment at the same time.

"Well, it was like this …" Daddy rested his hat on the table, leaned in, then simply said with a deadpan expression, "I was after Ol' Chester."

"Daddy, no!" I laughed with tears in my eyes as he explained while fixing two plates.

"Ol' sneaky thang had stolen my sandwich and was eating it right there in the middle of the road, lounging in the water-filled pothole. Suffice ta' say, I wasn't happy eitha and was gonna eat goat that day had I not run across ya beautiful mother."

Laughter erupted in the area. I couldn't believe it. Of all the ways to meet one another, my parents met because of that road and yet another silly animal. The sensation of warmth on my cheeks made me notice the good doc giving me a fleeting, casual glance. I shifted in my seat and said thank you to my father for the plate he set in front me as he sat back down at the table.

"See, this town is full of magic, baby girl," Nana Williams spoke up. "And though some thangs may not work out right in ya life, or with certain thangs, this town, it's people and ways, often make room for ya life ta work out as it should. In this case, history seems to be repeating itself, and you …" Nana Williams took my hands to hold them close to her, "are on a new path. I'm not sure what'cha got going on back up in Chicago, heard nothin' but good thangs for ya, but from the storm that trailed ya, sounds like it's time to come on home. I hope ya chose that, cus we gotta a'lotta work ta do and a'lotta history ta reclaim. Especially with Juneteenth. We need the hibiscus flowers from Gladys Norwood's floral shop, Floral Finesse, ready to decorate midtown, a lot of ya artwork, and we need 'So Truth' marching band to come on back, if we can."

Everyone in the dining room nodded in agreement. I sipped my cold glass of strawberry lemonade, then said, "I'll see what I can do."

"And I'll fuss at the rest of ma' children to come on home. The work is never done and can be done. We have a town to preserve," my father responded.

It was an hour later—after the town meeting and dinner—that I was outside next to my father's truck. Many of the elders stood around talking or heading out. It was a comforting scene to see how connected they all still were. For me, my shyness was playing at the edges of my stomach, making me ready to return to the inn. But I was grown, so I dealt with the old ways still tucked in my psyche and enjoyed the homecoming. In my hand was a yummy and moist 7up pound cake from Ms. Wilma—our town's second oldest elder who founded the airport nearby—various cards, some heavy with money, some with numbers of available sons, and a bag full of gifts and goodies from Grace and the rest of the town elders.

"Daddy," I quietly said while loading everything in my arms into my father's truck.

"Yes, my Willowshine?"

I took a moment to think, then closed the door. "Daddy, you know I can't stay too long."

"Uh huh, but it's nice to think about it, yes?" he replied.

"Yes, sir, but I can't stay. I have some things that I need to get in line that just blew up my world before I got here," I explained.

"Hmm, that's unfortunate, but I still feel that you can stay, you're just scared, and I understand that." My father focused his cerulean gray eyes on me in care, as if he knew something that I didn't, then it dawned on me.

"You're probably mad as well," he carefully stated. "But, once you settle, you'll be alright, I know it."

"Daddy, I guess you heard about—"

Hands flying in the air, my father interjected, "I only know what ya tell me and what my detective awareness tells me, baby girl, and from there I make my assessments."

"Oh." I looked down at my hands where the once massive 18-carat, white gold, round diamond halo ring with its twenty-six round diamond accents creating the band sat. I gave a deep sigh. "Well, I might just get it over with then. Hollis and I are over. Apparently, because of a case that I was working on making the news, causing issues for my employers, who forgot that we operate to protect our clients …" I shook my head and looked at my father with sadness in my eyes. "Hollis felt that I no longer fit his particular 'mold.' Aesthetically and socially since I confronted the state about the mishandling of my case. That was an issue for him. He said that basically my reputation for grassroot advocacy was now a problem. The family … mama's wealthy, affluent background wasn't going to be enough for Hollis's alderman aspirations."

When my father's eyes darkened to the tone of glass black marbles, I quickly opened the door to the truck and pulled out the cake. "Daddy, let's move on and eat some cake, yes?"

"No," he growled, taking the offering, and opening it to cut a slice with his switchblade.

I watched my father nibble on it while eying me. My father had a notorious sweet tooth, so I hoped that offering the cake would calm him a little bit.

Finally, he muttered, "I knew something was wrong when I saw that showboat ring missing. Knew somethin' was wrong when Sage called this mornin' angry but wouldn't say what it was about regarding ya'. I knew it. Never liked that opportunistic rat!"

"I'm sorry, Daddy," I said to his back.

"Ain't your fault, it's ya blessing. Nothing but ya blessing. He ain't never seemed to fit ya right but wasn't nothing I could say to change ya heart. That's how we are in this family. Quick to love. So, tell me why ya gotta go back, hmm?"

"Daddy, I—" I stopped when he gave me a stern look.

"Tell me why?"

I looked about, noticing the few elders still around, including the good doctor who was helping Nana Williams to his truck. I almost threw my hands in the air. My life was going to be in their minds for days. No one in the town gossiped but they sure thought of ways to help when they got wind of trouble. It was a sweet trait; it also was embarrassing for me in this moment.

Dropping my voice, I muttered, "I have no job because I stood my ground against the Chicago PD about a case that I was working on with them, which they botched. Because I pushed at the system, my state job was placed on hold, everything blew up in my face, Daddy. Like the bureaucrats they are, my supervisors 'politely' informed me that I was fired, and that my 401k was lost because of some bureaucratic error. Twelve years down the drain with Hollis and this mess with my old job, I have nothing. I'm a mess, Daddy, and … and … we also don't have the big house anymore so where will I stay besides the inn?"

"Don't you worry about that. I asked you here to help me with the center with your talent in art and your social work. I have a building right here on Main Street. We'll work this out, but ya not homeless. We came from survivors. We were reconstructionist union war vets and cowboys. I am ya foundation. There's no shame in taking a new path, my heart. Your mama would be proud of ya."

The arms of my father pulled me into a healing bear hug. I cried in his shoulders.

"We're here fa' ya, Willow," Nana Williams said in tandem by Doctor Kamal.

Tears that I thought I had gotten out of my system when I spoke to my twin last night fell. My life was a mess, not shambles, but a mess. However, I was home, and because of my father, I trusted his heart and words, I'd make it through. Sojourner Falls was healing balm.

Chapter 5: Kamal

"How long have you known about this?" I asked Mr. Walt.

"For about a month now." The expression on his face told me he was in a kind of pain that wasn't physical.

We were in the empty dining room at the inn. It was a little after nine and everyone else was asleep or in their rooms. The lone light on in the downstairs area showed a space that had been cleaned and prepared for guests the next morning. Place settings were already out, and fresh flowers had been placed in the middle of the long, rectangle, cherry wood table. The cream and golden tablecloth had not one stain. The pine and lemon scent wafting through the air made the place smell just as clean as it looked.

Mr. Walt was wearing pajama bottoms and no shirt. His robe was thrown across the back of a chair near us. His right arm was raised, and I studied the lump in his armpit with concern. He winced when I touched it and told me it had started paining him about two weeks ago.

"And it wasn't sore at first?" I asked.

He shook his head. "Naw. And then gradually it got so sore that I had to place a small rag under there to keep my arm from brushing against it. Been hard keeping them two ig'nant of it. Nita done started watching me more, and Ray done start asking me what's the matter with me."

"Have you told Doctor Martyn about this?"

Mr. Walt shook his head with a frown. "Naw. 'Cus if I do, he gonna tell Caridade, then she gonna tell Grace, and then all hell gonna break loose. I don't want to worry nobody 'lessen I really have to, ya know."

I gave a grim nod, hoping and praying that it was just a swollen lymph node. "Mr. Walt, listen to me, okay? Technically, you're not my patient. You have to tell Doctor Martyn this, and he can't say a thing to anyone else because of doctor-patient privilege. However, he needs to know so he can order a battery of tests. I can't tell you what this is just by looking at it, but I can tell you we should take it serious, until we know it's not."

The older man nodded, then glanced out the window. After picking up his robe, he put it back on, tied it at the waist, and picked up his mug of tea. "I just don't want to get my family all riled and worried if ain't nothing is all."

"We won't know what it is until you have the proper tests done, Mr. Walt. I understand trying to protect your family, but it would be best we tell Doctor Martyn about this as soon as possible."

"If you think it's best," was all he said as he walked over to the big, bay window in the dining room and looked out.

I studied him a moment, wishing there was something more comforting to say to him, but there wasn't. Truth of the matter was, it could be a simple, swollen lymph node, it could be cancerous, or anything in between. The 'what-ifs' would be up in the air until those tests were run.

I woke up the next morning with Mr. Walt on my mind. I planned to speak with Doctor Martyn as soon as I could. I knew older folk could be stubborn. I hoped that wasn't the case with Mr. Walt and that he would allow Doctor Martyn to do what was needed.

I looked around the room the town had put me in. The inn had themes for each of their suites. I was in the Coltrane Suite. There were two saxes that were on the wall above the bed's headboard. Several of his framed records decorated the teal and chocolate covered walls, including the album with him and Duke Ellington. A picture of Coltrane playing his beloved sax was on the wall to the left of the door. On the opposite wall was a framed newspaper article that chronicled the musical legend's life and early death. There was a record player with several Coltrane albums sitting on the stand underneath it. On the wall above the record player was a picture of the Duke and Coltrane, the Duke at the piano and Coltrane blowing his sax. I really felt as if Coltrane's memory was in the suite with me.

I'd let the window up earlier that morning as I'd gotten hot but didn't want to turn on the air. A cool breeze wafted through the teal, cream, and chocolate sheer curtains. The golden carpet with chocolate rings throughout had been vacuumed, but just like the bed would be changed to put on fresh linen, I knew someone would be in to vacuum the carpet once I left for the day. The bathroom sat off to the left of the room and was fairly big considering the cozy nature of the inn. The nook underneath the window held my medical books, some of the patients' records Hunter had given me, my laptop, and some of my other important papers. There was also a map of Sojourner Falls.

I didn't know if I wanted to move into an older house or have one built from the ground up. Blade and Hunter told me there was a lot of land that could be developed. I planned to take a drive near the shady groves to see what sat out that way.

Once I brushed my teeth, washed my face, and moisturized my chocolate brown, pencil-thin locs, I slid on my ironed jeans, plaid, button-down shirt, and brown cowboy boots, I pulled on my Stetson and headed down for breakfast. Normally, by 9:30 most of the guests had eaten and were out and about for the day. I was a bit late, but I hoped something had been saved for me.

Any other morning, I'd be down by 7:30. I didn't want to get up that early this morning. Didn't want to run the risk of Ms. Nita catching me. She always gazed upon like she could see everything I didn't want her to know.

"Nice of ya to join us this morning, young buck," a male voice greeted me.

I'd just made my way downstairs and was headed to the dining room. I looked to my right to see Mr. Clark. He had a dish rag over a shoulder, and another in his hand, wiping inside of a coffee mug.

"Long night," I said honestly. "Good morning to you, Mr. Clark."

He nodded, wise eyes studying me. "Morning. Care ta tell me what you and Walt was meeting about last night?"

Sighing, I shook my head. "Can't tell you that, Mr. Clark. I'm sorry."

He grunted. "All right. Ya food in there on the table. Should be still warm."

"Yes, sir. Thank you."

He kept rubbing the other dish towel around the mug in his hand. "Uh huh. One thang, though …"

"Yes, sir," I said.

The old man walked closer to me. "If there is something the matter with him and ya ain't telling, Imma be mighty pissed about it. Know why?"

I shook my head. "No, sir."

"Imma tell you why. My Nita gonna be upset and sad if something the matter with that man, too, and she don't know 'bout it. And ion like my woman being mad, sad, upset, or anythang like that. You hear me?"

"Yes, sir, I hear you."

"Good. Now go on eat. Leave ya dishes there on the table when ya done."

I said my good-byes, then turned to head to the dining room.

"Good morning. Sounds like you have some elder blowback on you."

I smiled at Willow. She looked as if she were ready to go pick sunflowers in a big, floppy hat, a long, flowing skirt, and a thin strap, lilac-colored shirt. The two pigtails she had draping down her shoulders gave her an innocent yet wise look. Her brown skin glowed, and the gloss she had on her lips drew my attention to them.

I took a seat on the opposite side of the table where my food tray was with a smile. "You can say that. They don't play at all, that's for sure. And good morning to you. You look beautiful."

She smiled, then averted her eyes before looking back at me. "Thank you, Doctor Brookhaven."

"Kamal," I said.

"Excuse me?"

"I'd like you to keep calling me Kamal, please."

"Good to know. I wasn't too sure after finding out you were a doctor if you were okay with me addressing you by your first name only."

I nodded. "It's fine. I dig hearing you say my name."

"Okay. I will. I like that name. Does it mean anything?"

I took the lid off my breakfast and felt my stomach rumble. "Yes. Perfection and excellence."

My mouth watered I looked at the homemade chicken sausage, fluffy, scrambled eggs with spinach mixed in as I'd asked, homemade hash browns, a big, fluffy waffle browned to perfection, and warm syrup.

"Wow! Your parents named you Kamal because they thought you were perfectly excellent?" she asked on a chuckle.

I looked up at her with a smile. "I never knew my parents. I know I was born in Riverdale,

66

Georgia and that I was adopted by family, but I'm told my aunt named me."

I said a quick grace then dug in. The meal was magnificent. The way Grace knew her way around a kitchen should have been a sin. The seasonings blended together so well, I could only close my eyes and savor the flavors.

"Yes, Grace's cooking will do that to you," Willow said. "This is my second helping. And I'm sorry about your parents. I shouldn't always assume things as such."

"It's okay. Trust me. How does it feel to be back home?" I asked.

She sighed, but there was a big smile on her face. "Surreal actually."

"Really?"

She nodded. "Yes, really. I haven't been here in so long and so much has changed, yet so much has stayed the same. It's crazy to walk around and see all the new construction going up. And all the tourists? It's like the town is bustling with life again. Something I hadn't really noticed before. When I left, things were not this rife with life."

I waited until I finished chewing the sausages and eggs in my mouth before responding. "I'm pretty excited about the farmer's market going up out near farming territory. That's going to be a huge hit," I said. "Also, I hear a new chef is coming to town, hence the work going on near the courthouse for a new restaurant. Not much on who the chef is yet though."

"See what I mean? It's amazing how we're expanding but still keeping the small town, family feel. I even heard they're revamping the library and school building. Daddy told me about the Heritage Fund being in the black for the first time since the seventies. And all of it is going toward the revitalization of the town."

I watched how prim and proper she was while we ate and talked. I'd never looked at a woman as she'd eaten and thought about how beautiful she was while doing the simple act.

"So you're single now, right?" I asked.

The question caught her so off guard that she almost choked on her apple juice.

I chuckled as I got up and rounded the table to pat her on the back. "You okay?"

She picked up the cloth napkin and dabbed at her mouth. I laid a hand on the small of her back, and then picked up her glass of water to hand to her.

"Gosh. No! You don't come right out and ask a woman that in the middle of her breakfast!" She tried to look serious, but I could see the humor in her eyes. "And thank you," she said.

"Are you?" I asked while taking my seat again.

She took a swallow of her water, studied me, then moved around in her seat. "Well, yeah … yes, I am."

"That means I can ask you on a date if so inclined?"

I got a kick out of the ruddy undertones of her cheeks.

There was annoyance in her eyes when she said, "You could ask. Doesn't mean I'll say yes. And don't you think it's too soon to be asking me out? Not only am I newly single, but you just met me. How do you think you even know enough about me to want to date me? You could be after me because of my name and my father's high standing in this town."

She said all that, then snapped her mouth closed as if she hadn't meant to say any of it out loud.

"I see …"

A few silent moments went by as I continued to eat.

"I'm sorry," she said. "I didn't mean for that to come out so …"

"Rude?" I said when she couldn't seem to find the right words.

"Snarky," she countered, cutting her eyes at me. "I'm just in a confused space right now. I have a lot to come to terms with is all."

I nodded. "I understand."

She and I sat and made small talk while we finished eating. Once done, I excused myself to my suite, picked up my laptop and patient files, and then headed back down. By the time I got ready to leave, Willow had already left. That annoyed me. I'd been planning to ask her to have dinner with me regardless of how she felt about it. I knew I liked the little bit I'd seen of her, the vibe she had. I also knew I wanted to get to know more about her.

I went about my day, making my rounds. It was a beautiful day in Sojourner. It wasn't too hot, wasn't too cold. It was just right with a nice cool breeze to match. The scent of freshly brewed coffee was in the air along with the smell of fried baked goods. I nodded and yelled out greetings to those who had done the same to me. Made my rounds in town first, then headed out toward the farmers and ranchers who lived farther outside of town.

By late afternoon, my nerves were fried. Some of my patients either refused to listen to me or take my recommendations, and the other half were excited that I'd found something wrong with them and then wanted to pay me in chickens, homemade butter, goat milk, or whatever else they could think of. I had to admit, if I had a home, I'd take them up on some of it. I chuckled as I sat in my office at the medical center. One patient in particular worried me. Mr. Whitman refused to let me even step foot on his property. Threatened to shoot me if I did, but according to Hunter that was just the way the man was. Still, he was on the list that Hunter had given me as a patient of his to check on.

My cell rang just as I was about to call it a day. I was happy to see it was Doctor Martyn.

"Doctor Martyn, how are you?" I greeted upon answering.

"I'd be better if they would quit delaying my flights home," he said, then chuckled. "How are things back in Sojourner?"

"Well, I'd like to tell you all is well, but … I think we have a problem."

"What kind of problem?"

"Well, for one, Mr. Whitman threatened to shoot me if I stepped foot on his property." I chuckled. "You could have told me the man was ornery."

He laughed. "It took me a while to get that old geezer to even let me check his pulse. He's going to take some wrangling, but once he lets you in, you're in. I mean, he's still going to be a stubborn mule, but at least you'll be able to check his health."

"If you say so. But on to that problem I mentioned earlier …"

For the next ten or so minutes, I ran down the details of what Mr. Walt and I had spoken about the night before.

"What did it look like to you?" Hunter asked.

"To be honest, I can't call it. It could be anything, but the fact that it is swollen and sore, and he said it had gotten bigger—"

"So it wasn't that big or sore to begin with? And my bad, I didn't mean to cut you off."

"No, it's fine. I understand. This is a town elder you love and respect. And according to Mr. Walt, it didn't start off sore or that large in size. It happened over time. He came to me because he said he didn't want you to tell Caridade for fear she would tell Grace and then Grace would tell his spouses. I assured him you wouldn't and couldn't do that, doctor-patient privilege and all."

"Yeah, that sounds like that old man. I should be there late tomorrow afternoon. I'll call to the inn and speak with him then."

For the next thirty minutes, he and I discussed other patients and then on to my plans for a home.

"Have you toured Shady Grove yet?" he asked.

"Not yet. I plan to this evening."

"You have to get on that so Marcus Legend and I can get together to discuss lumber and all the building material we'll need to get started. Whether you chose the old Fields' home or to build ground up, we need to know soon."

Once I got off the phone with him, I packed up for the day and headed back to the inn. It was four in the afternoon. That gave me a good four and half hours of daylight to use to explore the grove.

"Hello, Doctor Brookhaven," Mrs. Percy yelled as I walked down Main Street.

She had a tin watering pail in her hand as she walked to the potted flowers in front of her apothecary shop. She wore a faded pink apron, a chocolate brown dress, and comfortable, black Crocs on her feet. Her gray hair was in a bun at the nape of her neck, and her light brown skin looked radiant.

"Top of the afternoon to you, Mrs. Percy!"

"On your way in?" she asked, eyeing me curiously.

"Not quite. Going to head to the grove soon here."

"Ah! I see. Saw Walt talking to you at the town hall meeting. He alright?"

"As far as I know, he is," I said, not wanting to lie.

She studied me with that same curious smile on her face before nodding. "If ya say so. Gonna hold ya to it."

"I wouldn't have it any other way, Mrs. Percy. Hey, have to seen Willow Turner around here anywhere?"

She quirked a brow. "Seen her this morning. She was running around here with her pappy. Check at the sheriff station."

I took that info and went on about my way then stopped at my truck to toss my things inside. Afterwards, I planned to head toward the sheriff station until I was stopped by Lovey Davenport, the mayor's now ex-wife. Lovey had taken all of her weave out and now sported a Halle Berry type pixie cut. Lovey had lost some weight since the last time I saw her, too. She looked a whole lot better since divorcing her lecherous husband. There was a little boy with her whom I could tell was mixed race, but he looked more like the sheriff's kind of mixed race. He had shoulder-length, curly, blond hair and a mischievous smirk on his tanned face.

"Doctor Brookhaven," she called, running toward me. "Doctor Brookhaven! I need to speak with you!"

I really didn't want to be bothered with her. She was a helicopter mother who thought every minor scratch Chadwick got required medical attention. Still, I stopped and plastered on a welcoming smile.

"Yes, Lovey, how can I help you today?"

The woman was dressed in a cream skirt suit, with red stiletto pumps and a hat only a woman on the Mother's Board at church could appreciate.

"Come on, Chadwick. We can ask the doctor about it now," she fussed at the boy as she practically dragged him along. She took a deep breath when she finally got to me, then smiled wider. Sweat had pooled on her forehead. "Doctor Brookhaven, Chadwick here has gotten another rash. Think you can give him something for it?"

"Hello, Chadwick," I said.

The boy frowned up at me. "I don't want to talk to him. I want to talk to Doctor Kenya. I don't like him," he spat.

I chuckled as that wouldn't be the first time he'd said such a thing. He didn't like Doctor. Martyn either.

"Hush now," Lovey fussed, then turned him around and pulled his shirt up.

Across the boy's back were welts that I could tell were from an allergic reaction and scratches from where he had tried to dig at them.

My smile faded. I took an annoyed deep breath. "Lovey … have you given him shellfish again? Didn't Doctor Jones explicitly tell you to keep him from shellfish?"

"Yes, but … it wasn't so bad before, and last time he didn't break out at all. And he loves it so much—"

"Do you love your son, Lovey?"

She stood up straighter. "Of course I do. I knew I loved him upon first sight. It's why I fought so hard to adopt him. Why would you ask me—"

"Because, if you keep feeding him shellfish, you will run the risk of killing him. Do you understand that? I know I heard Doctor Jones tell you that even though he hasn't had a severe allergic reaction as of yet, if you keep this up, it's inevitable that he will." I yanked the door to my truck open, searched through my medical bag for my prescription pad, then quickly wrote out a prescription for two epi-pens. "If you truly love your son, stop feeding him shellfish. I don't care how much he loves shrimp and crabs." I tore off the prescription and handed it to her. "Go to the apothecary and get Mrs. Percy to fill this for you at the pharmacy. Keep it on you at all times and give one to his teacher. As far as the welts, ask Mrs. Percy at the apothecary can help with that, too. If you don't want him to have Benadryl, she can give you something to stop the itching."

"I told you I didn't like him, Mama," Chadwick whined.

After putting my pad back in the truck, I locked it. I left Lovey standing there scowling at me. I didn't care that I'd upset her. If she didn't stop giving in to him when he wanted shellfish, she would kill him.

I got to the sheriff's office and walked in to find Deputy Henderson there. He was a brown-skinned man with a bald head. He reminded me of Boris Kodjoe. He gave a terse nod when he saw me. He was one of the men who'd glared at me when I offered Willow my seat the last night. Before I could speak, the phone rang and he picked it up. I glanced around the small space. From the outside, it was a simple square bricked building. The old sign hanging on the right side of the door outside read **SOJO'S SHERIFF'S OFFICE AND JAILHOUSE.**

Inside was just as plain. There were three desks lined on one side of the exposed brick wall. There was a small office to the right of the room that read **'SHERIFF'**. Just beyond that office was a long hallway with six jailcells on each side. In the first one was a rotund man dressed in a green jumpsuit on a twin-sized bed with his back turned. I assumed he was the ex-mayor, Stacy Davenport.

"Can I help you?" drew my attention back to the front.

"Good afternoon, Deputy Henderson," I greeted.

"Doctor Brookhaven. Can I help you?" he asked again, Southern drawl thick.

"I came by to see if Sheriff Tucker and Willow were in?"

The man's black eyes turned to slits. "What you want with Willow?"

"That's personal. Is she around?"

"No."

I waited for him to say more. When he didn't, I asked, "Is Sheriff Tucker around?"

Deputy Henderson made a grand gesture of opening his arms and looking around. "Do you see him?"

Just as he said that, Stacy turned over on his bed. He looked at me, did a doubletake with wide eyes, then slowly sat up. He stood and walked over to the bars. The man studied me in a way that made my blood run cold. I didn't know what his problem was, but since Willow nor the sheriff were there, I left.

I looked for her at the bakery, at the flower shop, back at the inn, at the Green Pantry grocery store … I even went to the school. That woman had to be the hardest woman to find in a small town ever. In the end, I had lost darn near an hour searching for the woman I wanted to ask to ride with me to the grove. I supposed it wasn't mean for her to go with me, so I hopped in my truck and made my way to there alone. Maybe next time …

Chapter 6: Willow

The crooning humming of my father's voice as he sang along with Simply Red's "Holding Back the Years" made me smile in thought. While the music played in my father's truck as he rode through Helen, I crossed off items on our list of things we were buying to prepare for the Juneteenth parade. The smooth British soul song was a favorite of my parents. Whenever Daddy wished to connect to our mother, he'd play that or Phyllis Hyman's "When I Give my Love".

"Okay." I shifted my tablet in my hands and wrote on a sticky note I had laying on the corner of it. "Crossing off our prior visit to Legend Farm. Reminded them about the additional lamb for the BBQ and that they're hosting the history/founder tour and walk. They mentioned having the brick sidewalks be lined in lights at night, and the cowboy and gal carriage rides and light up bike rides that share the history of Juneteenth. Tammy wants to have skaters as guides, too. I'm just hoping we can get as many our families back home for this as possible."

Excited, I tapped my tablet, marking my p's and q's. "I also called Monae. She's going to check on my apartment in Chicago and visit our grans. I asked her to get an update on an order I put in for the town for some hot links, they have the best and it's a Black-owned business."

My father gave a nod as he glanced at me from underneath his Stetson. "Good job, baby. How is your cousin doing in St. Louis by the way? Might need ta' extend an invite to the, what y'all young people call 'em? Travel blogger?"

I laughed as we turned into the local big retail home and garden store with the blue dressings and huge, white lettering. "She's a travel journalist, Daddy, and she's ready for her next trip. Told me she might be ready to root somewhere after her trip to Bali."

"Uh huh. Speaking of Bali, time ta convince Sage to come on home, too. I need her military skills. Lookin' fa another deputy to help Henderson and Beales."

My eyes crossed at the mention of deputy Javon Henderson—not in annoyance, but in bated breath hoping my father wasn't trying to set me up, since I was single. Before my breakup with Hollis, Daddy had been trying to find ways to extend the long periods of separation between Hollis and I. Come to think of it, it made me wonder if he knew our break-up was inevitable. I hoped not. Javon and I used to date.

His family came from St. Louis, by way of Moline Acres, Missouri when he was seven. I told him I had a cousin from Florissant, Missouri, and we became close friends. When we became teens, he was snatch-your-heart fine and a sweetheart with a competitive bookworm spirit and track star gifts, so we started dating. He was my first everything but not first heartbreak. We naturally drifted apart due to leaving the town and college.

My twin, Sage, heard through the former kids of Sojo network that he had graduated from MIT. That was all I knew about my former boyfriend. Seeing him standing at the townhall meeting was the first time I had seen him in years. He was still easy on the eyes and dangerously tall, but I hadn't talked to him since stepping back into town. So, I wasn't even sure if his energy was still sultry, brilliant, and drawing. It didn't matter either way, a certain doctor had my unwavering focus.

"Sage is loving San Diego, Daddy," I started, noting on my tablet that Grace secured the DJ, and that all the red drinks were being outlined with Tammy.

"Doesn't mean a thing. I told you, I know things, as do the elders in the town. I felt my spirit needing you and that's what I'm listening to. My children, all of you, need to come home, even if it's part time. Now, what else are we getting on your list?"

I chuckled at my hardheaded sire and undid my seatbelt. "You need some supplies to build the hibiscus and willow Main Street canopy with Hunter. Outdoor activity game kits for the kids. We need some tassels and wrapping banners for flags. Oh, and Grace said her aunt, Kenya, needed a specific fabric we didn't have in town to work on the band and majorette outfits. Also, I believe I've I found your way to get Sage here, Daddy."

"How's that?" he asked with a twinkle in his eyes. "Sageheart is a petal in the wind sometimes."

"True. You have to hit her where her passions are to ground her. So, I was thinking working on the group will do that. She can handle setting up the streaming for our town website, using that Silicon Valley brain of hers. She's also the best designer I know, outside of being a marksman like you and the military taught her. So, maybe we can get her to take a red-eye to help with the outfits. Me and Grace are already talking to the elders to help sew, but …"

"It does help to have more young, fresh eyes on thangs, uh huh." Daddy swooped in to kiss the top of my head as only he could and grinned in pride. "Thank ya for joining me on out ride today and accepting my plan to get y'all all back home with me."

Laughing, I shook my head. "I knew I'd have to accept your shenanigans, and this is payback to Sage for calling you about Hollis." I winked while we walked into the store. "We may be twins and share the same eyes and smile, but that's as far as we go in looks."

"Baby, y'all have that twin psychic thang and mannerisms when y'all get back together, especially on the gun range, gawn somewhere with that." Daddy laughed, teasing me. "Use'ta drive me and ya mama up the wall with it. Would come in our room at night hovering, lookin' like the girls from *The Shining*, all cus y'all wanted to sleep in the bed with us. Gave me heart palpitations, gray hair, and forced us from stopping to sleep in the nude. Couldn't feel up on ya mama like I wanted to cus y'all'd pop up like *The Ring*."

My hands flew to my mouth as we laughed together. "Daddy!" I squealed.

"Now you know it's true and I got the video and pictures ta' prove it. All I know is, you and ya sista will get it back the same way as we got it, witcha' own babies and kids, same with my namesake. Now, speaking of kids …"

At that point, I was going to drown out Daddy's ramblings about grandbabies, until he mentioned his program. "Now, the Kwanza Kids program I co-run with Vincent and Kenya from up in Detroit an' down here?"

"Yes, sir, I'm familiar." I put items in our already overflowing cart, then kept walking.

"I think you should run our branch for it and make it yours. Now, before ya say anything, I dun already thought this out. I'll still be helping, but I think you could take the center I bought. The big, old iron cast and brick storefront? The one that used ta' be a furniture supply store and is a step over from the park? You could put ya old art studio in it, then teach and care for them kids." My father paused to add some outdoor lighting to our carts.

"A lot of them chil'ren are in the system, needing families, too," he continued. "So, with ya skill set, ya could also use the big office in the back for both businesses. I already put fancy black storefront windows in the front. There's a big kitchen I had Hunter put in. He fixed up to be a halal and kosher sterile kitchen, and there's even tiny safe spaces fa' kids to sleep in if needed. What cha thank? Shouldn't be nothing fa' ya ta move ya state license down here, Doctor Tucker, hmm? You could also use the spot to do ya dance sessions for the parade as well."

My head started spinning over my father's suggestions. I immediately latched on to the idea of having my own practice and art space. It was a long-lost dream of mine. To have it correlate with my father and Mr. Vincent's community program was a possibility I didn't see coming. How easily my father laid his idea out, made me think that he had planned this for longer than he said.

I wanted to be upset about it, about him manhandling my future. But honestly, looking back at what I just lost, the only thing I'd miss would be my work, somewhat my bougie grandparents, and the city life of Chicago. Those things could be easily replaced by the bustling city life of Atlanta, an occasional plane trip to Chicago, and accepting my father's plan for a new job. Helping children, single mothers, fathers, and families as a whole was a passion of mine and SoJo could use that help as well.

While my mind churned, I couldn't help but ask, "Daddy. Is that why you chose to give the house up and stay in the apartment over the station? Is this a part of what you and the elders have been planning as well?"

Outside of the store, my father directed a young, Black kid in loading two grill pits onto the truck, then looked my way. "I honestly didn't have an idea what my plan was for ya children. It took that storm on ya return home, and your confession about what happened ta ya, ta get all my pieces together. Yes, the town has been helping me use the funding to create that center, but that was done long before I thought about askin' fa ya help, baby girl."

"Oh. Okay, I'm glad," I gently replied.

"As for where I'm living, I know ya miss the family home, but none of y'all wanted to come home and buy it. That was my first attempt ta get ya back." Trent Tucker wiped his brow, then took off the work gloves he had slid on to help load the truck. "When that fell through, it just felt right to pass it on to the Legends. They needed it more than any of us since their home burned down. I can't be sorry fa' that, Willowshine."

"I'm not sorry that our home went to the Legends either. I just miss it and I worry about you. You're alone in that apartment and—"

"And I'm doing just fine. Got a whole town of folks lookin' after me. Hell, that Hunter made sure to renovate ma' apartment and made it smart, as if it was dumb before, I swear. Anyway, it's spacious, cozy, and nice with two big bathrooms and bedrooms. I'm just fine, baby. Besides, I enjoy being close ta' work to keep an eye on Stacy. I'm hoping the view of the center and garden that he'll have will help him remember the good man his family raised him up to be and that he abandoned."

My heart swelled at my father's words, but also ached. I could read between the lines and see the loneliness there. Elders who were strongly attached to their partners and deeply in love with them, often followed them to the grave months or years later. I didn't want to lose my father.

"Don't you want companionship?"

"Companion-what?" My father looked from under the brim of his hat to give me a hard side-eye. "Willowshine. I got ya mama in my heart, and though I'm old, I'm not ancient. I find ma' comforts when I want 'em, okay? Now I need that heart of yours to do the same fa' yaself while ya' step on that path. I'll be right there with cha'. Besides, with ya home now, I already know …"

My father's creole accent shone like a jewel in the sun at his ending phrase and I laughed. "Yes, sir, I know. I'll be there to bring you food, or cook, when the ladies in town aren't already doing so as is, or you're not at the center with your friends."

"Exactly. We have three years talking 'bout that and it ain't changed, baybe gal. We'll be just fine." Wrapping his arm around me, we collected the last of our things, which included a few five-gallon water containers as back up for any that didn't show for the parade. "Now let's get back to our town and enjoy ourselves. Besides, I just gotta text 'bout Doctor Kamal lookin' fa' ya? Hmm … what's that 'bout?"

Buck-eyed in confusion, I investigated my father's smiling face. "I-I don't know what that's about, Daddy, I promise."

My mind thought back to Doc Knight in Shining Armor Kamal asking me out. I lightly flipped out on him. I didn't want to be hurt or have my heart and time used for nothing. So, whatever reason that Kamal was looking for me, I prayed it wasn't bad, and I hoped … I don't know what I hoped.

"Uh huh. Well, ya better figure it out and enjoy yaself while ya do. Ya deserve something good in ya life, Willowshine, and not a foul wind based in Chicago. Let's get on back ta town. I'm hungry and want to visit the diner."

I adjusted my sunhat, and skirt, while my father gave me the keys to his truck.

"Don't go almost hitting any prissy cows and onery goats." My father hugged me and climbed into the passenger's side of his truck, immediately getting comfortable with the shift of his hat, and falling asleep.

Climbing in, I drove us home to the soft sound of Phyllis's crooning and sounding like my mother.

"Where are you? And why are you calling me sounding all huffy?"

Sounding huffy was an understatement. A sista was out of breath. I'd just finished bringing back groceries that I picked up in Helen on the way back after convincing my father to let me cook instead of going to the diner. I got an epiphany to avoid that spot because Kamal was looking for me. Now, my twin was in my ear fussing at me because I called her about needing help with bringing back the Juneteenth parade.

"Sis, of course I'm huffy. I've been out all day with Daddy, which was fun, and we've been dropping off items to everyone who asked us to grab them something."

I walked around my father's two-bedroom, loft-style apartment over the sheriff's station with one hand full of groceries, and other with my change of clothing, astonishingly impressed.

Daddy wasn't playing when he said Hunter gave him all the bells and whistles in renovating the old apartment. There was a huge flat screen TV resting on my old tall painting easels. On the brick wall next to it was the old fireplace. A large painting of Mama and Daddy in their twenties hung against the wall. Around it was smaller pictures of me and my siblings. I saw a teen TJ doing a smooth back lean with a whistle in his mouth, and a pole in his hand as Sojo band's drum leader.

Next to that was a picture of him decked out in a suit as an adult, handsome as ever, in his office. Following that, were pictures of me and my twin together. There was one of me messy with paint, painting in our old garden. One of Sage flipping in the air to dive in a pool for the swim team. Then there was our time as Sojo majorettes. I smiled in pride, especially as I saw our adult pictures, and one of Sage in her Navy attire and me receiving my doctorate cords.

We might not have our house anymore, but home was always with Daddy and his love.

"So, I'm tired, and was sweaty in my clothes. I needed to change, and I'm about to cook for Daddy who is napping. So, stop fussing at me, gal, and listen!"

It was close to five in the afternoon by the time we got home. I hurried to put everything away, then used the guest shower to clean up and change into a pair of ripped, skinny jeans and a teal tank. My painted toes were out, my hair was twisted into four long braids that brushed the center of my breasts, and I was now pulling out fresh chicken breasts, straight from the Legends' farm. I had plans to make Daddy crispy chicken parmesan with a small side of lasagna, garlic cheese bread, and a salad.

"I need you to take a red-eye home. It's emergent. I thought I'd do this for Daddy because the last time he called you panicked. So …"

"So, you want to do his dirty work, eh?" she laughed.

"No, I'm just saving you the anxiety attack. There's a lot going on here and it's piling up on me. I could use my mermaid twin's help is all," I explained. "And I'm trying to make sure Daddy isn't stressed out."

"What are you doing and why would he be stressed out? Wait—" Sage started.

"Nope. First of all, he'd be stressed because you told him about Hollis! I'm trying to keep him from flying to Chicago and killing that man. Second, the town wants to bring back the Juneteenth celebration and I need help since Grace is pregnant. I'm in charge of the 'So Truth' dance squad and we need outfits, banners, and … people! I called cousin Monae to help connect with the network today and bring back the kids, we need people first."

"Oh, gosh. You have lost it. You let the town suck you back in? Daddy's plan is working?"

I laughed at the fake panic in my sister's voice. "Eh. I must do something to keep myself calm as well. I have no job, remember? And … Daddy's idea is sounding sweet to me now."

"Okay, I know I slipped, hit my head, and fell into the sunken place," Sage replied. "Daddy's plan is sounding sweet to you? Break it down for me. I need to know said plan, and everything."

With a deep breathe, I gave my sister the rundown of Daddy's plan for me to run the center. "And, so, now I'm thinking of calling Monae and asking her to supervise transferring all my things here. I just have to find a temporary storage unit and then extend my stay at the inn until I can find an apartment here. But, I don't know, this is a huge change. I'm thirty-five and …"

"No and. Do it. Now," Sage ordered. "I'm going to get on that red-eye and come home to help. Let me book a room at the inn ASAP."

"Well, dang, Sargent. Just have to order me around?" I frowned in thought, contemplating telling her more about the good doc, too.

"Dang right. We all love Chicago; the city isn't the problem. The problem is your bosses, the cops on that case railroading you, and goat-mouth Hollis. The ancestors say that fresh water can change a stream, and that's what you need, sis. You overworked yourself, and sad to say it, Daddy is always right when he zeros in on issues in our lives. So, go with it. I'm the older twin, so you have to listen. It's time you live your dream. You always wanted to open your own art gallery and have your own practice. Well, you can have that, just streamline it and do it!"

"But—" I started to say.

"Do it," Sage repeated. "I'll be home soon, and keep Daddy in the dark. I want to surprise him and not let him know that I easily stepped into his plan or allowed the elders to start their own. Love you, fairy twin."

"I love you, too, mermaid twin. I'll see you—Oh!" I quickly added. "We also have to work on TJ."

"Ah, dang, we sure do. Now that might take all of Daddy's focus and maybe a horse," Sage joked.

With that, I hung up and focused on cooking, excited that my sister was coming. I had made my decision and I knew the town would start the parade early once they got the whiff of the news. In the meantime, I mentally made my list of what to do for the move, called my cousin again, then eventually sat down to a home-prepared meal with my loving father. Peace was coming, even in the whirlwind hurricane of my life.

Chapter 7: Kamal

"Hey there, baby," Ms. Sara said as she smiled up at me.

I smiled at the wise, old woman as I stood on her rickety front porch. It didn't match the cream and red color of her trailer. I could tell it had been built some time ago, as the wooden contraption looked aged and worn.

I took my black Stetson off and nodded. "How are you today, Ms. Sara?"

Her trailer sat on one hundred acres of land that had been in her family for generations. Just thinking about all that wealth and history that had almost been taken away angered me.

"I yet making it, baby. Yet making it. Ya here for my checkup?"

I nodded. "Yes, ma'am."

"Alright … let an old woman grab her bag and such and Imma be right on out."

"Sounds good to me, Ms. Sara. I'm going to stand on the porch and breathe in some of this fresh air. I love the smell of honeysuckle."

Ms. Sara snickered and walked back into her trailer. I looked out over her vast expanse of land.

Someone had been out to mow her lawn. I assumed it had been Marcus and his brothers. They tended to take care of the town's elders that way.

To the right, under a thicket of shade trees, was a makeshift hog pen that housed three pigs. Out in the field beyond that grazed four heifers, two bulls, and six calves. In a pen a few paces away from the hogs were seven goats fenced in so they couldn't make trouble I supposed. The last time I was out, two chased me around and headbutted me in the back of my knees at will.

About twenty paces behind her house was her first garden. I saw leafy greens but didn't readily know what they were from where I stood. Her second garden looked to have peas, beans, cucumbers, carrots, peppers, and the like. To the left of her front porch were lemon and pecan trees. She had a few peach trees lining the backwoods. I heard horses neighing out back where the barn was.

Taking a deep inhale, I basked in the sweet smells of the country and springtime. Honeysuckle was in the air along with the smells of berries and nature.

I looked behind me when I heard Ms. Sara coming out and quirked a brow at her attire. Normally, Ms. Sara always wore what she called a housedress around her home. Today, however, she had on a pair of worn denim jeans, a button-down, white shirt, some brown boots, and a big, straw hat with a picnic basket in the crease of her arm. Her pretty brown face peeked at me from underneath the hat.

I picked up my medical bag I brought with me. "Ms. Sara, I've never seen you in this getup," I said while escorting her down the steps.

"Well, an old woman needs to be comfortable for her checkup when she going to look on the sick and shut-in," she said.

"As you wish. Let me help you to my truck."

She shook her head. "No, son. Where we going, we gonna need a different kinda horsepower, yeah? We goin' na see an ole, cantankerous creature today, son. Follow me 'round back to this here barn."

We made the short trek in silence, minus Ms. Sara's beautiful humming. I found she always did that from time to time. As she got closer, two beautiful horses, a mare and a stallion, came out of the field and stopped to watch us. The stallion's coat was so beautiful and startingly black that it glistened in the sun. He was taller than the mare by at least three inches and built with lean muscle that I saw coil and roll each time he moved. The mare was just as beautiful. She was a rich, dark chocolate color that also shone bright underneath the beams of sunlight. She stood regal and swished her tail as the stallion pranced like a show horse around her.

"That there is Black John and Patty-Sue," she said with a wide smile.

I quirked a brow at the names. "Interesting names."

"Sho-you-right," she said on a chuckle. "Black John ain't gonna let no man ride Patty-Sue. She his woman, ya see, and he real persnickety when it comes to other males around her, human and horse. So you gonna have ta saddle up on him and I'll take his mate."

Ms. Sara wasn't lying when she said Black John didn't like males around his woman. When it looked as if I was getting too close to her, I saw the whites of his eyes and he showed me his teeth. His tail swished angrily, and Ms. Sara warned me to step back. I had no inkling to make the male angry, so I did as told, and waited until Ms. Sara had calmed him down to approach him.

"Now, Black John, you cut that fussing and carrying on out, ya hear me? This here is my friend, Doctor Brookhaven, and he don't mean ya no harm," she gently fussed as she rubbed her hand across the horse's body.

Ten minutes later, we were saddled and off. I kept my eye on Ms. Sara, noticing how at ease she was on horseback. The woman was over a hundred years old and was as spry as a woman thirty years her junior. This was all a part of her checkup. I couldn't treat her as if she was on the sick and shut-in listen. She outright refused to be boggled down by age and time. I often worried that she was doing too much. However, each time I came to see her, she insisted on accompanying me to one of her friend's homes to check up on them. It was a part of her medicine.

We kept a steady pace as we rode down the tree-lined dirt road. Wildlife skittered across our path, stopped and looked at us, and then kept on skittering. The smell of the fresh air, the smell of grass and pine on the wind made me realize that Sojourner Falls was rich with not just history, but land as well.

We stopped every now and again so Ms. Sara could pick blackberries, honeysuckle, plums, and wild sweet grass. I listened to her regal me with tales from days of old. She told me about how she was born to parents who had been sharecroppers. Her grandparents, who had been slaves on a plantation in Mississippi, were still alive when she was born. By the time she'd been born, they already lived in Sojourner Falls.

"I grew up a happy child for the most part, baby. Didn't know what it was to pick cotton and the likes. Knew 'bout slavery and all that, but this here place provided my peoples with safety and peace. My granddeddy told me 'bout how him, my granny, my mama and uncles ran from Mississippi clear up to that there Canada … then they got there and realized it weren't the promised land they was promised, ya see? So they had to make a slow trek somewhere else."

Ms. Sara stopped her horse to let her drink from a stream. I did the same for Black John.

"See, most folk know 'bout the escape north, but not many know about the flight of the runaways to Mexico. I mean the numbers of us who escaped to Mexico is far less than those of us who escaped to the north, but still … Anyhow, some who was escaping to Mexico went on foot, while others rode horses or were stowed away on ferries bound for the Mexican ports. I was told as a girl that Tejanos helped my people. The Tejanos was poor, but that ain't stop them from helping. My grands were in Mexico ten years before being told of this here place. My granddeddy said Mexico was good to 'em, but they was missing they peoples, ya see. And the US had started sending bounty hunters to Mexico to illegally steal people again and take 'em back 'cross the border. Then they met a man folks called Black John. The man's eyes were a crazy color they say. Some say gold with fire. Others say his eyes were so orange they looked like fire. Granddeddy and Black John got ta talking, told him about this safe haven he knew 'bout that not many other folk did. Granddeddy was said to have been skeptical at first, but something Black John said to him that made him trust the man. Either way, Black John got my people here and the rest is history." She looked at me and smiled with a twinkle in her fire-golden eyes. "Black history, son."

I smiled and took comfort in the fact I got to stay silent and listen to her talk. Being a doctor sometimes required that I always speak. However, Ms. Sara was doing doctoring of her own. I needed healing just as my patients did, just a different kind. I never knew my mother or father. Older women had always taken a liking to me. My aunt always said it was because I had a clean aura, an old soul, and a healing spirit. I'd never put much stock into it but being in Sojourner had taught me a few things.

We made it to Mr. Whitman's. We didn't come up his dirt graveled driveway like I had when I'd been in my truck, and he threatened to shoot me. We came up behind his trailer home from a well-used path that had been etched out with time and wear.

The rancid scent of cow manure assailed my senses as soon as we came up on the cow pasture on the back of his land. I took my Stetson off and fanned my face. That was one smell I would never get used to. I often wondered why Ms. Sara's cow pasture didn't smell as bad. His grass was also a few inches high which told me he didn't allow Marcus and his brothers out to cut it too often.

"I don't think this old man wants me on his property, Ms. Sara. Remember I told you he threatened to shoot me," I reminded her.

She smiled at me, stopped Patty Sue, then dismounted with an ease and grace that belied her age. "He just needs a strong hand from someone he can't bully, baby. Come on."

I dismounted and then tied Black John to a post next to his mate. After grabbing my black medical bag from the saddle, I followed her to the man's open backdoor.

"Cassius," she called out as she walked up a set of wooden steps.

I stayed behind just in case the man woke up on the wrong side of the bed this morning.

When she didn't get an answer, she yelled a little louder, "Cassius, now I know ya saw us ride up. You get on out here so the doctor can sees 'bout'cha."

"I don't need no damn fancy doctor seeing 'bout me," came an old, but deep baritone voice. "I want'im off my property, too!"

"Cassius, if you don't cut'cho foolishness, old man …" She crossed the threshold then said, "I'm coming in."

"I'm yet in my long johns, woman," he bellowed and sounded horrified.

"Yeah, well, I done seen worse and it's way past the time ya shoulda been decent for company."

My phone vibrated. Doctor Martyn had gotten back in. Said he was going to get his woman and son settled then go see Mr. Walt. I sent him a text to let him know I was on my rounds and would speak to him once I returned to town. I heard Ms. Sara inside fussing at Mr. Whitman and figured they must have had a friendship older than time because she was laying into him for not allowing me to check on him the first time I visited.

By the time she came back outside, I was curious to see if she had talked him into letting me examine him.

"Come on now, Cassius. We can let him check ya right out here under the fresh air. It's so beautiful out yonder today. Come on … You know Hunter wouldn't want ya giving the new doc a hard time."

She walked out first, and a few seconds later, a dark-brown-skinned man appeared behind her. I knew Mr. Whitman was eighty-five years old. All his children left Sojourner Falls almost twenty-five years ago. They rarely visited but they did send him letters and pictures regularly. The man was almost as tall as me, but time had stooped him a little. His bald head glistened under the sunlight, and his black eyes bore into mine. He had a beat-up straw hat in his hand and was dressed in a weathered shirt and denim overalls that had seen better days. On his feet were workman boots.

He scowled at me before taking Ms. Sara's arm and escorting her down the stairs.

Once to the bottom, Ms. Sara smiled up at the both of us. She pointed to the left of us where there was a small table and two chairs underneath a few trees. "Imma go sit up under the shade trees over yonder and give y'all some privacy."

Cassius glared at me, then back to her like he didn't want her to leave him with me.

He opened his mouth to protest I assumed, but she cut him off. "You get checked out, Cassius, or you can forget about our weekly dinner from now on."

"Now, woman, you listen here—"

"I mean it," she said firmly as she gazed up at him.

Whatever he had been about to say remained a thought as he huffed and grunted.

Twenty minutes later, and I had checked the old man's vitals and set up an appointment for him to come to the clinic for bloodwork. He grumbled and fussed the whole way, but he seemed to be in good health.

"Now, it's imperative that you come to town on this date, Mr. Whitman. We have to get your bloodwork drawn in order to be sure that you're in top health. Sojourner Falls loves their elders, and I wouldn't be doing the job this town pays me for if I didn't make sure all of you were taken care of and looked after," I said as I put my stethoscope back in my bag.

He mumbled under his breath about me poking and prodding, him then snatched up his hat and went storming down to his okra patch to fuss with Ms. Sara. They had an interesting relationship. One that made me wonder if they were sweet on one another.

Once back in town, the fact that I didn't have Willow's number weighed on me. It would have made looking for her the day before I lot easier. I was sure some of the elders had it, but knowing them, they got a kick out of me running around looking for her as opposed to calling her and asking her where she was. She didn't come back to the inn before I'd gone to bed.

I got up this morning, looking forward to seeing her, only to be told she stayed at her father's place the night before. Was she avoiding me? Had I done something wrong? I'd never been a man to chase any woman. I didn't think that made for good manners. If I put out feelers and nothing was reciprocated, I moved on. I always felt that if a woman wanted me, she would make it known.

Still, I wrote a note with my number on it asking her to call me whenever she got back in, then stuck it in her room's door. With the hope that she would call me in mind, I headed to find lunch.

I was in Jameson's Bakery, having a sandwich, coffee, and a donut when the sheriff walked in.

"Good day, Sheriff Tucker," I greeted.

"Good day, son. Heard old Cassius finally let ya check on'im," he said.

I nodded. "Yes, with the help of Ms. Sara of course."

The sheriff smiled. "Ms. Sara can 'bout get that old geezer to do anything. Mind if share a table with ya?"

I shook my head. "Not at all. Please, sit."

The sheriff took off his Stetson and placed it next to mine on the other side of the table.

"Get you a coffee, Sheriff?" Tammy yelled from behind the counter.

He smiled as he looked at her. "Yes, ma'am, and whatever this sandwich is he's eating as well."

"Coming right up," she said.

"It's called The Legend," I said, repeating what Tammy told me earlier. "She said her husband ask her make him a sandwich one night, so she threw together all the sandwich meat they had in the fridge with lettuce, tomatoes, onions, and some homemade dill mayo she'd made. I'm not too sure what's in the mayo, but this sandwich is pretty darn good."

"Looks it, too," he said. "So, got word yesterday that you was running 'round looking for my baby girl. What was ya reason?"

I didn't even pretend to be offended or taken aback by the abrupt change of subject. Since I'd met the man, he'd always been straight forward.

"Wanted to ask her to ride to the grove with me. Thinking about putting a house out that way," I answered honestly.

"You interested in my Willowshine?" he asked outright.

I wiped my mouth, then said, "Yes. Interested in getting to know her better."

"You try'na court her?"

"If she permits it."

Tammy came over with his coffee and sandwich. After placing it on the table, she rushed off to help her other customers.

The old man studied me, his gray eyes never wavering. "You just met her a couple days ago. How ya know ya really interested?"

"I was interested the moment I saw her stranded on the side of the road. I was very happy to know she was on her way to Sojourner."

"I likes you, son. Ya seem respectable and hardworking, but my Willowshine just got done over by a joker, and I don't want her hurting anymore or being blindside by underhanded thangs, ya hear me? You come courting her is fine, but I'll feed you to some hogs out at the Legend barn if you so much as break a nail on her finger."

I nodded. "I don't expect anything less, Sheriff Tucker."

He nodded once. "Good. She likes sweets and black-eyed Susans. She done loved them thangs since she was child. The rest ya gotta learn on ya own."

Just as he said that, a strong gust of wind blew through the town. The windows were up in the bakery, causing some of the napkins and other things fly around.

The sheriff stood. "Tammy, can ya wrap this up ta go for me?"

She nodded. "Yes, sir."

I noticed people walking out of their shops, looking around as if they were expecting something.

"I've gots to get to the town hall, son. We'll do lunch another time."

Once the sheriff grabbed his packaged sandwich and coffee, he rushed out the door. Curious, I went to stand on the walkway in front of the bakery. I saw townspeople milling about. Some in groups, whispering. Others shielding their eyes, looking toward the edge of town. I saw all the elders in town heading to the town hall. The wind didn't stop as it whipped up fallen leaves and grass. It blew the trees to and fro as clouds rolled in.

"It's called a wind of change," Tammy said as she walked outside.

"A wind of change?"

Tammy nodded. "Yes. It means something is afoot or someone new is coming to town. Only, this means they're bringing trouble with them."

"Sojourner Falls folklore?"

She nodded. "But every time we've gotten one of these, something sneaky was afoot. Last time was when Davenport invited those developers to town unbeknownst to the rest of us. Not real sure what this one means, but it can't be good."

I didn't know what to make of that. Didn't know what to say to old time superstitions, but I'd also learned not to brush them off as nonsensical.

Chapter 8: Willow

In my hand was a note, a simple one with the phone number of Doctor Brookhaven scribbled across the bottom. My spirit was bristling with anticipation. He wanted me to call him. I wanted to call him. Still, my nerves had me anxious.

Earlier, I took the time to visit the old building that had brick and cast-iron architecture my father was using as the children's center. It was soon to be my business and practice site. Seeing the foundational work that had been laid made my day. There was a stairway that led up to a cleared-out area that could be fitted to add more rooms. One I was thinking of making the kid's zone, another a multi-purpose area. The kitchen he had told me about was incredible, professional, and commercial chef level.

I mapped out areas where I wanted to hang art from Black artists I knew, and those in the surrounding area. I made note that I wanted a mural painted on the side of the building that was still distressed but would make sure the artist knew they had to respect the historic architecture and celebrated the history of the town. I had on tan work boots—that I was glad to have brought with me—jeans, and my old SoJo High T-shirt that I found in my father's storage room and was glad it fit my curvy frame. As I surveyed everything, I noted that I wanted the exposed brick wall for the kids to paint. I planned to use this place as a part-time art gallery, to sell and display works, but ultimately this was to be a home away from home for the children of SoJo.

As my father requested, I placed markers where I wanted easels, a kiln, and tables for sculpting, a weather-controlled supply storage and a dark room for photography. The area designated for my office was large, with two cast iron windows that I saw were frosted on the other side for privacy, but clear for my view. There was a bay window crafted and a butler's pantry with a spot for a refrigerator and plugs. Ceiling-high bookshelves. Amazing lighting framed by dark wooden beams.

I had secure storage for files and paperwork. I saw the wiring for internet and more. The office felt like a comfortable haven and a major change from what I was used to back in Chicago. Where I used to work, they set us up in a cubicle. Private meeting rooms had to be reserved for talking to our clients and/or families in private. With this space, I didn't have to worry about that. This building was incredible. I was thankful.

Before I'd realized it, I spent about four hours living in my dream and drawing out the blueprint of what I needed for the building. My father had edged me back into my first passion, and I felt ... calm. I stood by the window in the front of the center, looking at the town. On the framing were several names craved into stones, with two horseshoes and an arrow shaped compass. I smiled at the history.

Before this place was the town's furniture store, it was a stable and saloon. In the basement was a tunnel leading out of the town to the Nacoochee mounds and wooded area of the grove, so legend told it. Daddy had been clearing out the basement and former storage area, making sure that it was fixed up and safe. He hadn't told me if he found an exit route through. He did find old jugs of brandy, a few wine bottles, and moonshine, with old town newspapers and books. The history in the building reminded me of the SoJo Cowboys who would ride in the old Juneteenth parade.

Daddy used to be one of them, so I wondered if he might be willing to round up some for our returning parade. In thought, my feet thumped the wooden flooring of the building. I was on the phone with my landlord discussing my moving and getting my affairs in line. That included looking for a lawyer to discuss my "lost" benefits and 401k plan. Earlier, I called my twin and my cousin,

Monet, and let them know that I'd need her help in the next few months with the big move. My twin let me know that she would be touching down any day now and that made my day.

With a glance at the note in my hand, I saw a flash of Kamal's distinguished smile and dimples in my mind. A longing part of me missed hearing his silky voice and kind attentiveness. It was odd to me to feel this strongly for a man who I hadn't known long. Heck, I hadn't been in town long and my heart was already opening and singing an operatic tune of possibilities for the man. I knew this was due to what my father said. We Tuckers fell in love at first sight if it was the right person, and maybe because I was craving true intimacy again. It had been a long time since a man looked at me as if truly interested in me. Three years ago, when my mother passed, and my ex-fiancé refused to join me at her funeral, I became aware that I had been alone in the relationship for far too long. The way Kamal looked at me left me with a gentle warmth that I hadn't felt even with my former fiancé.

I realized that I had been ready to leave and find true, sincere love for a while now. My twin always called it out, but now I felt that clean break as sure as I was breathing. With that, I punched in Kamal's number in my cellphone and was about to press the call button when my phone rang. Outside, the town had a scattering of town folk heading to the townhall or leaving it. I focused on them to keep my temper from rising at the entitled voice on the other end of my phone.

"Hollis. How may I not help you this nice afternoon?"

"Very petty of you, Willow," Hollis declared. "But I assume that I should have expected that from you."

The nerve near my right eye twitched and I felt a headache on the rise. To move this along, I cleared my throat. "I have no reason to be petty, but I am waiting for you to tell me why you are calling me. Is there an issue?"

"I'd like you to return my ring as soon as possible, that is all." Hollis laced that request in a demand, then added, "I also received my things in a busted box? Is disrespect in your blood now?"

"Hollis, I'm not in a mood for your nasty mouth. I apologize if your items were returned to you in a disheveled box. I had no dealings with that. I can't be held accountable for how things are delivered. As far as I was shown, everything of yours was packed accordingly and sent your way. And I'll make sure to have your ring shipped to you as quickly as possible. Anything else?"

"Yes, I want it shipped today." Hollis used to have a voice like honey. Now it sounded like a tired cat on a hot, tin roof. "Once we hang up, take yourself to the waterhole of a post office you all have down there and send me my ring. Immediately."

Outside, I could see townsfolk rushing to cars, hurrying into shops, and others staring up at the darkening sky. A tightness and strain began to make me anxious in tandem to my ex-fiancé's rude tone. It seemed that whenever he called, some mess was sure enough ready to follow, and this windstorm felt like his doing.

"I don't have control over the time of your shipments, Hollis." *I need some protection crystals and sage from Mrs. Percy's shop for sure*, I thought while responding to the bully on the other end of the phone. "And this disrespectful tone of yours is not appreciated. I noted your requests and I'll make sure you have your ring. Don't call me again."

"Willow, I'm not done!" Hollis shouted.

"That's fine." I ended our call with the swipe of my finger. My mind circled at Hollis's aggressive tone.

I made a mental note to block his number. While I stared outside, I heard the quake of the store's windows. Banners, leaves, and flowers in the town whipped and thrashed, lifting in the air. It was May and spring seemed to want to announce itself again. A light frown played at the corners of my mouth. A storm was coming, or something else. Either way, the peace I felt earlier in the day was long gone and now replaced with worry. Something was coming and I wasn't sure what. I just prayed it wasn't harmful.

My father's truck was at townhall. I saw it from my window on the other side of the tiny park. I went to dial him and realized that I was dialing Kamal instead.

"Hello?" Kamal's weary, decadent voice answered my call, and I jumped.

"I'm so sorry. I meant to dial my father, Kamal." I heard the harsh wind on his end of the phone.

"So, you accidently called me? You found my note?" The bass in his tone melted away, leaving behind a gentle, comforting, jovial one.

Warmth spread through me, making me blush. My hand rested against my chest, and I turned my back to the window. "There's a storm that seems to be coming, and … yes I found your note when I went back to the inn. I was going to call, but I wanted to make sure my father was okay."

"I believe he is. He just left the Jameson Bakery and is headed to townhall." Kamal became silent, then added, "Are you safe?"

The sincerity in his voice helped me answer the question. "I'm safe. I'm close by. The building is near the apothecary. It's just across the street from the station and Elder Tree Fountain Park on the opposite end of townhall. My building is on the curve of the Main Street strip, near the three abandoned brick store fronts and the old, disheveled stone Victorian library."

"I'm relieved, and that is close. I think I know where you're talking about. I'm on my way."

I heard him walking, and when I looked by outside, I could see his tall, handsome self striding from the diner with a bag in his hand, crossing past the Elder Tree Fountain Park in the center of downtown. It was just a tiny, iron-fenced patch lot of green grass with a kiddy slide and spinner. He then crossed over to where I was. It was a quick walk.

"To be completely honest," he said while holding down his hat with one hand that held the bag and on his cellphone with the other hand; he was looking around to see which building might be mine, "I would be worried if you were caught up in this and no one knew. Which building are you in, woman?"

With a chuckle, I opened the door and felt it swing open out of my hands due to a gust of wind. "Geez, hurry in here. I didn't think the wind was this strong."

I moved out of the way, and Kamal hurried inside. He tucked his cellphone away. Then, with the light teal bag that had the Jameson Bakery logo on it hanging from the crook of his arm, he pushed the door closed.

"Finally," he sighed, locking eyes on me with a dimple grin. "We meet again, Miss Hurricane."

"Whoa, I did not cause this." Laughing, I held up both of my hands.

"Hmm." Kamal's warm, smiling gaze stayed on mine before looking past me into the rest of the old furniture store. He walked farther in while removing his black Stetson hat. "I'm not too sure about that. Also, I heard that the elders say this wind was a—"

"A wind of change," we said at the same time. We laughed, and I moved to sit at the bay seating that was attached to one of the front windows.

"I hope a tornado isn't coming." I looked outside. "Usually, they break up if they touch near the farmlands because of the mounds and trees."

"I hope not either. I was about to start my rounds in checkups again, but here we are." He chuckled, then looked at the bag. "Tammy heard me talking to you, so she made you a lunch. I don't want to rush you out of here. The windows seem to be holding up well in this building, but we should head to townhall just in case for shelter."

"You're right. We should go, though … Mrs. Percy's outdoor table just lost its um, umbrella." I pointed outside to where the pretty purple parasol was flying away.

"Do we have running water in here and a working bathroom?" Kamal asked.

"Yes, and we have electricity. I just tested the lighting today. My father bought this building and has been gutting it and fixing up the structure with Hunter, before Hunter left for his break."

"Then, we'll wait a little bit longer and see if the winds calm down a bit." Kamal walked over to a large, wooden worktable, dropped the bag of food on it, then pulled the table closer to where I was. After grabbing two wooden chairs piled in a corner, he waved me over. "It's safer to be away from the windows."

"Agreed," I quickly said. I turned on the main lights for the building.

Taking my seat, I did my best not to focus too much on the alluring man who smelled like the impending storm and the light, sensual, rich scent of spices, vanilla, patchouli, and cinnamon.

"Looks like we finally get to have a date, of sorts." Kamal sat once I took my seat, then he stretched out his long legs. "Tell me what this place is going to be. Oh, and enjoy your lunch, Willow. Tammy was looking out for you."

I caught his cute remark about this being a date and decided to hold off on a retort, then changed my mind.

"Only if I'm sharing this food." Smiling his way, I reached for the bag after hearing my stomach rumble. There was a small, roasted corn, southwest salad with grilled chicken, cheese, fried tortilla, red pepper bits with a salsa ranch sauce and BBQ sauce drizzle. Along with that was a chicken salad on croissant sandwich. My stomach rumbled some more when I saw the sweet butter pickle spear and a small container of glazed beignets. Setting a bottle of water that I found to the side, I opened the canister and closed my eyes. It was my favorite— iced chai chicory latte.

"Oh, my gosh, I love my girl. Tammy remembered and made sure that I'd be full," I muttered to myself, then remembered that Kamal had asked me a question.

Kamal studied me in amusement and patience.

"Looks like this is a date." Blushing, I divided the food out to share. "It's going to be a multi-purpose business. The children's center, my part-time practice to help the children in need, and my art studio and gallery."

With a chuckle, I added, "So says my father's blueprint for this property. He said he bought it with the town's children and me in mind. It used to be an old furniture store, and before that a saloon and horse and buggy stable."

"Every day I learn something about this town. I respect that. Sherriff Tucker seems to be a very intuitive man and doting father to set this up for you," Kamal said. "I also already ate and would love to watch you enjoy your meal in total, please."

Glancing at him, I pulled the portions back my way. "Say less. I missed breakfast today, so a sista is going to inhale this all. Please don't think less of me. Eating is good for me, and I can put away food when I want to. I'm not ashamed at all."

Laughing, Kamal crossed his arms over his chest. "Nothing to be ashamed about at all. You must eat, and how you eat does not worry me. I will say, I have a thing for feeding women I'm attracted to. That can be in any form, from me just paying for your meal, or …" I watched Kamal slide his chair close to me, pick up my fork, then hold out a portion of salad toward me. "Caring for your needs and feeding you. It's the most intimate experience I enjoy. Blame it on my profession to heal and care for others' well-being. Something you should know well, Doctor."

Blinking in surprise, I swallowed my hesitancy and took the bite while staring into his amber eyes. I was a sucker for a man who paid attention to who he was attracted to, including the nuances. I also was a sucker for the fall of attraction and this man kept me engaged. The heat in his words and simple act of feeding me took the wind out of me. I chewed, grabbed the canister, and poured myself a drink.

This man was something else, and he was causing a seductive heat to simmer in my body. Damn, my Tucker heart.

"This center fits you." Kamal handed me my fork and settled back in his leaning chair. The roar of the wind continued behind us. There was a change indeed coming and I felt it in my spirit.

"Oftentimes, it's hard for me to accept that sometimes, my father knows best, and in this, he was spot on." I laughed. "Don't tell him though. I'll never hear the end of it."

"I think this center and your businesses will be additional shining gems in the town," Kamal said with a chuckle. "I can see him teasing you for days. You might as well accept it though. You just admitted that you're staying in Sojourner. That admission makes my day. We can set up another date now."

"Another date?" I laughed and began putting my trash back in its bag. "Is that why you were looking for me yesterday?"

"That got back to you quickly, huh?" Kamal smirked. "I wanted to ask if you would accompany me to the grove. I'm thinking about purchasing a plot of land out there, maybe one with a house attached already."

"And you'd like me to go with you?" I asked, hoping that my excitement wasn't too apparent.

"Who better to go with me than your beautiful self?" Kamal reached for one of my remaining glazed beignets, then took a bite. "You'll be honest with me about what I'm looking at, and I'm hoping you'll steer me away from anything haunted."

The moment he said that I burst out laughing. "Keep you from anything haunted?"

He joined me in my laugher and dropped his head. "What? A brother has to be cautious?"

Kamal grinned, then added, "You have a beautiful laugh, Willow, and I aim to hear it again. And, just to let you know, I'm joking by the way."

"I see and thank you." I laughed, blushing. "I'll see to it that you won't get a haunted piece of land, and make sure it's a nice spot that fits you, once you tell me more about yourself."

Kamal stood and looked outside. "The medical office is close to here. We can have lunches without a hitch on any of our time."

"True. There's two back entrances if you want to dip into the center once it's done and hide from the elders." I pushed away from the table, noting he had ignored my statement. I hoped I hadn't upset him.

"I like how you think, Ms. Tucker." Kamal glanced down at me. We stood close enough to hold hands. Instead, the backs of our hands brushed each other, and the light intimacy was sweet to me.

Kamal's large hand encompassed mine. He guided it up and kissed the top of my hand. "As to knowing more about me," he started, "I'm an open book and eager to share with you whatever you want to know. I moved from Helen. I'm thirty-seven years old, and I'm single due to my own choice and devotion to my clients. I also hadn't met you yet. I have experience in horse riding, and I plan to court you."

Gazing up at him, my heart skipped a beat. I liked this tall, handsome man and his straight forwardness. I didn't feel a negative ulterior motive at all, and his hand felt like home as he held mine.

"I guess we'll be having another date then, so I can learn more about you," I expressed, grateful for being closed in with Kamal due to the storm. It felt like my ex had kick started the storm with his drama, but in the end, it helped me get closer to the man before me.

"We'll link up tomorrow for breakfast at the inn, then we can leave out." Kamal reached up and brushed a knuckle across my jaw. "It seems like the wind has calmed and the skies are clearing up. Walk with me and I can tell you a little more about myself, little hurricane."

Laughing, I began shutting down my future center. "I'd like that a lot, Doctor Knight in Shining Armor. This town is blessed to have you."

Chapter 9: Kamal

A whole week had passed since the "wind of change" blew through town, and while I was starting to believe that it just may have been Sojourner Falls' folklore, the elders and those who were born and bred here still behaved as if it was law. I didn't know what to make of it but didn't voice my opinion so as not to offend anyone.

Willow and I had been trying to spend as much time as we could getting to know one another, but with her helping Grace prep for the Juneteenth celebration in three weeks' time, it was if we were either playing phone tag or seeing one another at breakfast and not again until the end of the night. That could only be brief because the three elders who ran the inn kept an eye on us. I supposed it was because I was an outsider, and she was a hometown girl. Either way, every chance I got, I was finding a way to talk to her. One night, we fell asleep on the phone, and I felt like an overly eager, rambunctious teenage boy who had just found out what grown folk did when alone at night.

I had just walked out of the inn when I ran into Doctor Martyn and his son. The boy looked just like a Martyn, in height and facial features. Both his father, uncle, and great-uncle were well over six feet, and I could tell Hawk would be just as tall. He walked with his head high and shoulders squared as if he already knew he was the star in his father's eyes.

"Good morning, Doctor Brookhaven," he greeted.

"Good morning, Hawk." I shook his hand, noting it was firm for a kid his age. I extended the same hand to his father. "Doctor Martyn."

"Good morning," he responded.

"Headed to see Mr. Walt?" I asked, as I had noticed the man was up and dressed as if he were about to head out.

Doctor Martyn nodded. "Headed to Atlanta to have some tests run."

"What's he telling his spouses?"

"Said he told them he was headed with me to take care of some things for their upcoming anniversary."

I chuckled. "I bet they aren't going for that."

He shook his head. "No, probably not, but's he pretty adamant about keeping this on the hush until he knows for sure."

"I'm just glad you talked him into going. I pray it's nothing life threatening."

He and I chatted a bit more, then Hawk said he needed to ask me a question.

"Okay, I'm listening," I said.

"What would you buy a friend who you haven't seen in a while?"

"Hmm … I don't know. It depends on the friend."

I noticed a smirk on Doctor Martyn's face. "His friend is coming back with Uncle Vincent and Doctor Jones.".

Hawk looked up at his father with a slight frown. "Dad … I can tell him.".

Doctor Martyn nodded. "Okay, my bad. Carry on. I'm going to go in and see what's holding Mr. Walt. Be respectful and don't talk Doctor Brookhaven's ears off."

Hawk nodded. "Yes, sir." Once Doctor Martyn had walked inside, Hawk looked up at me. "Her name is Tessa, and I'm pretty excited to see her again. She's my best friend."

"Well, what does she like?"

He appeared to be deep in thought for a moment. "She likes ballerina stuff, but I've already given her those kinds of gifts."

"Anything else?"

"I don't know off the top of my head, Doctor Brookhaven."

"Well, you have to think on it some more. Gifts for special people should be well thought out to show that you care."

Hawk sighed. "Same thing my dad said. I'm going to ask Uncle Blade. He always gets Ms. Grace things she loves. Then she kisses him, and they get all mushy. Yuck," he said with a frown that made him look as if he were going to be sick. "I don't want to get Tessa anything that's going to make her kiss me. No way!"

I laughed. "Well then, you'd best get to thinking on a good gift that will make her so happy she won't be able to do anything but hug you."

He nodded, and then went into the inn. I needed to get to the bakery to pick up lunch for Willow and me. I had plans to take her to Shady Grove. I was to meet her at the same shop I had the week before when that so-called *wind of change* blew through. I had just taken out my cell to call Willow to let her know I would be there shortly when my phone rang.

I took a deep breath and calmed my nerves when I saw the number that flashed across the screen. I hadn't heard from her in months, not since she and I had a war of words about why she had lied to me all these years.

Still, she was my aunt. She raised me. I owed her at least the respect of answering when she called.

"Hello, Aunt Felisha."

***

"You're kind of quiet, Kamal. Sure you're okay?"

I glanced at Willow as the wind tossed her cottony hair. We were on our way to the grove. I'd picked up our lunch and hid it under some blankets in the backseat of my truck. I took my Stetson off and placed it on her lap. My locs were pulled back into a ponytail, and while I was a bit stressed, I wasn't upset.

"I'm okay. Just thinking. Got a lot to do, including getting into a home. Although Tammy is a fine cook, I can't keep only feeding you bakery food." I chuckled.

She smiled. "Hey, I don't mind eating it every so often."

"Yes, but I need somewhere to cook to show you my prowess in the kitchen."

"You can cook?"

"Yes, and I'm pretty damn good at it."

"You're going to have to prove that to me," she said as my truck bumped along the dirt road leading to the grove.

She was beautiful in her cut-off denim shorts and pink, ribbed tee. The fact that she had on cowgirl boots almost made my blood run hot. Her thighs were enticing. I couldn't help that my eyes traveled to her breasts as they jiggled ever so slightly every time we hit a bump. Her brown skin glistened with whatever she had moisturized her skin with and the scent emanating from her made everything male in me want to howl at the moon.

"I plan on it," I said, sending a slick grin her way before turning my eyes back to the road.

She giggled, and it was the sweetest, most innocent sound I'd heard from her since we met. The weather was nice. The sun was out but it wasn't so hot that it singed the skin. The wind whipped the trees back and forth, but it was needed to keep the air cool. Birds were chirping, butterflies and other winged bugs were in flight. Squirrels and rabbits could be seen peeking about the tall grass and ducking to run away.

As soon as I made a right at the fork, and passed the first Nahooche Indian burial mound, the grove was in sight. The dirt road was lined with big hardwoods of all kinds. Hemlocks, tuliptrees, basswoods, chestnut oaks, pine trees, and the like. It was a beautiful drive, one which we stopped talking long enough to admire the scenery.

Once the trees started to spread out, I saw a cluster of hilly earth and the remnants of what had once been dugouts and cabins. There were about five cabins, and the same number of dugouts. The only way I knew the location of the dugouts was because the grass had been freshly cut, and I saw what appeared to be narrow doorways. I slowed the truck to a snail's pace so I could take it all in.

"Back when we were kids, we used to take educational weekend trips out here. Pastor Pathwalker would bring us out here and tell us stories about how this was the original settlement of SoJo," Willow said.

I quirked a brow, then looked at Willow. "Really?"

She nodded with a smile. "Yes. Before this area was cleared out for lumber some years ago, this space was hidden by the grove of trees."

"So we're in the very spot where Sojourner Falls started?"

"According to the stories Ms. Sara used to tell, her grands told her it was as if the Great Spirit had shone the light on this space specifically. She said by the time her grandparents arrived, two of the cabins had been constructed."

"Any idea how they ended up here specifically?"

"Over in Helen, back then, most slaves were owned by the Williams family, who were descendants of the Ball family, one of the largest slave owners in South Carolina. The Ball slaves farmed and harvested what was called golden rice, making the Ball family very wealthy people. The Williams showed up to this neck of the woods around 1822, but unlike their family before them, the Williams' slaves farmed neither rice nor cotton. They logged timber, harvested corn, and cast rust-red bricks from foothill soil. Right now, if you go to Cleveland, Georgia to the White County Courthouse, one of the slaves Williams used to rent out was the main builder.

"But to answer your question, a few of their slaves stole away in the night; two families. One was a man named Solomon and his wife, Ophelia. The other was a man named Big Shadow—whose name was really O'ziah—and his wife, Lily May. The descendants of Big Shadow and Lily May are the Martyns. Solomon and Ophelia's descendants are the Clarks."

By now, I had parked the truck. She and I were out walking around the shanties. It was natural for me to take her hand in mine as she gave me a Sojourner Falls history lesson and tour. A part of me felt as if I were desecrating the land by even walking on it.

"Big Shadow built the dugouts after he swore his ancestors came to him in the middle of the night and told him not to move. He said they told him that this place, this land would be their refuge. Some time later—I think Pathwalker said two years later—another two families came rushing through the woods, looking for shelter from the dogs of the bounty hunters who were after them. Then, only the dugouts were around. No cabins had been built yet. The families had also escaped from the Williams' Plantation. Their names were Maise and Theo. Their descendant is Walter Bellamy. The other couple's names were Jasper and Caroline. Their descendant is Mr. Percy. Soon after, a family escaping from a plantation in Mississippi found this place; Luvern and Samuel."

My hand tightened around hers.

She looked up at me. "You okay?"

I nodded. "Yeah, just … in awe." It wasn't a lie, but it wasn't the full truth either.

She accepted my answer with a nod, then kept going. "Their ancestors are the Fields. That family …well, we don't have any more of them here …"

"Why?"

"Long story, but the gist of it is the town thought Felisha Fields had stolen all the monies, jewels, and valuables that had been entrusted to that family since Sojo's inception. All evidence pointed to Felisha when the money started coming up missing. The town felt as if they had no choice but to put her and the rest of her family out. The way it was told to me, Felisha begged and pleaded her case, but the town didn't want to hear it. They were told to pack up and leave. One sister moved to

London as she was ashamed of what Felisha had allegedly done. Their brother was killed in a hit and run … and no one knows where Felisha is after she was put in a ward for a time being. Her brother being killed drove her crazy they said …"

Anger that I thought I'd put to bed took residence within my heart. My left hand tapped against my thigh as we stood in the middle of Sojourner Falls' history. I kept my face stoic and my emotions hidden. We walked around the dugouts, but I didn't allow her to go inside one for fear it may cave in. The cabins, although in their original form, were surprisingly clean.

"The town keeps these up?" I asked her.

She nodded as we walked through the one at the end of the circle. "It used to be more often until we fell on hard times, but it looks as if the Sojo Preserve Society has started back."

"Who're they?"

"Older women who make it their business to keep this area, the dugouts, and the cabins clean."

It was Luvern and Samuel's cabin. I knew that because their names were carved above the door. The place smelled stale and looked as if it hadn't been touched in years. The wood cabin was simple. To the right of the room was a queen-sized bed that had seen much better days. The frame was solid wood. The mattress—if it could be called that—t had been made of feathers, grass, cotton, and hay. It was safe to assume the quilts were handmade. Time and age had faded the colors on it. There was a wooden, square table and two chairs to match. A small, stacked stone hearth was in the middle of the room. I could also tell meals had been prepared there because of the old pots and pans. On the other side of the room was a window with a tiny nook. On the nook lay a pile of thin books. I walked over to pick one up.

"Those are Samuel's old ledgers. When the families realized that it was possible they could indeed find safety here, they started putting all the valuables they had together to see what they could buy to help with food, seedlings, and things of that nature," Willow said as she stood next to me.

"Six gold coins, ten silver coins, and five dollars," I read from the legible handwriting. I glanced at Willow. "They had gold?"

She nodded. "Mmhmmm. Around 1831 most of the gold being produced in the United States came from the mountains of North Carolina and Georgia. Samuel had been taught to read and write by his first master. He was also taught how to keep books for his master. He had been well trusted and treated fairly well … as good as a slave could be treated during that time if you get my meaning. Anyway, things were going well for Samuel until his master died and the master's sons took over.

The oldest son wanted Samuel's wife and he wasn't having it. So, he hit the man over the head when he tried to violate Luvern. Killed him on the spot. Samuel knew he needed to go, so he grabbed his wife and they ran. However, the day the master died, Samuel took a bag of gold coins from his office."

I smiled. I knew the story, but I liked hearing her tell it.

"He brought that bag here with him. Also, legend tells it that we had this wild cowboy named Black John who robbed wealthy, white slavers, and when he found this place, he invested all the gold coins he'd stolen to help found Sojourner Falls."

"Ah! I've heard of Black John from Ms. Sara. So, the Great Spirit really did smile down on this place," I said as I laid the tethered book down. I felt my emotions taking over. "Hey, why don't you go to my truck and grab that big basket on the back seat as well as the cooler? I'm going to go relieve myself in these woods."

She chuckled and said, "TMI, Doctor!"

I laughed as we headed out of the cabin. I found a well-hidden area by a small stream to handle my business. Once done, I washed my hands in the cool water, then stood alone a minute to get my wits about me. The phone call from my aunt earlier had rattled me. It brought up old emotions that I tried to keep tucked far away, but hearing Willow tell me the Fields' family history, a history I knew all too well, reinforced it all. I felt my eyes burn with unshed tears but quickly got myself together.

I walked out of the woods to see Willow struggling with the cooler. I chuckled as I jogged forward to help her.

"Let me take that off your hands," I said, taking control of the cooler.

"What on earth is in that thing?" she asked, then took a deep breath.

"Cooking utensils," I said.

"Cooking utensils? For what?" she asked.

"I'm going to make us lunch, little lady," I said. "I went to Jameson Bakery, but then decided I'd rather cook for you so I headed over to the Green Pantry."

I dug inside of the basket she had already set down, grabbed the hand sanitizer, then put some on my hand.

She looked up at me with a laugh on her lips. "When you said you wanted to show me you could cook, I didn't think you meant out here."

"Well ... get ready, because I came prepared."

I returned to the truck, pulled the two folding chairs and a small, square, black folded table from the truck bed. After finding us a nice spot in the middle of the dugouts and cabins, a spot where the trees could shade us, I set up shop. From the basket, I pulled out a checkered tablecloth, placed it on the table, then pulled black-eyed Susans I found in a field of wildflowers, put them in a vase I borrowed from Ms. Nita, and placed them in the center of the table.

Willow's eyes lit up as I put one behind her ear. "These are my favorite wildflowers! How did you know?"

"A sheriff may have told me," I said, watching her as I found a patch of dirt to set up for a fire.

I took off my shirt when I felt sweat bead at my temples. The wind was still blowing, but all the moving I was doing made me hot. It took me no more than five minutes to get two fires going. Once done, I pulled out a cast iron skillet from the iced cooler, a small cast iron Dutch oven, onion, garlic, butter, steaks wrapped in butcher paper, long-stemmed broccoli, and potatoes. I then removed small, Ziploc bags of seasonings that I'd also gotten at the inn, thanks to Grace.

As I cooked, Willow and I talked about any and everything. I found I didn't care what she talked about, as long as I could hear her voice. I listened while she told me the troubles of her job before being let go.

"So, I know I did the right things, but sometimes, I get so sad thinking about the clients I lost, you know? Because it didn't have to end in such a way," she said with passion. "The detectives on the case outright refused to do things by the proper protocol." A deep frown creased her brows.

"Were any of the cops reprimanded?"

"If they were, it was a slap on the wrist. I even sent a formal complaint to the governor. I doubt anything will be done, but still. That mother did all she could to keep her and her children safe, and in the end, the people who were supposed to protect her, failed them."

I could tell that talking about it caused her great pain, so I changed the subject.

Once the food was done, we sat at the table to eat while nature serenaded us.

"Great time of day. You really can cook," Willow said as she put the last of her cut up potatoes in her mouth.

"And you really can eat. I can't believe you put away that whole steak." I laughed.

She joined in with me. "Listen, when the food is as good as this, I'm going to eat and feel absolutely no shame about it."

"I enjoyed watching you eat. I like that you aren't afraid to eat."

Pouring us more cold water, she said, "Keep cooking for me like this and I will stalk you once you get your place."

I chuckled as I watched her lick particles of water from her lips. "Don't tempt me with a good time, woman."

"I am so not joking," she said.

"Neither am I. Stalk me anytime you want. In fact, I insist."

I reached across the table, cupped her delicate chin, then rubbed the pad of my thumb across her bottom lip. There was a craving for her that I couldn't stop. I just met the woman two weeks ago, and I already wanted her in my bed and my life.

"No way a woman as beautiful as you should be single. Your ex must be out of his mind. Your mind, your brain, your beauty, your talent … your body. My God, woman."

She glanced away, then back up at me. "Stop it, Kamal. You're making me blush here …"

"That's not all I'm trying to make you do." I stood, and she gazed up at me expectantly. I held my hand out to her. "Walk with me?"

Smiling coyly, she nodded. She took my hand, and as we walked, she regaled me with tales of her youth. She told me how although she and her twin didn't look identical, from a distance people still mistook one for the other. I found that comical.

"You mean to tell me there is another woman walking around here just as breathtakingly beautiful as you are?" I asked.

140

Willow playfully swatted at me. "Stop that," she whined with red cheeks.

I laughed. "But I don't want to. I like making you blush, little lady."

We had stopped in a field of white, fluffy dandelions. As she looked up at me, I realized that yearning I was feeling was my need to kiss her. I pulled her closer to me, tilted her chin, then took my time savoring her lips. Her phone rang. She ignored it.

Willow had plush, pillow soft lips. The kind a man wanted to feel on his body. Her tongue was smoothly and velvety. Her kiss like nectar. I held her close to me as if she were my woman. In that kiss, I made sure she could feel the ways in which I longed to know her.

My phone rang. I ignored it. I let both my hands roam over her voluptuous backside. When she moaned and leaned farther into the kiss, my nature stirred around behind my zipper. I cupped the back of her neck with one hand, then ran my fingers up through her wild mane. I felt her breasts against my bare chest and found I wanted to touch her in all the ways a man could touch a woman. I didn't know how long we stood there kissing, but I knew I had to stop lest I behave like an inexperienced adolescent.

"We should clean up and head back," I said, gazing down at her.

She looked spent. She looked like a woman who wanted to surrender to the rampant lust running through her veins, lips so kiss swollen that I wanted to take her right where she stood. Alas, I knew I couldn't, not until I told her the whole truth about who I was.

"Do we have to?" she asked, then stood on her toes to take my mouth with fervor.

She fisted the back of my shirt as she kissed me, pulled my locs from the leather tie holding them, then ran her fingers over my scalp. That was something I hadn't allowed anybody to do, not even the women I'd dated. I thought I lost a bit of my natural-born mind in the moment. I lifted that woman around my waist, my hand roaming areas and places her father would shoot me for.

I pulled away. "Willow … we have to stop."

In my arms, she breathlessly peered down at me. "Do we have to?" she asked again.

I chuckled. "Yes … unless you want your father to shoot me and then feed me to a Legend's pig."

She threw her head back and laughed. "Fine," she sighed.

I had to be careful putting her down, lest she think I was trying to be fresher than the moment called for. After easing her to her feet, I guided her in front of me so she wouldn't be embarrassed by the bulge in my jeans.

Both our phones rang at the same time. "I think we'd better answer," I said.

She nodded in agreement as she pulled her phone out. "Yeah, I think so, too." She turned to me. "It's Grace."

I held up my phone. "Your father."

"Must be an emergency since he called me first."

"Doctor Brookhaven," I answered.

"You got my Willowshine with you?" the sheriff asked for a greeting.

As he did, a strong gust of wind came roaring through the grove.

"Yes, sir. We were having lun—"

"You and she get back here now. There are two new faces in town and they're asking about her. I don't get the feeling these are friendly faces either."

Chapter 10: Willow

Lunch was …

I had no words, but to make it light and general, it was amazing and genuine. My spirit and heart were floating. I was fully aware that this was fast, but I couldn't stop it, nor wanted to. A somewhat common joke in my old college social circle was that it was passé for my generation to fall in love at first sight. We don't do that.

But it was clear that that was a fable. I was falling for a man with healing hands, eyes bright as polished copper in the sun, and with a sensual, brilliant personality to match. A cool breeze carrying the scent of budding summer, yet still spring, grass, and flowers of the grove circled us. It calmed the blooming heat in my body for Kamal.

I studied the shift of his body language and how he tried to hide an inclination of tension.

Something was going on. I could read it in the way his hold on my hand became tighter, then relaxed. An undertone was there in how he laced our fingers in a protective manner. The change was there by how his jawline clenched with the slight tick of a nerve. I studied his darkening distant gaze while listening to whoever was on the other end of his cellphone before his gaze shifted on me. Those brazen eyes glinted as if flames, then calmed when he gave me a gentle, dimpled smile.

"Is everything okay?" I asked in worry.

I had years to study my clients' body language, especially children. Sometimes it was a simple thing to catch, that someone was lying or trying to protect themselves or loved ones. With Kamal, I wasn't sure what was going on, but whatever it was, I hoped that it wasn't something damaging to him. I genuinely liked this man, cared for this man, and I didn't want anything to hurt him, or what we were attempting to build.

"We need to get back to town, my hurricane." It was the first time he had used the possessive term for his little nickname for me. "That was your father on the phone. There seems to be some people in town asking about you."

I blinked for a second to comprehend, then I shook my head. "I know that it better not be Hollis. That disrespectful sycophant wants his ring back. I mailed it to him first class a couple of days ago."

Kamal caressed my chin. The pad of his thumb outlined my cheek, then lower lip. A sweet blaze of passion ignited in me, and I wanted this man as if lost in a desert looking for water. I needed another kiss. I wanted to feel how good his hard body felt against mine, how right it felt and fit. Yet, at the same time, my nerves took over. I really hoped Hollis wasn't here with another person.

"I'm not sure who they are, but your father didn't recognize them, nor did the rest of the town," Kamal explained.

Quiet in thought, I tilted my head, racking my brain. "Then one of them wouldn't be Hollis. Daddy knows him in great detail, while some elders met him a few times in passing, so he couldn't come into town in secret."

An alarm on my cellphone sounded. I hurried and turned it off, looking at Kamal.

"Good. If he had come through, I'd introduce myself immediately and thank him for sending you my way," he teased and winked down at me.

I laughed with him. My hand reached up to lay against his chest and I sighed. "I genuinely like you. I like what we're starting, regardless how fast it's going, and I wish we could kiss a little longer, by the way. Thank you for this sweet change. It's refreshing. Anyway …" I smoothed a hand over Kamal's hard bicep. "We should go. That was my alarm reminding me to go to the children's center and galley. Grace and Sage have the banners made, and thanks to Sage setting up the town's website for the parade since arriving last week, she was able to get more of us older SoJo kids to come home with their kids."

I leaned up to brush my lips against Kamal's. I savored the memory and sensation of his lips. From how firm, yet lush they felt. How expert of a kisser he was. Sighing, I stopped myself from deepening it.

When his large palm warmed the small of my back and his long fingers held me close, I added, "Everything for Juneteenth is coming together. I'm supposed to help my twin with planning a dance and marching routine. Grace has some of the children in town waiting on me. I'll keep an eye out for these newbies. If anything happens, I have my gun."

"And you have me, your father, and this town." Kamal's voice flowed like rich molasses. "Thank you for our date, Ms. Tucker, and for sharing the town's history with me. I wish that we had more time. I want to stay here and kiss you until the sun sets." He chuckled, then moved to lift the back of my hand to his lips and leave a kiss. "But we both have things to do, so let me get you safely to town, as you said. Besides, I think your father might barrel up here if I take too long getting you back, and rightfully so, we're on high alert."

With that, we began to pack up everything, giving each other fleeting, longing looks. Then, we headed back to town with the bear mounds, grass knolls, and precious cabins behind us.

"Call me if anyone approaches you. Just let me know if you feel something isn't right, my hurricane."

With a glance around, everything appeared as always—sleepy, little Sojourner Falls. It felt protective and not out of the ordinary.

"I promise I will. I sent my father a text that I was at the center. He said he should be showing up with, of all people, my big brother," I explained, holding up my cellphone.

Kamal watched me as he rested a hand on the steering wheel of his truck. "Then I won't worry too much. Have dinner with me at the inn tonight? Unless your family wants you to themselves."

"You're invited if they try to snatch me away. I'd like you to meet my big brother and officially meet my busy twin since she was MIA at the inn."

Kamal chuckled. His copper eyes lightened to gold, which let me know that he was slightly relaxed and not worrying too much about me.

"Then it's another date, wherever it is. I'm off to the medical center. Enjoy the center and kids."

"I will. You don't let the elders run you around too much. Bye, Doctor Knight."

After kissing Kamal good-bye and him watching me walk into the center, I smiled at the voice of my twin.

"These banners are perfect, Grace! I love the crimson red wax print Kente to represent the town and Juneteenth, along with this Muscogee-Seminole textile print cord sewn into the freedom star. Miss Nita will be proud of your work. Heck, so will Past'a Chief Pathwalker. The historic attention to detail is spot on."

Smooth jazz rent the air. Kids played near the back of the center; some grabbed snacks or drinks from the adjoining kitchen in the back. The wooden floor was buffed, dark brown, and shiny. The walls were prepped for future artwork. Everything was coming together. I was proud of the rapid progress in the restoration and building of the center.

While I walked into the still in progress center, Sage stood in the middle of the place admiring the flag. She ran her fingers over it to inspect the stitching while she spoke.

"I'll work on the rest of these to give your fingers a break. You know Miss Nita would fuss at us both if we messed up any stitch work." Sage laughed, then waved the flag. "This will work great for us flag dancers, and the bigger ones will look amazing as banners. Let me test the flag. Kids, watch my routine closely. Some of what I'm doing is the old SoJo line moves with some of the updated dances you all voted on, so check it out."

Waving the dance flag, Sage gave a countdown, then the music in the center created a vibrant pulse of energy in the room. My twin's fluffy hair was a coiled halo around her head and shoulders, and a bright smile spread across her face. She kicked her legs up in a perfect dancer pose, toes pointed, then spun. In her own groove, she dropped it low in a hip shaking pop of her pelvis and thighs with the flag proudly waving around. She moved around in a sports bra and yoga pants that bore the name of her former Navy unit.

A few of the older teenage children stood by watching Sage's routine, soaking it up. She paused to show them the moves and poses to follow. Which reminded me to look into getting wall mirrors installed upstairs for the dance area.

Once Sage made sure that they had the moves down, she stopped, then waved at me. "Sis! About time! Remember the grove stomp? Check me!" Sage clapped her hands together in a rhythm that matched her stomping feet.

I watched on, feeling a rush of childhood memories, then felt myself fall in line with my twin. We moved in dual grace and style, stopping so that Grace could slide in line to pose with our hands by our sides saluting Sojourner Truth.

Hand against my chest with bated breath, I laughed. "I can't believe that we remembered! Whew, it's been a long time! And, Grace, go sit down!"

Grace laughed, taking her time to sit back down with a hand against her swollen belly. "I love it that you're both back. I missed you! Willow, come look at the outfits Sage sewed together. She updated our old uniforms for the kids."

I did as she said, occasionally glancing back at my twin teaching the kids.

"Missed you, too, GiGi. The outfits look incredible! I think the elders are going to love the look. I'm still jealous at how good you and the twin sew. That was not my gift."

Clapping and stomping started. The teens who were watching were following Sage's dance routine with the younger children in tandem. My cellphone vibrated, and I took a quick glance. It was my cousin, Monet, texting me that our grandparents had helped with packing up my apartment. The next step was to arrange a time in the coming month to move everything into a storage pod and ship it to town.

Monet also let me know that she would be coming down to visit and celebrate Juneteenth with us. Excited, I smiled until I read her next text. What I read made me hold my breath in worry. She explained that some men had come to my apartment asking about me and that our grandmother cursed them out and sent them on their way.

"Girl, please," said Grace, who was looking down at a banner she was sewing.

It pulled me out of the spiral of fear growing within me. I wasn't sure what the heck was going on for people to be looking for me, but I was effectively unnerved.

I looked to Grace as she waved her hand, dismissing my earlier comment, and sat the banner down. "Sage outdoes us both with her eyes closed in that area. I just get by like you, and I had the time, since Cari, my husband, and my brother-in-law all keep demanding I lessen my workload now that you're here."

"Well, I believe you should listen to them. I'm just saying, beautiful." I laughed and sat by her side, picking up items. "I love how you're glowing. Where's Cari? I sent a text asking if she and Tammy needed anything extra for refreshments and elder's street seating set up."

"Thank you, this little one is being sweet to my body, and I'm thankful. With Blade and your father handling the legalities and permits and sorting out the finances for this parade, the stress of it all has been lifted off my shoulders. As for Cari, I heard her talking about getting that set up with Tammy. She should be back on her way. Marcus Legend and

Hunter were distracting her about your text to bring back the SoJo Buffalo Riders for the parade. This parade planning has her running around like you. She's helping me open more space in the inn. She also just brought over one of the SoJo-Kwanzaa Kids, Tessa."

Grace waved over an adorable, little girl who was in the back with the other children her age learning the routine. "Little flower just landed with Mr. Vincent and Doctor Kenya from Detroit. Tessa? Come meet Miss Sage's twin sister, Willow. She's helping with the outfits and bringing everything for the parade together."

When my eyes settled on the little girl rushing our way with a large duffle bag, everyone and thing in the room seemed to slow. It felt as if the winds outside had picked up and my heart skipped a beat. My eyes immediately looked at my twin, who was watching me. She gave me a nod, and I knew that who I was looking at wasn't a figment of my imagination. I didn't know this little adorable girl from Adam, yet my spirit felt that it did.

I stared at a little girl who looked just like my mother as a child, but slightly different. It was uncanny. I almost rushed the little girl to wrap her in a hug, that was how powerful the pull was. I wished she were mine by just a look and that frightened me. The Tucker inclination to fall in love at first sight was there again, but this time for this little girl with the adorable, big, fluffy puffs of dark afro hair, big cheeks and lips, rich mahogany clear skin, big, brown eyes, and adorable smile. She looked no more than eight or nine years old, and she wore a pale-yellow shirt with a Black ballerina Barbie doll dancing, jeans, and Spider-Kid Nike shoes.

"Hi, Tessa, it's very nice to meet you," I managed to get out.

Tessa, oblivious to what I was feeling, held out a hand. "Hi, Miss Willow. I really like your center! I'm having the best time! I can't wait to see Hawk and teach him the dance Miss Sage showed us. Miss Sage said you were her twin. You two do kinda look the same and really pretty."

A sweet smile spread across her adorable face, and I almost reached out to hug her again. I had to get myself together, so I playfully sucked my teeth while embracing her little hand, before letting it go. "Pfft, I'm the ugly one. My mer-twin took all the pretty."

Tessa covered her mouth and gave a carefree, shy laugh, then whispered, "I think you both are pretty. Why do you call her a mer-twin?"

I looked around, then leaned in. "Don't tell a soul, but she has gills. She loves the water and always swims. It's why she went into the Navy. She wanted to study the ocean animals, but her big brain made her work on an ocean project in Silicon Valley instead."

"Really? I mean the swimming. No ways she has gills!" Tessa laughed again.

I gave her a wink and smile. "Honest and cross my heart, everything I said is true. You should go over there and see. She'll show you. She loves dancing, too."

Tessa looked Sage's way and turned back to me. "Was she a ballerina?"

"Yup, we both were."

Incredulous, Tessa gasped. "Are you a mermaid, too?"

"Oh, no. I love water, but not like my twin. I'm a fairy. I paint, play with clay, snap pictures, and listen to anyone who wants help or to talk. I also love gardens."

Tessa quirked a brow as if she had a million bubbling in her mind, ready to explode. She opened her mouth to talk but stopped and stared past me. It happened so quickly that I was almost scared. My mind went back to the men who were looking for me and I abruptly stood up.

"Amazing, isn't it? She looks like our mother," I heard in a low, forlorn tone.

When I turned, my eyes landed on the tall six-two, bronze-brown, thirty-eight-year-old carbon copy of my father—cerulean gray eyes, and all—plus, a touch of our mother. Trent Tucker Junior.

My arms flew up and wrapped his lean, muscled frame. His dark hair with the natural red highlights, which showed up in the sun, was in a kinky, tapered fade. His chiseled jaw was covered in a thick, groomed beard, and he stood there in a long, dark grey jacket, black, button-down shirt, dark jeans, and brogue boots.

I squealed. "TJ!"

"Surprise, little sis," TJ said, holding me in a tight rocking hold.

We stayed like that for a second before he let me go. We hadn't physically seen each other in over a year.

"He was on the plane with me," I heard by my side, then remembered Tessa was still there.

I chuckled, wiping at my eyes, happy to have my family here.

"We were seat buddies. I taught her spades and told her how her favorite Sheriff Tucker tricked me to coming to town," TJ explained. "Said Mom's horse is sick, and that mom's spirit would be heartbroken if I didn't come check on him and the horse. Although I told him that I knew about the parade. Now, he has me running around loading his truck with items for the parade. Old man made me go over who will be the new SoJo drum major and the moves that I have to teach."

My brother's contorted face had both me and Tessa cracking up.

"I want to learn," Tessa whispered.

Her volition made my brother and I look on in pride.

By that time, Sage rushed forward to hug our brother in joy.

"If my other sister lets me go," TJ grunted with a chuckle. "And I talk with Mr. Percy about the band musical arrangements, then I can work with you and the other kids with that. Besides," TJ took a knee, then pointed behind him while he spoke to Tessa, "I think the friend you told me about is behind me."

Tessa's eyes widened and she rushed past us to the opening door. When she did, she giggled, then quietly closed the door to wait.

"Who is she waiting on?" I asked in curiosity.

When I looked through the glass door, my heart swelled with joy. Cari, who was the youngest of original SoJo kids, was there looking as gorgeous as ever in overalls that accented her curves. She had plump twist braids with cowrie shells and a few flowers braided in each strand. By her side, I saw the tiny, mirror image of Hunter. He stood near a truck with items in his little arms, frowning at another kid who I saw was Chadwick.

"Her friend who she talked about a lot on the plane ride over, Hawk Martyn," TJ explained but I lost focus.

Two unfamiliar men in business suits stood on the street outside of the center next to the boys and Cari. The men seemed to be annoyed about something, and that something seemed to be annoying the boys. Because the outside windows of the center were tinted, no one could see inside, but I could see outside. As the two men held something out toward the boys, I could see Hawk trying to move around the men while shrugging, which caused the men to change their positions.

Chadwick was equally annoyed, based on the expression on his face, and his loud, "I don't know who that is!"

Cari's face went cold. I could see her saying something in anger as well while pulling the boys behind her and made out the words, "This is disrespectful!"

Both men bristled and moved back. Because of that I was able to see in their hand a cellphone with a picture of me outside of my Chicago apartment. A knot formed in my stomach. The commotion from the boys and Cari caught the attention of Vincent who was on the other side of the truck bent down unloading. It took only one stony look from a rising Vincent, whose face was a mask of fury, for the two men to leave as fast as they had appeared down Main Street.

Nerves on edge, I watched the men disappear, and my spirit said be careful.

I was in danger, and I wasn't sure of why.

Chapter 11: Kamal

I saw the men as they questioned the children. That was a red flag of itself. Any adult who walked up to children they didn't know to question them had an ulterior motive in my book. I sat in my truck, parked on the side of the sheriff's station, and watched. One man had a scar lining the right side of her face. The other one, white, looked like Nick Nolte. He had a cigarette dangling between his fingers as he tried to get Chadwick to look at the picture he was showing them.

What they hadn't counted on was Caridade and Vincent being within earshot. That also showed how careless they were. One look from Vincent had the men cowering out of his line of vision.

A sharp rap on my window caught my attention. It was Sheriff Tucker.

"What's your thoughts on those two?" he asked as he nodded to the two men making a hasty retreat to their vehicle.

We watched as Vincent stared the two men down as they drove away. Once they had sped out of the town, Vincent glanced our way, then gave the sheriff a nod. Sheriff Tucker took off his Stetson and nodded back. A silent signal had been passed between the two.

I glanced at the sheriff. "I think Willow stepped on a hornet's nest before she left Chicago." I told the sheriff about Willow saying she'd gone to the higher ups about the mishandling of her clients' case.

"She tell ya of anyone hounding her before she left?" he asked.

I shook my head. "But I know those types. They're flunkies sent by someone else who wants to silence her."

"Willowshine done ruffled some feathers."

"More than likely."

The sheriff put his hat back on, then rapped his knuckles against my door. "Come inside. Wanna run something by ya."

I walked into the station to hear Davenport fussing about having to eat another sandwich.

"You're lucky you got that," Deputy Henderson told him.

"I've still got rights," Davenport yelled.

"Barely."

Both men got quiet when I walked in. Stacy's beady eyes shot to me, then a slow smirk crossed his features. Deputy Henderson's cut his eyes at me with his nose turned up like something stunk.

"That's all well and dandy," he barked at Deputy Henderson. He walked over to his bed, picked up a newspaper, then nodded at me. "When I get my day in court, I'll air my grievances."

"Stacy, sat down and quit making useless noise," Sheriff Tucker said as he stuck his head out his office door, then waved me in.

"Tell me, Sheriff," Stacy croaked in all his pomposity, "y'all ever think the reason such bad luck fell upon this place cuz of what ya did to them Fields?" He chuckled as he shook his head.

I cut a glare at the man.

Sheriff Tucker said, "You ever thank the reason ya behind them bars is because you the reason it happened? Ya left ya woman out to dry all them years ago, and ya knew full well you was the reason all that money and them assets was missing. You a coward, Davenport. A potbellied coward."

Stacy grumbled something under his breath, then turned to me. "Who yo peoples, boy?"

"I'm nobody's boy," I said, a bit cooler than intended.

"Yeah, but who yo peoples?" he asked again, a slick smirk on his face.

Deputy Henderson looked in my direction curiously. "You say you from Helen, right?"

I nodded. "I am."

The deputy got ready to say something else before the sheriff cut him off and called me into his office. I was happy about that. I wasn't ready to reveal who I was just yet, and something told me Stacy knew that … just as I suspected he knew who I was.

Just as the thought crossed my mind, a text came through on my phone.

I'm coming home, was all it said.

The bottom of my stomach hollowed out. I didn't know what to make of my aunt's text, but I knew with the strangers looking for Willow, and Aunt Felisha making her way back to Sojourner Falls, the winds of change everyone was talking about were definitely on the horizon.

***

I didn't make it to Sheriff Tucker's for dinner that evening. After brainstorming with the sheriff and his son, Trent Junior, whom I met after he came to the station, about how to keep Willow safe, I headed to the medical center to get some work done. Doctor Martyn stopped in to go over patient charts with me but left soon after.

"Now that she's done with her tasks for the Juneteenth celebration, I have to help my wife study some algae down at one of the lakes," he said, then chuckled. "A doctor's work is never done when he's in love with an agricultural engineer."

"What exactly is she doing for the celebration?" I asked. "I saw her directing the

Legends with a truck load of soil and other things a few days ago."

"Ah! She's in charge of the Ancestor's Grove. It's a small area of Shady Grove we're clearing to plant trees in the name of all of our ancestors who lived, breathed, and died in Sojourner Falls. She spent most of this spring studying the grounds to find the perfect place to plant the trees. She chose the white oak. We're getting the shipment of them two days before the celebration."

"There hasn't always been an Ancestor's Grove?"

He shook his head as he placed paperwork in his satchel. "No. This will be something for new generations and those thereafter."

I was set to ask something else until his cell rung. He tapped his Bluetooth. "I am walking out the door now, love," he said to who I assumed was Cari.

He gave me a nod, then headed out. Not long after, I packed up and headed out as well. A few hours had passed since lunch and my stomach was talking to me. Made me regret not making it to the dinner Willow invited me to. I had plans to go, but figured since her brother had just flown in, I wouldn't intrude. Besides, after meeting him earlier and listening to the way he spoke of his twin sisters with pride, I knew he probably wanted to spend time with them and their father alone.

I laid in bed, tossing and turning. I couldn't sleep. Couldn't get Willow off my mind. That was on top of thinking about my aunt. I didn't know how I was going to tell Willow who I really was. I'd had no plans of ever living in Sojourner Falls.

"How did I let those old folk talk me into coming here?" I shook my head.

I looked at the moon shining through my window. Thought about Willow some more. I wondered if she was sleeping. She'd told me the truth about my family's history in this town. I had never mentioned it to anyone. I knew to do so would open a whole other can of worms. Still, I'd fallen for Willow from the moment I saw her. I hadn't planned on that either. I didn't know what the woman had done to me, but I couldn't help the attraction I felt.

I threw my legs over the side of the bed, then sat up. I was happy for the carpeted floor as I didn't want to put on slippers. I trekked to the bathroom to use the facilities, washed my hands, then sat on the bed. It was only nine in the evening. Normally I could fall asleep no problem. I picked up the phone and looked at the text exchange between my aunt and me again.

I'm coming home, was the last thing she sent to me.

I didn't know how to take it, but I knew what she meant. As a kid, my aunt told me stories of the all-Black, small town that was founded by people who had run away from the shackles of slavery and freedman. She always spoke about Sojourner Falls as if it was a magical kingdom. As a kid, I dreamed of one day running away to said town.

I didn't remember my father, even though he'd been in my life up until he died when I was very young. My aunt had plenty of pictures of him, but that was the gist of what I knew about him. My mother didn't want to be saddled with raising a son alone. She was prepared to give me up until my aunt stepped in. Auntie Felisha had to fight for me as the state was worried about her mental well-being. However, after her psychologist spoke on her behalf, I got to go home with her.

My mind traveled back to Willow. Why did I miss that woman so much? I'd just seen her at lunch. Maybe there was something magical about Sojourner Falls. That was the only way I could explain why and how Willow had my nose open so soon.

Hey, I sent in a text.

Hey back, she responded.

How would she react when I told her the whole truth?

I texted, **You asleep?**

Not really.

Can we talk?

Yeah. We are talking.

I chuckled. **No, I mean can I come see you and talk? I miss you.**

She didn't respond right away, leading me to believe I may have been too pushy. That was the last thing I wanted to do.

I miss you, too. Sure, come over. We can talk, but not for long. It's late and…I don't need you getting the wrong ideas about me. Imma lady. 😊

An easy smile spread across my face. I still didn't know how to come out and tell her who I was. I had a good mind to tell her now, but seeing as it was going on ten o'clock at night, I didn't know if that kind of conversation was fitting. Still, I found my slippers, pulled on my robe, then slipped out my room.

Willow was in the Zora Neal Hurston suite at the opposite end of the hall. I was just about to knock on her door when someone clearing their throat behind me caught my attention. I turned to see Mr. Clark standing there with a mug of something steaming his hand. The steam rose as his brown eyes studied me. Mr. Clark stood at six-two, he was brown as the richest bourbon and stocky. He may have been older, but I still didn't think I wanted to see the old man in a fight.

"Something ya need in that there room, son?" he asked after taking a sip of whatever he was drinking.

"I was just going to see if she was asleep," I said.

"Ya couldn't call?"

"I could have, but I wanted to see her, too."

He grunted and took another sip from his mug. "It ain't fitting for a unmarried man, any man to be honest, to be at a single woman's door in the middle of the night, son."

I chuckled, then pushed my locs back. "Mr. Clark, you have me out here feeling like a hormonal teenager. I just wanted to see her and talk."

"Call her," he said firmly. "You just got to town. That young woman in there is a hometown girl."

In that moment, I realized that being in a small town had its setbacks. While I appreciated the fact that he wanted to protect Willow, I had to admit, I was annoyed that he was cramping my style.

"Mr. Clark—"

"Ya heard me, son. I ain't for too much repeating ma'self either."

Just as he said that, Ms. Nita's voice carried up the staircase. "Ray, baby, what's taking ya so long ta come back down?"

He kept his eyes on me as he answered, "Caught the good doc here sleepwalking I 'spose."

Ms. Nita walked up the stairs just as Willow's room door opened. Willow rubbed her eyes as if she had been sleeping. There was a slick smirk only I could see and a mischievous twinkle in her eyes.

"Mr. Clark, everything okay?" she asked, and even produced a yawn.

I ran a tongue over my teeth, then smiled. Willow was hanging me out the dry.

"Everythang's just fine, Willow. Right, Doc?" Mr. Clark asked.

I nodded. "Everything's fine, Mr. Clark."

"Ray, why ya up here messing with these young folk like you wasn't sneaking 'round my window when we was young?" Ms. Nita fussed, swatting at her other husband.

Quirking a brow, I chuckled. "Is that so?"

Mr. Clark cut his eyes at me. "Mind ya business, son. Ya wanna talk to Willow, get downstairs to the dining room. Otherwise, you get back to your room and she gonna be getting back to hers. Ya hear me?"

Ms. Nita was laughing. "Y'all come on down to the dining room. Ray here just messing and being old fashioned."

With that, she took his arm and urged him down the stairs.

I looked at Willow. "That was cold. To leave me hanging like that?" I said, and she laughed. "I'll get you back, my beautiful hurricane."

She sobered, then gazed up at me. "Come on. You know that was funny."

"And you knew Mr. Clark was probably prowling."

She laughed again while nodding. "I did know. I had just called him and asked for fresh towels. It's what took me so long to respond to your last text."

I ran a tongue over my teeth, then chuckled. "I will get you back."

Sobering, she walked toward me. She was breathtakingly beautiful. She also had on pjs but no robe. The top was spaghetti strapped and fell loosely over her breasts. The bottoms were just as loose but couldn't hide her full-figured hips and thighs. Her hair had been braided into two plaits, and she was a picture of perfection.

She stood close enough to make me have to look down directly into her eyes, then stood on her toes. Her lips brushed mine when she said, "I look forward to it," before heading downstairs.

My blood heated and raced through my body like electricity. I rolled my shoulders to stave off the primal instincts trying to take root with me. Running a hand through my locs, I knew I was going to be in for a few long nights if I didn't get a handle on the hot-blooded reaction I had anytime she as so much as looked at me. After tasting her kisses today, there would be no way I could keep my hands to myself. It was at that moment I was glad Mr. Clark hadn't allowed me to go into her room.

Chapter 12: Willow

My little jest with Kamal made my night slightly better. Before his text, I was up dealing with anxiety and a need to work it out through getting everything in line for the Juneteenth parade. A lot of the planning was moving along quickly thanks to Grace's earlier outline of things that needed to be done. That was on top of the outline that I made. Food vendors were set. Red velvet cakes were in cue to be made for the event. Lamb and other meat for the big barbecue was also being seasoned and prepped for storage.

I typed all night, sending emails to the savvy Elders Council and writing requests to those who didn't mess with cellphones. I let everyone on the town council know who had been assigned to the event cleaning board. I laid out the parade routes Daddy had given me during our family dinner. I made note to let the elders know that everything for the parade would be crafted to be sustainable. Solar panel gardens were going to be created.

Trash and recycling bins were set up. Food waste bins for compost were ordered. A clean space positioned on an open lot that used to be a building before it crumbled away was created for cooling stations and converted buses that were showers with bathroom stations. These unique, green zone areas were being brought in thanks to the SoJo network group that stretched across the nation and overseas.

In thought of my mother, I had an idea to decorate our ancestor's cemetery with garden lamps, pictures, flowers, and plot offerings/gifts. I made another note. Cari would be the best person to talk to about the greenspace specifics in the morning. I ended my emails and notes on the plans for the SoJo marching band, and the SoJo Riders' tribute to the elders, vets, Buffalo soldiers, and founding Civil War vets.

By the time I had lost myself in the parade management work and wrapped it up, I realized that it had been a welcomed distraction. But I was still anxious as heck. My mind drifted to the strange men in town. My father let me know that the town was watching and recording everything. The fact that the two men has been foolish enough to talk to children in the town had only helped out the situation more. I figured they had done so in belief that the kids would readily point me out due to their innocence.

But all it did was make everyone in town go on high alert. I was thankful for that and appreciative for the layer of security given to me. However, I was still scared as hell. This situation was grating my nerves. It bothered me that I could only assume that these men wanted to 'talk' to me because of something transpiring between my being fired in Chicago. Or could it have had something to do with Hollis?

Hollis had been rubbing his elbows with important political dignitaries who I had riled over my complaints about the state and my job's botched involvement in my forensic social work case. So, there was a high possibility that this was linked to that, which I had shared with my family at dinner. With my mind in a flux, pacing back and forth in my room, I called downstairs for some towels for a relaxing bath, then Kamal texted me.

"Dinner go well with your family?" Kamal's smooth baritone drew me out of my thoughts as he said, "I apologize for missing it."

I stood near a Yoruba carved armoire table positioned against a wall in the dining room. A Chesterfield sofa sat near a silk-draped bay window framed to the left with a bound of white orchids in a large floor vase and on the right a small table full of books with a lamp. Framed artwork and photos hug decoratively on the cozy, painted wall. Pictures of the inn in the past, old Sojourner Falls, several pictures of famous Black musicians and actors in the town drew my attention. Next to the displays were the smiling faces of the current Bellamys and past Bellamys. Sojourner had a rich, vibrant, and sometimes complicated history.

"It was great to be around my family as always. I forget how much I miss them when we're not together. Would you like a cup of coffee?" I asked Kamal while still in thought.

"I'd like that a lot," he replied.

Distracted by my thoughts, I grabbed some cups. On the table was a coffee maker and a heating plate that held a kettle of hot water. In a glass and wooden carved box were a selection of teas, both bagged and loose. There was a fresh pot of Mr. Clark's famous cinnamon chicory coffee, as well as coffee pods for other variety choices. In a small, Geechee weaved basket were individual creamers and various forms of sweetener packets, including honey and brown sugar.

In the glass mini refrigerator that was part of the table there were chilled water, juices, and various types of milk. I knew that when there were guests in the inn, this limited table offerings were set out at night for night owl guests. Bowls of fruit, cereal in glass sealed canisters, with bowls, or muffins would be set out as well. Tonight, there were just drinks. I guessed because it was just me and Kamal in the inn and we were trusted to go into the private kitchen to cook as we willed.

"Are you worried about the men looking for you?" Kamal asked in a manner that told me he was concerned.

"Hmm?" I glanced over my shoulder with a smile. In my hand was a cup for Kamal and tea for myself in the other hand.

Kamal sat at a large, majestic mahogany dining table with several wingback chairs. Each leg held intricate carved designs that matched the grand fireplace behind him. Designs representing the artisans of Sojourner Falls. Kamal looked like a relaxed king to me. Butterflies danced in my belly because of his nearness and gaze. He had captured my heart in such a short time that the shock of it was not going to go away anytime soon.

"You seem a little distant now that I have you to myself," Kamal shared. "Are you worried? I promise you, I'll protect you by any means necessary."

I studied my knight in shining armor. Handsome, with warm, concerned eyes and something else. Possibly parts of him that I still needed to know, wanted to know. The black tank he wore with his black sweatpants made me fantasize what he looked like without his shirt. His muscled arms were magnificent. The way his shoulder-length locs crowned his face made me mesmerized by his calm.

"You can read me already?" I sighed but held my smile. I loved the care he showed. "I'm more so anxious and angry. I don't know what this is all about, but I have my assumptions … Anyway, I smell baked apples. Mr. Walt must be baking," I added as I sat in a chair by Kamal's side.

"Thank you for the coffee." Kamal took a sip, then nodded at the pleasure in that sip. "Talk to me. I missed your voice and presence the rest of the day."

My hand found his resting one that sat on the table. Our fingers entwined, and I smiled in joy. "I missed you as well. You, mister, had me smiling at your text like I was in high school again. I'm not sure how I feel about that completely, but … it's really nice."

Kamal's smile lit up his golden eyes. Blushing, I took a quick sip of my tea, enjoying the warmth spreading through my body, caused by the tea and Kamal's closeness.

"We had my father's famous fried chicken. I made honey sweet potato biscuits; Sage made ham hocks with sautéed green beans and cabbage. My brother, TJ, replicated our mother's peach cobbler. I packed some away for you and stored it in the kitchen," I explained.

"Okay, I really am sorry for missing out. That's my type of spread. Thank you for bringing me some, Miss Hurricane." Kamal lifted our clasped hands to kiss the back of mine.

I blushed and reached up with my free hand to caress his jaw. "It's no bother, and again, no need to apologize, you're a busy doctor. It's expected that you'd be working sometimes."

"You take my breath away," Kamal explained. "Do you know that, Willow? I mean, whenever I'm around you I lose my center of gravity. I've never had a woman enthrall me the way you have, and I just can't grasp the how and why of it. Not that I'm complaining by far. I just, enjoy our time together and want to …"

For the life of me, I didn't know how I ended up in Kamal's lap, but I did. My arms were wrapped about him. His large hands sensually held my waist, then slid across my back. We stared into each other's eyes, feeling our breaths sync until our lips met. Sweetness and the light bitterness of the chicory coffee Kamal had sipped made our sensual kiss heaven. We savored each other's caresses.

The heated pressure of the weight of our mouths dancing against each other was pure bliss. My fingers laced themselves in the length of his locs. I sighed. He moaned. The vibration traveled through my body, finding the sweet spot of my haven.

Yes, I could feel how much we missed each other on an intellectual level. But I could now say, we'd been missing each other a passionate, intimate level. To have him in my bed was a must. I could have stayed there forever, and I felt the heat of him under me, speaking the same desire I had.

We kissed a little longer, until he promptly moved me to my seat and huskily said, "I hear someone coming."

Lips swollen, eyes hooded, I smiled at Kamal's passion-laced face. I did that and I was proud of it.

"Nice save," I whispered.

"If this were a historical romance, a brotha such as myself would say, compromising a good woman of the race, is not akin to polite règles de société." Kamal's golden eyes burned with desire.

My own wanton gaze widened at the ease of French sultry spilling from his lips as he added, "But since we're in the now, Miss Willow, I'll have to say, I'm not trying to get my behind whupped by the elder gentlemen in this house. A brotha enjoys breathing comfortably."

A bubble of laughter spilled over, as I shook my head. "Kamal, you are surprising as heck."

"Thank you. I enjoy keeping you on your toes." Kamal smirked, then gave a nod to the door. "Mr. Walt, glad to see you up with us night owls, sir. Let me help you."

Holding a large, wooden tray in his hands, Mr. Walt Bellamy strolled into the dining room, dressed in linen drawstring pants, and a white, short-sleeved tee that wasn't too big or too small. He wore a cooking apron which sported the monogram of the Bellamy Inn. His honey brown skin seemed a little flush. My gaze ran over the white beard crowning his jaw, then over his face. He seemed tired. My gaze went to Kamal as I also stood to help him.

"Whew. It's hotter than pepper jam and juke joints in that there kitchen." Mr. Walt wiped his brow with a cloth towel he had hanging over his shoulder. "Cookin' at night usually don't make it so hot, but this here global climate sho is changin' everythang' I usta' know 'bout the weather."

The moment Kamal reached for the tray, Mr. Walt snapped a stern eye on him and shook his head. "I got this, young man. You both sit'cha selves down right now."

When we didn't budge, his smile turned into a deep frown.

"Yes, sir," Kamal and I said in quick unison. We fell into our collective seats and looked around like chastised children.

"Now. I got my Nita's favorite apple cinnamon muffins fresh out that oven. You two get to taste it first. I also made carrot cake cinnamon rolls.

There's one of each for ya. The rest ya get with ya breakfast in the morning."

To break the awkwardness, I found myself grabbing a muffin with a thank you and a town historic factoid. "Kamal? Did I tell you that Sojourner was inflicted by a riot, around the same time as Greenwood, Oklahoma's Black Wallstreet massacre?"

My gaze was locked on an old black and white picture of the town hanging on the wall behind Mr. Walt.

"No, you didn't. I had no idea," Kamal gently stated, grabbing a cinnamon roll.

"Mmhmm. What Willow said is true. I wasn't born then but it happened 'bout six months after Black Wallstreet. Our little town might be magical and blessed, but we been through a lot to keep it 'round and protected." Mr. Walt moved around the room to take a seat near the bay window on the couch. "Had it not been fa' the large number of soldiers that survived the attack and made their way to SoJo ... as well as the fact that the town was sparse and needed for labor work in the surrounding counties, our little area might had not have made it. Missy Sara could tell ya the story in more detail than I can."

Kamal took my hand while we ate. I smiled at his sweet gesture, then told the little that I knew of what happened. "Daddy explained that had it not been for bear mounds and secret tunnels, a lot of the elders back then were afraid that everything they had built would have been wiped out."

"That's absolutely true. No one today knows how to access them there bear mounds, except Miss Sara I believe. But she 'axes like she dun't remember. Just like wit' the secret tunnels. My generation lost that information 'bout how the mounds and tunnels function and where all of them were. Little bit we did know came off like old wives' tales. Seems like the ancestors been ready to reveal more of the town's secrets by the more you youngins keep coming back. That makes me happy. Why'd that come to ya mind, baby gal?" Mr. Walt asked.

"I'm not sure," I said in thought. "I think with how we found a tunnel in the soon-to-be youth center and my art studio-gally, old stories Daddy would tell me came to mind. That wind of change also made me think of it. That's what supposedly signaled everyone to hide and to protect the buildings, right?"

Mr. Walt looked over Kamal and how he held my hand. I swore a smile played at the corners of his lips before he leisurely stood.

"You got a lot of the griot ways in ya, little Willow. I'm very proud that ya back. It's been long overdue." Mr. Walt headed to the door, then glanced our way. "Enjoy them muffins there and don't cha both be staying up in here too long, hob nobbin' and nuzzling like ya young people do when in lov— in like. I remember them days and enjoyed them. But ya both betta keep my dining room clean. We have more guests arriving in the morning."

I gasped and held in my laughter.

Kamal dropped his head, chuckling. "Mr. Walt. We're just talking and catching up on a few things."

"Uh huh." Mr. Walt looked down his nose at us with a raised brow. He was not one to be fooled. "Catchin' up on a few thangs is how me and my Joy created our children. Catchin' up on thangs is how me and my spouses found our love again generations later. Mmhmm. I know 'bout that catchin' up. I'm an old soldier. You can't pull one over on me, Doc."

"Mr. Walt, you wound me. I'm just being a gentleman. Willow was going over some of the parade information that we hadn't gotten to talk about yet."

"Uh huh, by sittin' on ya lap and you givin' her mouth-to-mouth resuscitation?"

Kamal choked on his muffin, then calmly wiped his mouth. "I … uh, she had … we were just … she bit her cheek, and I was looking for a cut?"

I laughed at both men's witty banter. I said, "Oh, my Loa! That was bad, Kamal."

"Yes, it was, but he's quick with the comebacks," he whispered, then chuckled.

"I sure am," Mr. Walt said with a sly, brilliant smile. "By the way, if I'm remembering correctly," Mr. Walt casually slid his hands into the pockets of his pants while standing in the dining doorway, "the ones that lead everyone to the bear mounds back then were the Fields. That family came from underground conductors and healers. Willow, yo' military trained family gathered up with the SoJo Riders and vets from Greenwood to hide near the buildings and protect it. It was a change in the winds that sparked it all."

The history that came from Mr. Walt lit my spirt and reminded me of the resolve of the town.

"My father said that in the early founder days it was my marshal great-grandmother who suggested the old emergency clause to use the townsfolk who could pass and trick anyone who may be a threat to the town. The idea was to use them to make the surrounding areas think that this was a majority white granted town," I explained.

"That there is the truth, too. 'Appear' and 'granted' is important. I rememba' Miss Sara telling us kids that. With the protection of where we sit, the mounds, and the fact that we were so small that we didn't 'appear' to be a threat to Ol'Jim, helped us. Havin' townsfolk that people assumed were white, look like the deed owners of the town, also helped us. Once it was set in the white folks' heads in the past, when the town mayors and others got darker, it made them folks no neva mind. The old clause Willow's gran suggested, and all those other protocols is what kept the whole town from being burned down again. The first town was moved from where it was, to where it is now because it was attacked during Reconstruction. Gotta lot of complicated magic, history, and Black military security in this town. With a lotta unity, blessings, and love. Y'all have a good night and focus on some of what I shared in that there parade."

With that, Mr. Walt left Kamal and me to ourselves.

"I plan to listen to Mr. Walt and Ms. Sara and work with the historians to put plaques around the town, sharing the history of Sojourner Falls. But our secrets will stay within."

Kamal looked toward where Mr. Walt had once stood. He then slid his arm around the back of my chair to pull me closer. He had a distant look in his eyes again.

"What's on your mind, good doc?" I sweetly asked, tracing his jaw with my fingers.

"Hmm ..." Kamal gazed into my eyes. "Seems like the town is working us both with the history," he said. "I'm just soaking it all in … We should call it a night, but not before one last kiss."

"I want to know your mind, Kamal, but yes, one more kiss. Then breakfast in the morning?"

Pulling me out of my chair, Kamal slid me onto his lap, brushed his lips against mine, then deeply muttered, "Mmm … breakfast in the morning sounds good, sweet hurricane."

Chapter 13: Kamal

Three whole days passed without one sighting of the men who had been looking for Willow. It was odd in a sense. No one knew where they had been staying as it was clear it was nowhere in town.

"I think we should mount a posse and head out to the wooded areas, see if they have set up camp anywhere just to be on the safe side," Blade said as we all sat in the town hall.

It was the first time he had actually sat down and had a talk. Since he'd been back in town, Grace had him running here and there in preparation for the celebration. However, the mayor said he'd told his fiancé that tonight, he had to sit in on this meeting.

Most of the young menfolk in town had come to the meeting. A few were still in their work clothes as was evident by the caked-on mud and dirt from a hard day's labor. Blade had put out a call to arms to all the men who were available. There was no doubt in my mind I would be the first one to attend.

We all stood in various places around the room, about a good fifty of us. Some of us had coffee or tea. Some had something stronger in their tumblers or mugs.

It was surreal to see all the men come together in defense of Willow. I had no doubt that they would do it for any of the women in town. It did my heart some good to see us Black men in a position to defend a protect our women, children, elders, and the town. We had come a long way in the fight for freedom. Race relations were still raggedy in America, but Sojourner Falls was our slice of the so-called American pie. A place Black folk had carved out for their own. It was good to see we not only had the means to protect it, but also to do it by any means necessary.

"That's not a bad idea," Trent said. "I don't like the idea of my sister having a target on her back and we not know where the proverbial shooters are."

The man was just as tall as I was and was the spitting image of his father, only Trent was phenotypically Black. He stood with the same sense of pride as the sheriff did, and the frown etched across his features said he was worried.

Blade continued. "Some of us can take off on horseback and the others can use ATVs for the more rugged terrains."

"Let's check out near the dugouts as well as the groves and near that dilapidated bridge out by Cassius's place," Sheriff Tucker suggested.

Blade nodded. "The rest of us can take the main highway."

"We should check out near the Freemans' place as well. Lots of trees and wooded area to hide in," Hunter cut in.

"Would also be best to send out two different scouting teams; one during the day and one at night," Marcus Legend added. "That way, if we miss any signs during the day, at night he will need fire, the night team would be able to spot the glow the blaze."

"Also might be a good idea to mount a security team to be on detail at all times," Blade added. "Men like that won't hesitate to hurt elders, women, and kids."

"That's evident by the fact they tried talking to children in broad daylight," Vincent Martyn said.

Just then, we heard a man's loud yell. The way he howled in pain told us that something or someone was hurt. We rushed outside to see what all the ruckus was about. The night was cool, and the wind whipped around. Rain was on the horizon. I smelled it in the air. Lights on the walls of the store fronts lit up the night and gave us a perfect view.

On the ground was a man, balled in fetal position, with an angry Mr. Percy glowering down at him. In Mr. Percy's hand was a piece of wood so thick, it could probably crush a diamond. It resembled a wooden baseball bat. On the business end of that piece of wood was a splash of blood.

"Caught this scoundrel lurking around the woods behind my house. My woman, child, and grandchild in there," he spat, then actually spit by the man's prone body. "I introduced him ta Malcolm X here." He patted the end of the bat-like piece of wood in his meaty palm. "Onna you docs may wanna take a look at'im."

Hunter's eyes went wild. "Are Cari, Hawk, and Mrs. Percy okay?" he asked.

Mr. Percy nodded. "Sho'is. Left Caridade and her mama with my shotgun and rifle. They been told that if anybody come 'round, shoot first and ask who it is later."

Hunter visibly relaxed. "I'm going to head down to check on them anyway."

Before anyone could stop him, he jogged off, headed to his truck.

"Who is that?" Trent asked as he walked over, then turned the man on his back. "Yikes!"

"Good grief, Mr. Percy," Blade said. "You clobbered the man."

"Knocked the piss out of him, too," I said, pointing to the man's soiled breeches.

The right side of the man's face was covered in blood. My guess it was where Mr. Percy had connected with Malcolm X. As the man groaned in pain on the ground, the rest of the men surrounded him. Mr. Percy was a big bear of a man. No way I'd want to run up on him in the dark. The man had hands the size of baseball mittens. Sure, he may have been an elder, but just like with Mr. Clark, I didn't want to square up with him either.

"It's onna dem jokers who was looking for ya Willow," Mr. Percy said to the sheriff. "The Black one. Caught him trying to sneak up on my property. I hit 'im then made 'im walk here. He passed out here, then I kicked 'im for good measure."

Sheriff Tucker signaled for Deputy Henderson. "You got'cha cuffs on ya?" he asked once the man had strutted to the front of the crowd.

"Yes, sir," he said.

"Cuff him, take him in. Put him in the cell down from Davenport," Sheriff Tucker ordered. "I'll see if one of the docs will have a look at him. Don't want him dying on my watch."

"That takes care of one of them," Blade said, shaking his head as he watched the deputy half drag the man down the road to the station.

The man limped and lumbered along as if his legs refused to work.

"For now anyway," Sheriff Tucker said, then looked at Mr. Percy. "You go on back home. It's probably best the rest of you men get back to ya families, too. We can catch up in the morrow."

After a few more conversations about the times and places we would all meet up the next day, I headed in for the night. I wanted to see Willow. I needed to see her, but my mind was all over the place. I was falling for her, probably had already fallen and refused to admit it. Still, I couldn't start a relationship based on lies. And yet … I didn't quite know how to tell her. Not only did I need to tell her, I had to tell a few others as well.

I turned back around, happy to see the sheriff and Trent were still about, along with the mayor. The other men had already walked off, heading to their vehicles to head home. That was all right with me.

"Hey, do you three have a minute?"

Chapter 14: Kamal

The next day, at breakfast, I got Willow alone before she went on her duties for the day. I'd noticed she had been having that little girl, Tessa, tag along with her. Tessa seemed to be just as taken with Willow as Willow was with her. So much so, that the little girl had eaten breakfast with her for four days in a row. In fact, she low-key scowled at me when I asked to speak to Willow alone.

"Willowshine," she called in her small voice.

Willow smiled at the little girl. "Yes, Tessa-Belle."

Tessa giggled. "That's not my name!"

"Yeah? Well darn, it sure does sound pretty to my ears when I say it."

"Like Sheriff Tucker said he feels when he calls you Willowshine?"

Willow nodded with a smile. "That's exactly what I mean."

"Do you have to go with the doctor?" she asked Willow.

Willow glanced at me, then back to Tessa. "I don't think so, but let me make sure just in case."

"If you have to go with him, may I come, too?"

Willow glanced my way again.. "I don't see why not. Doctor Brookhaven wouldn't take me anywhere you couldn't go." Willow held her hand out to the little girl.

Tessa hopped up from the table, walked over to Willow, took her hand, and then they turned their eyes to me. .

"Hey," Willow said. "Everything okay?"

I took note of the glee in her eyes when she was around the child. There was something akin to love there. Willow always joked that her family fell in love easily. Was it possible she had already taken a liking to the child?

"Yeah, everything is fine. I just wanted to know if I can speak to you alone this evening? It's important."

Her smile faltered a bit, but she caught herself and plastered it back on. "Sure. What time?"

"I'm with the day patrol today until about six. Does seven work for you?"

She nodded but studied me as if she was trying to figure out what I needed to tell her and if it was something bad. "Yeah, that um … that works."

I stepped closer to her. "Everything is fine, Miss Hurricane. Stop looking at me as if I'm about read you your last rights." I dipped my head to kiss her.

"Ew," Tessa squealed.

I pulled away to see her nose turned up as if something stunk.

She said, "I thought you said he was your friend, Willowshine? I don't kiss my friends. I'd never kiss that toad Chadwick, and I'd sock Hawk good if he ever tried to kiss me."

I laughed, remembering that Hawk had said he didn't want to get Tessa a gift that would make her kiss him either. The innocence of children was unmatched.

Willow's cheeks were beet red as she glanced from me to her new best friend. "Um … this is a lesson for another time, sweetheart. Why don't you go ask Ms. Nita to wrap us up some muffins to take to the center?"

Tessa had taken off before Willow could even finish the last part of her sentence.

I looked at Willow. "I'm on day patrol, going out near Ms. Sara's and Mr. Whitman's place with your father … and your twin of all people."

Willow gave a playful brow raise. "Is it because she's a woman that it shocks you?"

I decided to be honest. "Actually, yes."

"Are you sexist, Kamal?"

"Sexist? No. Traditionalist? Yes. For some reason, I like the idea of Black men being able to freely and openly protect their women and children."

"I get that, but don't forget some of those same women, and even the children, are also capable of lending a helping hand. Sage is just as good at firearms, hand-to-hand combat, and scouting as the rest of you men."

"I figured as much, but … I don't know … thinking about the history of this town and the sordid history we as a people have with this land … I take pride in seeing those men, young and old, mounting up to be sure that one of their own is protected, something we as Black men haven't always been able to do."

She cupped my cheek, then lovingly rubbed my face. "Again, I completely understand it, but I need you to understand that because of that same sordid history, Black women haven't always been able to protect their children, their husbands, their brothers, not even themselves, same as Black men. Some of us still love healthy gender roles. There are those of us who are even as dainty as our white counterparts. And that's okay. However, some of us are as brash and bold as our menfolk. Some of us said gender roles be damned and started doing our own thing. Some of us have had to be strong because the world left us no choice. They took our men and left us to fill the void for generations. I'm sure you know this," she said, then stepped closer to me to take my hands in hers.

It was the damnedest thing to have a woman show me affection and understanding as such. Again, it wasn't that I was unused to it; it was that I had never experienced this level of intensity with it. The primal instincts in me wanted to pick her up, throw her over my shoulder, and run off to some secluded area, and then make love to her until neither of us could stand it anymore. However, the man that I was gazed into her eyes and saw the beauty, truth, and emotions behind her words. I appreciated her more in that moment than ever. It gave me hope that when I told her the truth later, she wouldn't shut me out.

"All I'm asking," she continued, "is that you release some of the pride and extend a little of it to Sage Tucker, because if my hind parts were in a bind, it would be her I wanted on my team. And I'm not just saying that because she's my twin. No, Sage really can throw hands and knives, and bullets, and so on ..." Willow chuckled. "She is our ancestors' wildest dream."

Smiling, I nodded. "I'll check my ego and male privilege and respect the warrior your sister is."

Willow's smile widened. "Thank you. That's all I ask."

"Willowshine! Willowshine, I got the muffins," yelled Tessa as she came running to Willow, a covered picnic basket in hand.

"Thank you so much, Tessa-Belle. Now, we have to get going so Doctor Brookhaven can go about his business as well."

Tessa glanced over her shoulder, then looked back at Willow coyly. Since Willow had taken the basket, Tessa had placed both hands behind her back and was twisting side to side the way children did when they were nervous.

"What's the matter, sweetie?" Willow asked.

"Um … I know I was supposed to help you at the center today, but um …" She looked over her shoulder again.

I smiled seeing Hawk standing near the mudroom. He had two fishing poles and a small tacklebox in his hand.

"You coming, Tessa? If so, you better hurry. Uncle Vincent said the fish are biting good down near the creek! There are even crawdaddies!"

Tessa turned sad eyes to Willow. She looked like she didn't know who to choose to hang with for the day.

"Tell you what," Willow said as she knelt, "why don't you go hang with Hawk? I'll set up at the center, and then we can meet up later for dinner."

Tessa's face lit up with excitement as she nodded, then kissed both of Willow's cheeks. "Yes, ma'am! And I'll bring you back a whole mess of fish," she yelled over her shoulder while running toward Hawk.

He gave her one of his poles, then pulled a small, pink bucket hat, or fishing hat as we called them, from his pocket for her. There was a black ballerina on the front of the hat.

Tessa beamed, then whispered, "Thank you, Hawk," as if she were in awe.

I watched as he helped her to put it on. "Already the young gentleman," I said. I looked at Willow to see her smiling on with watery eyes. "Are you okay?"

She nodded. "Yes. It's just … I mean … well, look at them. Aren't they adorable?"

"Are you one of those dainty Black women you just spoke about?" I asked in jest.

She laughed and playfully swatted my arm. "Oh, hush."

"Hawk, you and Tessa about ready? Uncle Vin is waiting on us," Doctor Martyn said as he walked in.

Before Hawk could answer, Chadwick came rushing through the inn's front doors with Lovey in tow. "I want to go fishing," he yelled, casting a sullen look at his mom.

"Oh, Doctor. Martyn," she screeched while waving wildly and dragging a grinning Chadwick behind her.

Doctor. Martyn took a deep breath and rubbed a hand over the back of his head while Hawk and Tessa scowled at Chadwick.

Hawk groaned while mumbling to Tessa "I told you to hurry. Knew he was gonna try to butt in."

Doctor. Martyn tried to hide a grin. "Hawk, that's not nice," he said, then looked at Mrs. Davenport. "We have room for him, but he isn't dressed for the occasion, nor does he have a rod."

Mrs. Davenport waved a hand frantically as she pulled Chadwick back toward the front doors. "Give me ten minutes," she yelled. "Just ten!"

"How is she running like that in those stiletto pumps and why does it always look as if she's dragging the child along?" Willow asked.

"The better question would be, why she act like a mad woman when it comes to that boy?" Ms. Nita said as she came around the corner, drying a plate. She shook her head. "She done already spoiled him rotten and she ain't even had him a year."

"Why does it seem Hawk and Tessa only tolerate Chadwick?" I asked.

Ms. Nita said, "Last year that boy used'ta pick at Tessa something fierce. Hawk had to put him on his backside about it."

"What?" Willow asked in disbelief.

Ms. Nita nodded. "Socked him good right outside Jameson Bakery Hawk did."

She watched the door for a few more seconds, then went back to the kitchen. Willow and I confirmed our date for later, and a few minutes later, went our separate ways.

By noon, the team and I had searched high and low for any signs of the other man who had been looking for Willow. We found no tracks out near Ms. Sara's place or Mr. Whitman's.

"It did rain recently. Whatever tracks could have been out here are long gone now," Sage said from her mounted stallion.

She was dressed in tight jeans and a plaid, button-down shirt. Her hair was pulled back into a ponytail, and she wore brown cowgirl boots on her feet. She sat astride the horse as if she had been born a cowgirl. Sure, Willow had told me they looked nothing alike, but there were some striking similarities. In the right lighting, Sage could be mistaken for Willow. She was even the exact same size as her twin sister.

"Has the other man said anything?" I asked the sheriff.

He shook his head. "Naw. Even after Doctor Martyn patched him up, the urchin refused to utter a single word."

"Not even to ask for an attorney or a phone call?" I asked.

"Not even that. The clown just stares at the wall all day."

"When I got in last night, I reached out to a friend in the FBI in the Chicago area," Trent said. "Gave him the man's name Pops locked up last night. Tobias Pine is wanted in several states including Alaska. Armed robbery, assault with a deadly weapon, felony assault, arson, and a whole slew of others. According to what Agent Singleton told me, Tobias normally hangs with a man who goes by the name Jessie Dalton. He, too, has a rap sheet about three miles long and is just as dangerous. I also asked Agent Singleton to see if any of his informants on the street to see if they had heard anything."

"Any luck?" I asked.

"Seems that my little sister ruffled some feathers with the way she went after the cops and other case workers behind her clients. According to one of his informants, they know the two men who have been asking about Willow. They're bounty hunters."

"Bounty hunters," Sage quipped. "What, are we in 1865 or something? Bounty hunters?" she repeated, a frown marring her beautiful face.

Trent nodded. "Yeah. Apparently, Willow has a bounty on her head and they're the men who got the job. They're dangerous and have been known to take out anyone who gets in their way."

Silence settled over the group. My mind turned a mile a minute. A bounty on Willow's head? Anger coiled in my gut, but also something I wasn't familiar with took a stronghold there as well—fear.

"I'm going to trek ahead and see if I can find a firepit or any signs of a campsite. The rain may have washed away footprints, but I think I can still tell where vegetation has been agitated or cleared out," she said.

"If you run into any trouble, whistle," Trent told her.

"Or … I can just shoot." She tapped the Desert Eagle on her hip.

"Sage," Sheriff Tucker called out, "these are dangerous men. I'm well aware ya can handle ya'self, but—"

"Yes, I know, Daddy. I'll whistle if I run into trouble," she said, trudging her horse ahead.

"Have you told Willow the truth yet?" Trent asked as soon as his sister was out of earshot.

I shook my head. "Not yet. My plan is to tell her this evening."

The sheriff studied me a long time but remained quiet. It was the same thing he did last night after I revealed my truth to them.

"Better late than never. If you're going to be courting my sister, at least we know your intentions are honorable," Trent said just as a loud whistle rent the air.

Whatever else we were about to say was forgotten. We galloped toward Sage.

"Found something," she yelled as we rode up.

She was standing near the mouth of what appeared to be a small cave. "Someone has been hunkering down in there based on the tracks, cold fire pit, and leftover cans from the food they've eaten. Come take a look." She nodded toward the cave.

We dismounted, then walked in behind her. She had been right. There was a cold fire pit in the middle of the small space. Empty tuna cans, bean cans, and other types of canned food were strewn about. Plastic water bottles that had been emptied sat against the back wall. On either side of the cave, we saw an area that looked as if someone had been sleeping.

"They didn't even bother to clean up," Trent spat in disgust.

"Ain't nobody been in here for at least two, three days," Sheriff Tucker said.

"Think the other one was scared to come back after his buddy got hemmed up?" I asked.

"More than likely, and look at this," she said, moving back outside.

We came out to see her pointing to a trail of broken leaves, grass, and branches.

"Looks like they made a trail here. This isn't a game trail as there is no immediate water source in the area. Those leaves and grass are also not compressed enough for prolonged use. I suggest we follow this trail and see where it leads."

Sheriff Tucker nodded. "Tie the horses and let's go on foot.".

We followed that trail for an hour. Besides evidence that someone had walked it, there was no evidence of anything else. At least that was what I thought until we came upon a small hill that overlooked where Sage pointed south. "Look there.".

"This one of the Fields' old property," Sheriff Tucker said. "How in hell would they know to find this place?"

Trent frowned. "Thought no one has been out here in years."

I looked around at the grass that hadn't been cut recently … the overgrown vegetation and vines that had overtaken one side of the house. Where a big garden had once been showed it had been taken over by grass and weeds, but I could still see the sticks leaning where beans and other vined vegetables had been planted. The big, manor-style house looked as if it hadn't been live in for decades.

My gut twisted in knots, and I felt the burden of shame my family bore for years settle in my bones. My eyes narrowed as I felt as if I could see people actually walking around …

"Tire tracks leading to the old barn," Sage said. "Bet any kind of money, their car is parked there."

"Yeah … but again, how would out of towners know to look there for that house?" the sheriff asked.

"Thought all of you elders told us that this place was hidden specifically because of who the Fields were and what they had hidden under their home," Trent said.

"No way someone who didn't grow up here would know 'bout that there place," he told his son. "Unless …"

The sheriff's voice trailed off for so long, I had to look over at him to see if something had happened, only to find him and Trent looking at me, with Sage glancing between the three of us.

Chapter 15: Willow

"Ooo, I like this color, Miss Willowshine!"

I smiled down at the attentive, quiescent girl by my side.

Tessa and I were standing under a large, airy tarp partition connected to the side of the children's center. A susurrous breeze from the fan and outside air kept us all comfortable with the work we were doing—clearing away strewn bricks in the grass lot and picking out paint to begin the massive mural stenciled on the side of the brick wall of the center. Someone nearby played "Bustin' Loose" while water bottles were being handed out by volunteers to everyone entering the partition.

"This color is called haint blue," I explained with a gentle smile. "It's a precious color for the ancestors here in Sojourner Falls. You can spot a little of the color on the town hall building. You can see it near Freemans Gourd, the water mill, and falls. It's also near the grove and on the welcome sign to the town. When me and my sister were your age, and my brother was a little older, we'd go to the welcome sign and follow the street path out, finding tiny, blue-painted, polished stones lining the roadway side."

Every now and then, I could see a cowboy hat wearing, town deputy walk by checking on us, this one was a woman. The hat made me miss Kamal. We hadn't talked yet, though he had sent me an invitation for dinner tonight. The random walk through by various town deputies also made me aware that Daddy was making sure we all were protected, mainly me.

"Why was the color important?" Tessa asked.

"It kind of looks like the water in Jamaica, Tessa," Hawk chimed, looking down into the paint can. "Remember when I told you Uncle Vin took me and Auntie Kenya there?"

"Looks like the sky, too," Chadwick said by my side. He picked up a brick, then looked my way.

"Hey, we should paint the bricks and make a path, too," Tessa suggested.

My heart swelled at her suggestion. It was something I was working my way to suggesting in explaining the history behind the color, but the bright little minds around me were steps ahead of me. Behind me, old friends from my high school days worked on my stenciled wall mural, following the color plans I had laid out. They had their own children helping other town children from the town to paint. All the kids eventually formed a crowd around me listening.

Earlier, after enjoying herself with fishing with her best friend, Hawk, and her friend-enemy and arch nemesis, Chadwick, the three amigos showed up at the center smelling like fresh cut grass and fish. We practiced some of the dance routines for the parade. I listened to Hawk and Chadwick fuss over what instrument they were going to try to play with the band, which just ended up being drums, as they watched a video of my brother instructing the drum movements for the song and additional musical 'punches' he comprised for the younger kids that would link with the adult dance line and bands.

Tessa and I worked with some of the Jameson and Legend kids, including a few of Chief Pathwalker's grandchildren and other children. We practiced the drum major and majorette routines my sister and brother put together. Tessa's love for dance made her shine bright like a star, along with one of the Pathwalker girls, and Jameson boys. We had a solid kid dance line group here and it made me proud. With how fast the kids picked up the routines, I knew that in a few days here, Trent could choose his duo heads for the kid drum majors.

In the flurry of all the busyness and parade work coming along, I decided then and there to have them all help me outside to air out a bit. I adored their cuteness and closeness, but the active kids that they were demanded something else for them to do.

"Everyone grab a brick and paint it with the haint blue. When it dries enough, I want you all to write your name in white or your favorite color, then place it on the edge of grass of this lot. We're going to make this area our art garden with flowers, sitting, and everything."

Children roared in joy and asked if they could add decorations to the bricks, which I said was a wonderful addition.

"To answer Tessa-Belle's question," I began, waving a hand to gather the children around as they picked their red bricks, "this color protects us and hides us, so the elders told us as kids."

With my thick hair high on my head in a plump, braided knot, I stood in my old paint-splattered and scuffed black military boots and thigh-shredded, blue overall jeans. Under it was a simple white tank. I was sure my face had traces of paint on it because my hands were covered in various vibrant colors due to my work. I loved my art.

The wall behind me showed the faces of our ancestors' past, and elders present. The names of all the lost ones and elders. There was a graffiti-style splash of haint blue and railroad, representing the river followed by our ancestors and First Nation people who helped lead us to the area. A gallant horse framed by the town's flag, standing on its high legs in grandeur, was starting to take shape on the colorful wall representing the farmers and SoJo riders. Flowers, musical notes, children, food, buildings, the gourd, the grove, and other town landmarks were in the mural as well.

I had worked hard at night and throughout the days of my time back in town on the mural and it was shaping into a powerful, beautiful piece. "Haint blue is a color of protection for us, and so much more. This color is no normal pale teal or sea-green because of the way the blue mixes into it."

Walking around each child, I watched them gather and sit to paint. Hawk and Tessa swapped bricks back and forth, showing the other how they were designing it, while Chadwick happily made swirls of the color.

"Our town has a deep Gullah, Geechee connection." As I showed the children some design swirls to use, I looked up to see Cari walking toward me with a barrel of plants, chairs, and other items. With her was my cousin, Monae, who handed chairs to the few men standing around them. Chuckling, I waited for them to get closer so that I could hug them tight.

After kissing each one's cheek, I stepped back, "It's great that you both are here!"

"Whew, with all the things Grace threw my way, and my mama, I swear I wasn't sure that we were going to make it in time," Cari explained. "You know every time my mother gets near my car, we end up at someone's store or big chain hardware store. Luckily, Ms. Gladys and Ms. Nita distracted Mama. Ms. Gladys's daughter, Topaz, has returned! She got the group invite and texts while in Bali working. She helped me with the plants and flowers you asked for from Mrs. Gladys."

In her hands, Monae held a blossoming, tall plant with leaves and sheafs of violet flowers. "Cousin! I think we came right on time for your story about haint blue."

"I think you both did as well," I replied in excitement.

My favorite cousin was here! Which meant my storage pod was probably here. I could settle down now.

"I love what I'm seeing with the mural. I always loved your art. It's like you capture the sempiternal power of the spirit," Monae shared in awe while studying the artwork, then turned my way holding out the potted plant. "Here you go."

Taking it, I nodded. I was happy that she was here for the parade. I took a seat in front of the kids and positioned the plant in front of me. "We'll all talk in a minute here. The hot links and hot dogs you shipped are here. Mr. Vincent has the majority, and we have a few here for the kids. Go eat."

Both ladies gave me a knowing smile as I went to explain the history of haint blue. "Cotton, corn, and rice are all around Sojourner, but this plant is something that you can only find in the freeman fields."

"Ooo, what is it?" one of the children asked.

"Indigo," I explained, setting the plant down in front of us. "Haint blue was made from it and used as a dye. Our ancestors would paint the color on the ceilings of their porches, or homes. Others would paint it on their shutters, or on stones and bricks like you all are doing."

"Why?" Chadwick asked.

"It was a tradition of ours, thought to keep us protected from negative forces and to scare away ghosts, or what they called haints …"

"Ghosts! Keep that away from me and give me the paint," Chadwick yelled.

Hawk let out a laugh while Tessa hid a smile behind her hand.

"Chad, it'll be okay, sir, I promise you. Sometimes it's those of us who have a deep connection to the spirits, who like to protect the most. But that's another story. Anyway, you all were right about it looking like the sky or the sea. The ghost or evils would think they were near water, and they couldn't cross into an ancestors' homes."

"Really? We need some back in Detroit," Tessa exclaimed.

"Uh huh," Hawk said. "I remember a lot of kids in our group used to have nightmares at the group homes."

Tessa looked up at me and softy added, "But it got better when Mr. Vin and Ms. Kenya created the program."

There was a tone in her voice, one that worried me, and one that made me want to pull her closer to me.

"Yeah, got even better when we came to Sojourner Falls," Chadwick shared, flipping his now blue brick in his hand. I noticed that he had a talent for art because there were white lines and swirls on it that reminded me of Loa veve. Where that little boy knew how to draw that astonished me.

I took a look at Tessa's brick; her name was painted in beautiful pink script, with a brown ballerina dancing on a cloud. "Oh, Tessa-Belle, this is beautiful. I love the bricks you all painted. I see we have artists in the mix. Hawk, I love the leaves and tribal designs you made."

Hawk looked up at me with a big smile, then went back to paint as he talked to his brick. "Ms.

Denise used to take us to the art galleries up in Detroit and taught us some painting, too."

"Well, I hope she comes back to town to visit. It would be great to talk to her and show her your artwork," I said. I remembered that Ms. Denise was the Kwanza Kids Detroit chapter chaperone. I made a quick note to double check with her to see if she'd be bringing the rest of those kids down for the parade.

"So, once you all are done and eat some lunch, I want you to place those brick on the grass edge of the lot. The rest of adults will fill in the empty spots, until you all want to paint and design more bricks. Miss Monae, my cousin, will watch over you and bring you my way when you're done. Right, cousin?"

"I sure will! I'm gonna share how we celebrate Juneteenth up in the Lou and tell them how I drank a whole pitcher of strawberry lemonade at their age during our parade and ended up being chased by a horse around my father's caddy driving in the parade, all because I had to pee."

More exclamations of excitement went up in the area by the kids while I laughed and stood up to take the indigo plant outside of the partition where the rest of the plants were.

"Miss Willowshine?"

I stopped my exit to see Tessa by me. "Hi, sweeting. What's going on?"

"Can I come with you?" she asked, staring up at me with big, brown eyes. "We ate while fishing."

"Good, I was wondering, and you sure can. What about Hawk and Chadwick?" I held out my hand. Willow took it, and we stepped out of the partition.

"They wanted to add some pictures to the wall," Tessa explained. "They're going to come after they finish."

My heart swelled for this little sweetheart. She reminded me of so many things I've missed out on in my thirty-five years of life. One of them was experiencing pregnancy and having children of my own. I had delayed having kids, not because of my career aspirations, but because Hollis wasn't ready. Plus, a quiet part of me never felt he would be the right man to have children with, especially when at thirty-three I was told that I may need to freeze my eggs due to a health issue related to polycystic ovarian syndrome.

Hollis wouldn't help me pay for the procedure, I didn't want to ask my grandparents or father for the money, and the savings that I was going to use was pushed to the back of my head when work took over. I never had my eggs frozen. I never had children even when my fertility doctor happily let me know a year ago that I would be able to, albeit with fertility monitoring. But I knew with my work in child protection and forensic sociology, that I would adopt a child at the blink of an eye.

Glancing down at the little girl who held my hand and smiled like my mother, my heart hummed. My spirit said, my daughter. So, with that, I began another plan—I needed a house instead of a small apartment here in SoJo. And even though Kamal and I were building something, the conversation about children would take some time. However, me being an adoptive parent could happen as soon as I talked with Tessa and her social worker about it.

"What are you going to do with it?" Ahead of us was Cari. She sat on a lush spot of grass with plants around her, planting and turning soil. Framing her were a few of the children's blue-painted bricks lined up in rows drying in the sun.

"I'm going to talk to Miss Cari about a special project and I think you'd be a wonderful help in that."

"Great! I love helping you, Miss Willowshine," Tessa said, walking ahead of me with her hands behind her back and studying my face. "I like hanging with you."

"I like that, too, and love your help, Tessa-Belle. I think we make a great team!"

With that Tessa turned on her heel, then ran up to Cari to hug her and tell her that we were there to help.

"Hey, lady," I said, hugging Cari once I reached her. I sat down.

"Whew, I love how busy we all are with this, I'm tired." Cari laughed, holding her gloved hand out for the plant.

She took it and checked it. She had a gift with plants. If Mrs. Gladys wasn't already our town botanist and owner of the plant boutique, I was sure Cari would have found a way to take it over and combine it with the apothecary. Cari's love for agriculture always made her an advocate in the care of the town's land and the earth. I knew talking to her about my idea for the grove was the smartest choice.

"So, tell me about this idea you have for my Ancestor Grove project?" Cari asked in interest. "What do you need me for, or this plant of indigo?"

Tessa sat by my side watching us in curiosity. I laid a hand on the top of her head, then explained, "I'd love for it to extend to our cemetery. I want to lay down these painted bricks to mark the start of the cemetery with new gates and new headstones. And … I want to plant this indigo at my mother's grave, along with some hibiscus, lilies, your trees, and fruit trees included. I wanted weather protected pictures of our lost loved ones and town elders at the graves with hanging lamps and safe candles that won't burn the place down. I'd like this to be a new tradition added to yours for Ancestor's Grove. What do you think?"

"Hmm …" Cari—who sat in jeans and a fitted T-shirt that said 'SoJo Preservation Committee'—clasped her chin, then looked at Tessa. "What do you think, Ms. Tessa?"

"Can we kids plant some of the flowers and dance?"

My heart swelled again, and tears lined my eyes. "I love that suggestion," I whispered.

Cari glanced at me with caring, knowing eyes, and gently said, "I think that was an excellent idea as well, and I love us coming up with new traditions for the next generation. So of course we can add that to the plan, Willie."

My eyes rolled at the endearing nickname that only she was allowed to say. "Charity …"

Cari laughed and winked.

"Willie?" Tessa asked.

I groaned at her sharp ears. "It's a childhood nickname Charity gave me when I used to babysit her. Only she is allowed to call me that."

"Uh, huh," Cari muttered. "And Trent. Anyway, let's quickly outline this because Monae is supposed to handle talking with Javon Henderson about the stage set up for the music acts and the permit for it. I had to make sure that she didn't slip some Nelly and other STL rapper's segments for the DJ because the elders would lose their minds, flip some tables, and shut the whole thing down."

Tessa let out a cute laugh, and we all joined her. In her hands where new painted bricks that she laid out in the design I had etched with a stick in the ground. While she did that, Hawk and Chadwick showed up to help her while Cari and I talked.

"Mo is a trip. I know she loves to sing, so she'll be a great additional music advisor with that," I said, still laughing.

"Great, because I didn't know what to do if she was serious. Luckily, she said that she'd get some jazz and blues music to be added along with some soul and funk that mixed in Georgia, STL, and Chicago groove."

"I love it. We're almost done," I said, watching Tessa fuss with Hawk and Chad about where to lay more of the bricks. As she directed, more kids their age showed up to add to the bricks.

"And I can't believe that you were able to take over for Grace and get everything flowing. She needed the help and breather," Cari said, then looked at me. "And you … you and Doctor Brookhaven? How is that flowing?"

Rolling my eyes, I laughed. "I want to plant this indigo plant here where Tessa made the circle with the bricks."

"Uh, huh … answer my question, or when Sage shows up, I'll have her and Monae tag team you!"

Cari made me remember how much I wanted to shake her at times for her pockets of nosiness.

"It's fine." I flipped my hand in the air. "The man is fine, tall, delicious, smells good with lush, shoulder-length locs that I can't keep my hands out of. He has a smile that should be labeled illegal because it's bright and sexy. When he stands near me, the alluring heat of his body pulls me in and feels like home. He's also a freakin' doctor. I just …"

"SoJo hits again! You're in love like you Tuckers always end up in at first sight … well, except Trent. Oh! I love it." Cari giggled.

"Whatever … you're caught up." Standing, I wrapped my arms around myself. I watched Tessa, Hawk, and Chadwick carefully turn the earth to mix in nutrients for the indigo plant that was in a bucket near Cari, then plant the precious plant, along with a cotton plant. Once they were finished, they placed three bricks near the circle with their names.

"Kamal and I are just learning each other, and we're busy with the parade plans and his work. Besides, I'm sure I'm bringing too much drama his way, and I think he's holding back from us for some reason I'm not sure about. I also have no house, so I need to get that going."

"Hmm … sounds like excuses and denial," Cari said in care while watching the kids now practice their drumline dances. "But I understand that. Personally, I went through similar emotions with Hunter about our sunshine, Hawk."

"That surprise rocked me back when I found out. He is a little teddy bear spirit and so wise! He's definitely a wonderful mixture of you and Hunter," I said, standing near my best friend.

"I agree … it took the magic of this town, the elders, and Hawk's special wish to shake us all up and bring us together. I know the town will do that for you, too. It's definite. You deserve loyal, healthy love."

A breeze wrapped around us as the sun faded and the town lights began to turn on in the warm fading horizon.

"Thank you."

Suddenly, Hawk rushed us.

"Mama? Can Tessa … and I guess Chadwick come have dinner with us? I told her you were making mac n cheese, and a yucky seafood and oyster mac n cheese. Chad didn't believe me and wanted to see."

Cari laughed as she hugged her child and kissed the top of Hawk's head. She looked my way with a wink. "Uncle Vin is testing a Juneteenth recipe. Us Black folk used to eat oysters during the celebration with lamb. I'm making a roasted lamb, and ham for the kids."

"That sounds so good. Daddy makes a mean baked oyster," I said, feeling Tessa's hand in my own.

When I looked down at her I could see she was conflicted because we were supposed to have dinner. So, following suit because it felt natural to my heart, I kissed the top of her head and said, "Enjoy dinner with your best friends. We can have lunch or breakfast at the inn any time. I'm not going anywhere, and I hope to keep you around as long as you like."

"You mean it? It's okay? And you do?" Tessa seemed to be floating in enthusiasm.

I adored it. "I sure do."

"Will you be okay?" she quickly added. "You should eat. We worked a lot here."

Laughing, I felt my mother's spirit in her words as I hugged her. "I sure will be fine, Tessa-Belle. Besides, I'll ask my friend to have dinner with me."

"Doctor Brookhaven?" Tessa asked, then made a face. "You gonna kiss him again?"

My eyes crossed as I choked. Laughter spilled from Cari. All the kids had disgusted expressions on their faces.

"I plan to have dinner, that is all, I promise." I crossed my heart over my chest and hid my crossed fingers behind my back.

Satisfied with that promise, we all packed up. I looked at the indigo plant that had a blue brick painted with my mother and father's name in gold by it. I then made my way to the inn to clean up and change for dinner. When I reached Kamal's room, I wore my thick hair in curls down my back, an off-the-shoulder, curve fitting, light pink dress that stopped at the top of my ankles and made the top of my bosoms plush. Light pink, red bottoms were on feet, and I held my purse in my hand.

I hoped Kamal could have dinner. I was ready to tell him about my desire to adopt Tessa, finding a house since my things were in town now, and share with him how much I deeply cared for him. I also wanted to take him to my mother's grave to plant my other indigo plant. Either way, I was excited and ready to see my Doctor Knight in Shining Armor, so I knocked and waited in hope.

Chapter 16: Kamal

"Willow," I called from the top of the stairs.

I saw her when she came from her room. She was stunning. For a few seconds, I had to stand in awe of her beauty and her body. I knew the in thing these days was to be attracted to bodies made in factories, but as a Southern gentleman, born and bred, I loved every inch of her thickness. The dress she had on accentuated every winding curve she owned.

When she saw me, she took a sharp inhale as if her breath had caught.

"I hope that sharp intake of breath means you approve of my attire for this evening?" I said as I removed my Stetson.

"I have never seen a man dressed in all black who makes it look as good as you," she replied as she sauntered over to me.

I quirked a brow with a smile. "It's just a black button-down with black jeans, black cowboy boots, and a black blazer." I chuckled.

"Yes, but you make it look as if you're an Instagram model or getting ready for a spread in *GQ* on Black cowboys."

I eased one arm around her waist when she got close enough for me to reach out and touch. With the other hand, I cupped her chin to tilt her head. I studied her eyes, looking for acceptance. Something I knew I could never fully get until I told her the truth. I kissed her. Brought my lips to hers and savored the energy that passed between us. When she moaned sexily and it landed in my gut, then traveled south, I knew I had to get her to dinner, or we would never make it.

"So … let me get you to dinner or we won't be going anywhere," I said once I pulled away from the kiss.

She gazed up at me with dreamy eyes, kiss-swollen lips, and desire riding the aura around her. "Do we have to?" she asked.

We laughed in unison.

It was the same thing she had asked the first time we kissed out near the mounds. Taking her hand, I escorted her down the stairs.

"You two have a good time, ya hear?" Ms. Nita said as smiled and waved at us.

"You brang her back the way ya taking her," Mr. Clark added.

I nodded, trying to ignore Willow hiding a grin. "Yes, sir."

"Ya got'cha pistol, son?" Mr. Walt asked.

"I do."

"Then y'all get on. Take care of each other."

Once outside, I helped her into my truck before walking around to the driver's side to get in.

"Where're we going?" she asked. "I assumed we would be dining at the inn."

I laid my Stetson on her thighs, cranked my truck, and pulled out. "I called in a few favors. Wanted to take you some place private so we could enjoy the moment and the night."

I glanced at her to see she was smiling. On the drive to Hunter's folks' old cabin, she and I talked about different things. She asked me about my childhood. I didn't mind answering certain things, but other topics were still a sore spot.

"I'm going to be honest here, some things about my childhood are pretty sensitive. My aunt and I aren't really on speaking terms … kind of," I said.

"May I ask why?"

I took a deep breath before answering. "To make a long story short, I feel as if she didn't do enough to introduce me to who I really am."

"What do you mean?" she asked in a tone that told me she was confused. Her voice had hitched, and from my peripheral I saw her head tilt and brows furrow.

"There are things she left out … about our family." Seeing the cabin come into view, I smiled. "Look ahead, love."

Willow looked out the windshield and gasped.

"You like it?" I asked.

"I love it …"

I gave a silent thank you to Sage. I asked her, at the last minute, to put fairy lights around the cabin, set up the table and chairs, and set the table. I was running late getting to the Martyns to pick up the food I asked Grace to cook, and knew if I didn't ask for help, the date would be half-assed.

I pulled into the cobbled driveway. The yard was manicured, and a cobblestone walkway had been constructed. On the right side of the yard, underneath a big oak tree, sat a round table with two chairs. A golden tablecloth adorned the table along with a dinner set. Globe-like lanterns hung on a few of the branches on tree.

I hopped out the trucked, grabbed something from the back, then rounded to open her door.

"Oh gosh … Kamal," she said when saw the bouquet of tulips in my hand.

"I didn't know which color to pick … so I got one of every color they had," I said.

"It's the perfect bouquet." She sniffed the flowers, then took my hand.

After helping her down, I extended my elbow. She slid her arm through mine as I led her down the stone walkway. Once at the table, I pulled her chair out, then helped her to sit.

"Let me know if you get cold." I kissed her shoulder. "I've got a shawl for you."

"Okay …"

"That tray next to you is for you to place your flowers."

Once at my seat, I pulled my blazer off, then placed it on the back of my chair.

"You've thought of everything," she said with a warm smile.

I gave a nonchalant shrug. "I tried to at least."

As soon as I took my seat, the front door to the cabin opened and out came Sage and Cari. Sage, dressed as if she were a waitress, had a tray of food perched on the palm of her hand. Cari carried an ice pail with a bottle of the best chilled Riesling.

Willow quirked a brow at her twin and laughed. Then she peeked around at Cari. "Okay, how did you pull this off?" she asked. "I was with Cari earlier and she didn't hint around to a thing!"

I grinned. "My Southern charm …"

"Really?"

I nodded as Sage placed food on the table. Fresh, wild trout with a lemon-garlic butter sauce was paired with buttery, stone-ground grits from the LaRue Company. Once Cari and Willow were done serving, they kissed either side of Willow's cheeks then disappeared back inside of the cabin. I knew there was still a man on the prowl, and while I wanted to show Willow a good time, I was no fool.

Several men that her father deputized were on horse, surrounding the wooded area.

I unwrapped the utensils, took the spoon, scooped a bit of the sugar Sage had set out with the condiments, and then sprinkled some on Willow's grits.

"Did Sage tell you I like sugar in my grits?" she asked on a laugh.

"Nope. Did my own research." I winked. "Take a sip of your Riesling and tell me if it's to your liking."

"Okay, come on, Kamal. You know my favorite wine, too? What kind of research did you do?" she asked as she picked up the wine flute.

I chuckled.

She took a slow sip, then gazed at me with wonderment. "Where on earth did you get this?"

"As a negotiant via auction."

Her brows arched in curiosity.

"I happen to love a good wine. In my spare time, I participate in wine auctions. The last one I went to was at the High Museum Atlanta Wine Auction. This bottle is an Egon Müller Scharzhofberger Riesling Trockenbeerenauslese."

"Not to be ill-mannered or nosy, but how much does something like this cost?" she asked, then took another sip.

I told her. She darn near choked on her drink. I went to stand but she held up a hand to stop me. After setting the flute down, she picked up the white cloth napkin and tapped it against her lips.

She caught her breath, then said, "Excuse me? You paid what? For one bottle of Riesling?"

I nodded. "It's from the Mosel region, one of most important to Germany's wine reputation. Get this, I also got it from a Black-German wine sommelier as well."

"Wow, Kamal … and you did all this for me?"

I nodded.

"Why?"

"Because I like you. I'm pretty sure I want to love you, too."

I smiled when she blushed and averted her eyes before turning her attention back to me.

"We just met a few weeks ago. How could you possibly know that?" she asked.

"I may not fall in love at first sight, but I know what I feel. I know how you make me feel. I want to take whatever this is we're doing—"

"Courting," she cut in. "You're courting me like the men of old in those novels you mentioned a while back."

I smiled. "Okay. I'm courting you, and I'd like to keep courting you. I know you just ended something with that jackass you were with, but I want to get to know you in ways that will take generations to unravel. I want to know what you like and what you don't like. I want to know what makes you laugh, what makes you cry. I want to learn more about your favorite foods and the things you like to drink. I want to go shopping and bring back different paints and canvases and brushes, do the type of things that make you so excited that you squeal and jump and down. I want to watch you carry life we created within your womb if you so desire that as I do.

"I want your father and brother to know that you're as safe with me as you are with them. I want your sister to be able to rest easy knowing her twin is being loved healthily and properly." I took her hand and intertwined our fingers. "I want to be able to tell when something is wrong with you with just one look. Your mood swings, your moon-cycle, your quirks and idiosyncrasies … I want to learn them all. So that, as a man, as *your* man, I can pour love into you in ways that make this life a little easier to live."

She picked up the napkin with her free hand, then dabbed at her eyes. She got ready to speak, but I held a hand up.

"Before you respond, I need to be honest with you about a few things first."

"You're not about to tell me you're an axe murderer, are you?"

I knew she was joking, but I needed to be serious. "I don't know any other way to say this than to come right out and … say it. My family has history here."

She placed the napkin down. "Here, as in—"

"*Here*, as in Sojourner Falls."

Her brows furrowed. "How so?"

"Felisa Fields is my … aunt," I said.

Willow's eyes widened. "What?"

"Yes. When her brother died, the state allowed her to have custody of me after her stint in a mental facility. Losing him was too much for her on top of everything else our family endured. I was in foster care for a short time after his death. My aunt flew back from London for a few months. She visited me three times a week and two weekends out of the month, or so I was told. I don't remember much from that time. I recall being told her brother was my father and that she didn't really know my mother."

I didn't know what I expected, but when Willow's eyes softened as she squeezed my hand, I felt hope that she wouldn't walk away from me.

"I'm sorry about your parents," she said. "That had to be tough growing up."

I nodded. "It was, but my aunt is a good woman. She took great care of me. I went to the best schools, never wanted for anything. Even when she had to do without, she made sure I didn't.

At one time, she had three jobs and still managed to help me with homework, a hot meal was always on the table, and how she managed to make sure I always had the best clothes and shoes is beyond me."

"I imagine being here must be tough for you, especially knowing what happened with your family …"

"It has been tough since I didn't have anyone to vent or just talk to about it. I was actually nervous to even tell you."

"Why?" she asked.

"Because I didn't know what your reaction would be. I didn't know if you would feel as if I was trying to do something underhanded and sneaky."

She chuckled. "Why on earth would I think that?"

"I don't know, but I believe your father and brother may have thought so earlier."

"Wait. They know?"

"Yes, I told them the night all the men had that meeting in town hall."

"And what did they say to make you think that they thought you're up to something?"

I told her about what had happened when we all did the scouting and patrol earlier.

"They thought maybe I, or my aunt, could have had something to do with the men being in town and knowing where my family's old home was. But it was fleeting. Your father and brother are smart men, but they are cautious right now is all."

Willow studied me for a long time. She stood, then walked around to stand by my side. I wrapped an arm around her waist. When she cupped my face in both her hands and brought her lips to mine, all was right in my world. I knew by the way her tongue slowly searched for mine that she would give me a chance to love her openly and freely.

She gazed down at me, searching my eyes for any signs of deception or lies I suppose … "Thank you for opening up and being honest with me before we take things further. That means the world to me. And just so you know, I plan to let you love and get to know me in all the ways you wish. I also plan to pour that same love, care, and affection right back into you." She kissed me again, ran a hand through my locs, and then went back to her seat.

"There is more I need to tell you …"

She nodded once. "Okay, but let's eat before all this good food gets cold."

As we shared dinner, I opened up more to her about family.

"I meant to ask you," she said after swallowing a forkful of grits, "why aren't you and your aunt on speaking terms?"

"Oh … That." I took a deep inhale. "Remember when I told you she hadn't been completely honest with me?"

Willow nodded.

"Right before I accepted the job and moved here, she told me the full truth of my parentage. She's not really my aunt … she's my mom. And, I hate to even admit this part, but Stacy Davenport is my father."

Willow let out an expletive that caused me to quirk a brow.

She slapped a hand over her mouth, then removed it slowly. "I'm so sorry. Please excuse me." She cleared her throat. "Allow me to rephrase … I know you're freaking lying!"

Laughing, I shook my head. "I wish I were."

"How did *you* … come from a vile, loathsome, pathetic little man like that?"

She was so serious, the incredulous expression on her face so perturbed, that all I could do was throw my head back and laugh heartily. I laughed so long and hard that she started laughing, too. It was in that moment, as I watched her cackle at a joke that she and I hadn't even shared but somehow knew the punchline to, that I knew she was the one.

Chapter 17: Willow

Black-owned heritage, organic, locally sourced and affordable with an abundance of love was the motto of the establishment I currently sat in. Jamerson Bakery and Diner, the epicenter of the town's culinary history, was teetering in its own energetic, yet comforting vellichor. The place was packed. Old, young, and surrounding area Sojourner townies were in the house! The place was abuzz with the talk of the upcoming parade. And now that it was June 8th, people were excited about the prospect of their businesses and the town flourishing.

Last night's date was on my mind and made me smile over all the surprises that came with it. Doctor Kamal Brookhaven was technically a Fields-Davenport. My Doctor Knight in Shining Armor was the freaking shady and former Mayor Stacy Davenport's *son!* My hands still shook from that reality as I lifted a cup of comforting matcha latte to my lips. I missed his kisses, his warmth, and the feel of him holding me.

But again, Stacy Davenport was his *father!*

Never in my life did I ever think that I would be associating myself with anything or anyone Davenport. In high school, it was one of the things us kids were happy to not have to deal with, any extra Davenports. Especially at that time when slimy Stacy was vying to be the high school principal and getting on everyone's nerves. No one was sure where Stacy's aspirations for being mayor came from, but us kids were just relieved we didn't have to deal with his glossy goat stare of authority. Instead, we gained an amazing new principal, Deputy Javon Henderson's mother who moved here with his father, from St. Louis, Missouri after answering an advertisement Elder Sara secretly sent out to an old department of education friend.

Sojourner Falls was indeed working its magic to correct wrongs, clear misunderstandings, foster renewal, and maintain its legacy. The ancestors were truly something special.

"Here you are, sis, and little Katherine Dunham." Tammy Jameson-Legend's sweet voice, along with a piping hot plate of food pulled me from my thoughts.

"Thank you, Ms. Tammy! And who is that?" Tessa asked in innocent curiosity.

"Well, Katherine Dunham was a well sought out, Black, classically trained dancer who opened her own school and had her own dance technique.

She worked with Alvin Ailey and other Black dancers and ballet dancers. I think Sage and Willow can tell you better than me."

"Oh! Will you tell me more, Miss Willowshine? I want to be the best ballet dancer, even better than Misty Copeland!"

A sweet love spread in my heart, and I nodded. "I sure can tell you more, especially about Raven Wilkinson, who was the first Black ballet dancer credited for dancing with a major classical ballet company. But I think my sister is better in that education. She took dance in college when she wasn't on leave for the Navy for her marine biology work or focused on her tech hobby."

"And you will be top tier prima ballerina, Tessa-Belle, better than Misty," I replied in joy because I believed and meant that. "Tammy, thank you again. Everything looks exquisite as usual."

"Don't eat too fast," Tammy said with a wink, then headed back to the kitchen.

Fresh butter from the Legend's Farm melted in shiny, fatty praise near savory cooked, thick-cut bacon, and plump sausage. Next to it were a few fried green tomatoes and fluffy, scrambled cheese eggs. Warm, bourbon-laced maple syrup and regular creole butter praline syrup from the Jameson's Farm sat in glass town crafted jars. The custardy vanilla and cinnamon crème brûlée fragrance of the French toast with buttery, fresh-whipped cream sat in front of me and my guest. The alluring scents made my stomach dance in tandem of the little happy child sitting across the table from me.

Throwback tunes from my youth mixed in with the clinking for utensils and plates, along with the busy murmurs of patrons and returning faces of old Sojourner Falls adults, families, and children who were now adults. Tessa and I threw down, eating our wonderful breakfast. Every now and then I'd catch Tessa watching how I'd use my utensils or drink. She'd then mimic me, which made my day.

"I've been thinkin' 'bout cha … *la, la,la!* 'Cus in my heart … *la, la, la!*"

I laughed at the little girl wearing white shorts, and a pink, crop T-shirt with an adorable My Little Pony ballerina wearing the same afro puffs that she wore. Tessa's coily hair with two beaded braids had pink glitter hair pins that I had brought her. Adorning her crown was an African wax print headband that was pink and white. It matched the watch she wore. She ate in peace while singing, making up her own words, and rocking to one of my favorite teenage songs back in the day.

"I like your song, Miss Willowshine," Tessa said with a big, syrupy smile and a fork in her little hand. "I might have to sing it to Hawk just so he can know the song since he likes to sing."

"I do, too. Me and my mother used to rock to it," I shared while chowing down on my food and glancing over the paperwork I requested from Tessa's social worker. A couple of days ago, I contacted the state about transferring my forensic social worker license. My plan was to move that along as quickly as possible so that I could be the Sojourner social worker liaison worker for Kwanza Kids' foster program. I'd be working with my father, Mr. Vincent, Ms. Kenya, and Ms. Denise who was over the Detroit section.

"I'll have to play it for you and Hawk later then."

"Oh, I'd like that! Thank you for taking me to see your old house, too. I really loved your mama's garden, and the house was so pretty," Tessa said.

Regret about losing the family house filled my heart again. Though it was with a better family, I still missed home. "I love and miss that beautiful, grand, old house. It was in our family for a long time and built by family's hands. Me and my siblings didn't think we'd come back for it. But it's being cared for by an amazing family, the Legends."

"Are you my mentor?" Tessa's warm eyes settled on me as if memorizing me.

As a social worker, I was familiar with that innocence, quiet question of worthiness, care, and desire for family.

"Hawk and Chadwick got mentors when they first came. Are you mine?" she repeated.

"Hmm …" Taking a moment to send off the information that was asked of me on my tablet, then texting Monae, Cari, Sage, and Grace, I closed it down and nodded. "I think that I am. We have fun hanging together, and you've helped me a lot with the parade and learning your parts. Would it be okay if I were your mentor?"

"Yes! That would be the best. Like, Hawk and Chadwick get on my nerves sometimes. Well, really Chadwick does. It's fun having someone like you to go around with." Tessa's big, brown eyes focused down on her play as her tiny voice softened. "Maybe … maybe, I'll be good enough to adopt? Like … like Chadwick and Hawk did. Well, Hawk found his birth parents because he made an awesome wish, but you know? Maybe I'll find a nice family because of you?"

I slid my hand across the table to take hers. I had made my promise to her in my heart a few days ago. All I could do was hope I got word back in time to officially start the adoption process.

"You just might, Tessa-Belle." I held Tessa's eyes and I felt the spirit of my mother again. "There's magic in this town that surprises everyone, including myself. You're full of magic, so the elders are looking out for you, too, just as I am."

"Thank you, Miss Willowshine," Tessa softly replied.

I held her little hands. "Hey, I made a promise to visit my mother today and I have a special project in mind for that. Monae is taking care of the center today, which leaves me time to do some final errands for the parade and look at town listings for an apartment or house. You want to go with me? Sage, Miss Cari, and Grace will be there."

"Uh huh! I want to go. I know my dance part already and you need a house, a big one like your old family one!"

"Great!" I reached into my purse to pay. "Let's get going before we both get the 'itis from eating this good food. I'll order a picnic basket for lunch, too."

We climbed out of the booth, and Tessa took my hand as we headed to the ordering counter.

"Now tell me why I need a big house, Ms. Tessa-Belle. Hmm?" I peered down at her as she looked up at me. "It's just me."

"I don't know." She shrugged, then smiled. "You miss your old home, so maybe you'll find one just like it or better! And … and maybe it'll be the right size for me and the kids to visit you?"

My mind went to the three-bedroom, loft apartment above the upstairs hostel apartments for future kids or families who may need it, connected to the children center and my art gallery and studio. The thought had flown from my mind. Daddy must have purposely built it so I could be close to work and to lure me home.

"You know what that sounds like?"

"What?" she asked in excitement.

"The children's center. There's a perfect place just for me right there."

"Ooo, yes! Live there. We'll always visit there." Tessa bobbed her head, then waved at Tammy while holding our lunch basket.

As she did so, she kept her back to me while dancing in a ray of sun. She then said in a matter-of-fact tone of divine wisdom, "Then maybe the big house you want with the garden will find you and you can live there with your friend."

Stunned, I stopped in my tracks to look at Tessa. We were outside by my father's truck he had lent me. She casually set the basket down to show me a twirl on her toes. "Look, Miss Willowshine!"

My eyes watered while I looked on in pride. "Very good, Tessa-Belle. Sage would also be proud of your form."

I told Tessa that magic was in the town, and I meant it. Especially, when I said magic was in her, too. Therefore, seeing her so carefree with the grace of my mother's spirit all around her shook me.

Whatever the plan this town had for me or for the little girl in front of me, I could only pray that I'd honor her rearing. That was all I could truly ask and pray for; outside of wanting Kamal.

While we climbed into the truck, in the distance near an empty lot and abandoned cottage house in the distance stood a hidden, watchful, unknown, dangerous figure.

"With the little bit of housing that we have in town, there's really only fixer uppers on this list, Willow," Grace said while walking by my side with her hand against her swollen belly in a breezy maxi dress and tennis shoes. "Blade has been working with Hunter on restoring more of the elders' homes that are alive, as well as reaching out to some of the former SoJo kids that work in housing development and a few of their trusted, old college friends to outline new buildings."

"Oh, wow! This is really happening, huh?" I said in amazement.

"Yes, it is. It honestly just kicked up because of you. When you reached out to me to talk to Blade about housing, it was like a rainfall descended on his office." Grace laughed, then paused in her slow walking to look around Ancestor's Grove and old, fading headstones.

Ahead of us was Tessa, Hawk, Chadwick, Cari, and Sage. Cari pushed a cart of flower bulbs, water, tools, and potted flowers ready to be planted. One was the indigo and black-eyed Susans. Both women were directing the children to headstones that were fading away. In the kids' hands were big, blank pieces of paper. I told them to take big crayons and shade over the paper to create headstone rubbings. It was my hope to pick up as much information from the old stones, then add plaques in front of the fading stones.

"Thanks to Sage redoing our town's website and adding all the savvy tech things and firewalls that we needed, more of the original SoJo kids were able to reach out, the ones that don't have elders here in town anymore. A lot of them were calling the old school, and Principal Henderson needed to route them to town hall just to get it in order."

"It's amazing how the elders' prayers kickstarted this regrowth. I know that it's been a long time coming, and is taking time, but the prospect of the growth is astonishing," I shared as we walked. "We'll need to covert more of the old district buildings … which wraps me around to the small housing listing. Daddy built an attached apartment loft on the top level of the center. I'm going to move in there since my Pod storage is already parked behind the building parking."

"Great idea!" Grace clapped her hands together, then hugged me, her adorable belly lightly pressing into me. "I so am excited that you're coming back! I wasn't sure that you would stick around with how good Sheriff Tucker was trying to get you to stay."

I laughed, then sighed. "Life shook me hard for a moment there, but I went with it. I had no choice to do anything but try something new, or Sankofa my life and return home. The winds of change dictated, and I couldn't fight against it."

My eyes focused on the little girl who stole my heart. She was moving away from one of the graves, carefully laying flowers around with a crayon-rubbed, grave-marked paper in her hand. "Besides, my work as a forensic social worker insists that I advocate for communities and families in need. I'm needed here."

"Yes, you are, and you were missed, girl, very missed." Grace linked arms with me. I rested a hand against her forearm and walked toward my mother's grave.

"I'm going to plant some flowers on my parents' grave as well. I'll be right by you," she said, then waved when Chief, aka Pastor Pathwalker, walked her way. In his hand was sage, water, and other items used to anoint the grounds. One of his older sons was with him chanting and praying.

"Sageheart, ready to plant the indigo?" I yelled to my twin, then stopped when I saw my smiling cowboy up ahead.

Kamal stood with flowers in his hand. His large Stetson hat was hooked low over his copper eyes. Twin dimples played in his cheeks with his subtle smile and today he wore blue and white.

"Sis, you step away from that hustler right there! Do you know who that man is? That man who made my heart do the Tootsie Roll every time he's near. Hmm?" I said with humor in my voice.

"I sure do, but he's the better version of the hustler line, I say." Sage winked, then went to grab her flowers. "Don't you two kiss too long. I can't believe this plot twist if you paid me."

Kamal and I laughed.

When we heard Tessa's, "Ewww, kissing? No," we laughed some more.

I walked up to Kamal and took the hand that he held for me. "You came."

"I had to. I refuse to miss our dates unless it's emergent and, in this case, this date and meeting is what was emergent to me." Kamal looked down at me. His hand pulled me close into a hug, and I melted against him. "My sweet hurricane?" I heard muttered low in question.

"Yes?" I looked up into his eyes and saw a hint of humor there.

"Ms. Tucker, I feel your gun," he said with a smile.

Embarrassed and laughing at the same time, I quickly kissed his lips and stepped back. "Had to be cautious, especially with having Tessa with me."

"But of course. I like that fire in your spirit. I'm learning more about you every day. Now ..." Kamal took my hand, then stepped to face my mother's grave. He took his hat off, placed it against his heart, and bowed his head. "Mrs. Tucker, it's an honor to stand before your resting place." Kamal took a knee and laid flowers around the headstone of my mother's grave. "I see the beauty of your love in your daughter. Thank you for guiding us together. I heard the story of how you met Sheriff Tucker, and I can only believe that it was you who brought us together that day."

Tears framed my eyes. "My mother would have fallen in love with you, Kamal."

I knelt by the soft plot of grass. I turned to look for the indigo and saw Tessa standing there. She stared at the grave with a soft smile while Sage laid a caring hand on her shoulder.

"Thank you, Tessa-Belle. I'd like to introduce you and Kamal to my mother."

"She was pretty," Tessa exclaimed.

"I agree, she truly was," Kamal added.

Tessa beamed in pride. "Yup, pretty like Miss Willowshine, Miss Sageheart, and Mr. Trent! I think she was probably really kind. She looks like it."

I glanced at the cared for grave in agreement and watched Tessa sit by my side. On the intricately carved stone was a picture of my smiling mother. Under it was a set of flowers, poem, a glass of rosemary water, two plums, and a bit of fresh burning incense. My father had been here.

"She could sing like Phyliss Hyman, Tessa-Belle … I'll have to play her music for you soon," I explained. "She could play the piano like Beethoven and make the best peach cobbler around. Daddy also taught her to ride, and we still have her horse."

"You think I can learn to ride, and ride her horse?" Tessa asked while helping me and Sage plant the indigo and black-eyed Susans.

"I think so. Maybe Sage and the older riders can teach you. We're all going to ride in the parade in memory of our lost loved ones." I explained.

"Really? Then I can't wait," Tessa exclaimed. "I like your mother's name, too. Monica Emory-Tucker! Grandma Monica, I hope to one day get a mommy just as nice as Miss Willowshine who smiles like her and has your kind eyes. That's my first Sojourner wish!"

"An almost Juneteenth wish," I choked out, wiping at my eyes.

My twin and I held each other's hands where we knelt, and Kamal rested a gentle hand against my back as we spoke a prayer to the ancestors, one traced back to West Africa. As we did so, the loud scream of Hawk and Chadwick's strained, scared voices drew our attention.

An unsettling rush of my heart beating fast made me run in a panicked rush, with Kamal by my side. Laid out on the plot of her parents' grave was Grace. Surrounding her was a bushel of colorful flowers. Cradling her were a crying Hawk and Chadwick.

"She said she needed to sit, a-and we tried to help, but she fell over, Miss Willow," Hawk cried out. "Doctor Brookhaven, help, please!"

Without missing a beat, Kamal let out a loud, purposeful whistle. Breaking through the manicured line of forest trees came his majestic horse. After quickly checking Grace, he placed his hat on his head, gave us all a nod, and scooped up Grace in his arms. "We'll get her to the health center immediately. Let's ride."

Chapter 18: Kamal

"She's stable for now. Ms. Olivia said it's more than likely Grace is exhausted and has overexerted herself because of the celebration coming up," I told the mayor as he studied me with worried eyes.

"So why can't I see her?" he asked.

While Willow and Sage had driven Grace to the hospital, I hopped on my horse and made a beeline for the medical center. I got there five minutes before they did. Still, it was enough time for me to have Ms. Olivia prep our prenatal triage area for Grace.

"Because you're antsy. She's crying and already afraid something's wrong with the baby even though I've assured her that the baby is fine. If you go in there with that expression on your face, with that kind of energy, she will panic, and we will be back at square one. Her blood pressure has spiked. If it doesn't come down, we may have to induce her. Do you understand?" I spoke slow and even, needing him to feel the gravity of my words. I needed him to calm down so that he wouldn't go into that room and trigger his fiancé into another panic attack which could spike her blood pressure more.

Blade nodded. "I understand … I understand. But she's okay, right? I'm glad the baby is okay, but I need her to be out of the woods as well," he said emphatically.

"For now, she's okay. However, we need her blood pressure to come down before I can say she's out of the woods."

"You said you would induce to deliver the baby if it doesn't come down, but what happens to her?" he asked.

"I'm going to be honest with you, if her blood pressure doesn't come down and we don't induce quick enough, she could very well be in trouble."

"And by trouble you mean—"

"She could die."

"Oh Lord, no," I heard behind me.

I whipped around to see Ms. Nita, Mr. Clark, and Mr. Walt standing there. I didn't even know they had walked in.

"What you mean?" Mr. Clark asked, his brown eyes darkening.

Mr. Walt had a deep frown. "Die?"

Blade stepped in. "No … I mean, Grace is fine. The doctor was just telling me what would have happened had they not got her to the medical center in time. She is fine, and so is the baby. She just tired herself out, was doing too much and it caught up to her."

"Ya sure, baby?" Ms. Nita asked, gazing up at Blade with wet eyes.

He guided her to sit in one of the chairs in the hall. "Yes, I'm sure. I don't want any of you to worry," he said, glancing from Ms. Nita to her husbands.

I felt a comforting hand on my back, then turned to see Willow with Tessa by her side. "You okay?" she asked.

I nodded. "I am. However, Grace scared me for a minute. Ms. Olivia is fussing up a storm."

Willow chuckled. "I know. I heard it all when we brought Grace in. I ain't had a fussing out like that since my mama caught me and Sage stealing from the Green Pantry as kids."

My eyes widened. "My fair lady, you were a thief?"

Tessa squealed. "I don't believe you stole something, Miss Willowshine!"

Willow nodded while laughing. "We didn't want to wait until Mama got to the store to get us snacks, so we took some candy and some chips. Mr. Clark wasn't going to tell on us, but Mama happened to be coming around the corner as he gave us a lesson on why we shouldn't steal. She laid into us something fierce. I think I'd have rather she whupped us. Her being disappointed in us hurt worse."

"I'd be sad if you were disappointed in me, too," Tessa said.

I smiled at the woman who was putting a move on my heart. I saw my future in her eyes. I was about to ask her plans for later when she frowned.

"Crap," she said.

"What's wrong?" I asked.

"I forgot that Marcus Legend is supposed to stop by the center to pick up the invoice for all the cuts of meat Mr. Vincent needs for the celebration."

"I thought he already had all the meat?"

"He does for the most part. These are just some last-minute cuts that Grace and Mrs. Percy had asked for to go in side dishes and things like that."

"Will I see you later?" I asked.

She smiled. "Yes ... yes you will."

I kissed her before watching her sprint out the front doors, and then laughed at Tessa screeching, "Ewwww," as she ran behind Willow.

It was six-thirty in the evening by the time I got to leave. Grace was stable, but Ms. Olivia and I agreed that she should stay overnight just in case. Doctor Martyn agreed, and so did Doctor Jones. I headed to the inn to shower and prepare for dinner. By seven, it dawned on me that I hadn't heard from Willow since that afternoon. I tried calling her cell twice but got no answer. I went to knock her room door, but she didn't answer there either.

My gut clenched in a way that told me something was wrong, but I didn't want to panic just yet. I thought about Tobias Pine still in jail. I remembered the sheriff saying he had refused to talk. My heart did a somersault at the idea of Willow and Tessa being in danger.

"Did Willow come in?" I asked Mr. Clark once I jogged downstairs.

He and Mr. Walt had come back to the inn about an hour or so ago.

He looked up from his guestbook. "Naw. Ain't seen her since she left the medical center earlier with Tessa. You ain't heard from her?"

I shook my head. "No. I'm going to head over to the center. She said she was supposed to be meeting Marcus Legend earlier."

As soon as I said that, Marcus walked in. "Willow here?" he asked.

The bottom of my stomach hollowed out. "No. You haven't seen her?"

"I did earlier. She gave me this list, but I realized she forgot to put the quantities on here. I called her but she didn't pick up. Figured she was busy at the center, so I stopped by. I saw the light on in her office, but she wasn't in there."

"The door was unlocked?"

Marcus nodded. "Yeah, I thought that was a bit strange. That's why I came here."

"Go get the sheriff and Trent," I told Marcus. "I'm going to check around and see if anyone else has seen her."

My heart pounded in my ears, and I ran full speed from the inn. Why did I allow her to leave by herself, knowing there was another man out there who had ill-intentions? Why had I been so lackadaisical about letting her trot off alone? Sure she carried a gun, and I had no doubt she knew how to use it, but she was up against hardened criminals who'd made a life out of hurting people. I'd foolishly assumed that after Tobias had been arrested, his associate would leave town. I should have known better.

I rushed into the center, then up to her office. Nothing looked out of place. Not even a chair had been knocked over. Her desk sat against the exposed brick wall with papers piled atop it. Paint, canvases, stencils, and the like sat against the walls.

Cans of unopened paint sat by the door. I left her office and headed back downstairs.

Near the basement door was a little, Black girl figurine in a ballet post. Tessa must have dropped it. I opened the basement door, then went down. I searched the wall for a light switch, found one, and flipped it up. There were boxes lined up along one side of the wall with old liquor crates. There was poster of a Black man on a black horse. He had eyes so golden they looked like fire as the horse reared back in all its glory. Old school bank bags were in a basket in the corner. Battered and weathered doors that looked as if they once belonged to a saloon.

I found myself frustrated that everything was where it was supposed to be. Why hadn't there been a struggle? Did Willow not put up a fight because Tessa was with her? Why didn't she leave something behind? Something for me to follow. Was she okay? Had the man hurt her and Tessa? I was going to drive myself mad trying to wrap my mind around all of it.

Twenty minutes after asking everyone who was still in town if they'd seen Willow and Tessa, and I was back at square one. No one had seen them. No one knew where they could have gone. My gut told me Jessie Dalton had taken her and Tessa.

"We're all going to fan out," I heard Sheriff Tucker say. "It'll be dark soon, so we need to move fast. Half of us will search the surrounding area, the rest of us will search the secret areas, the areas unknown to outsiders and those areas that are underground but easy to find …"

Most of the people from the town had gathered in the small park on Main Street. Even a few of the older kids were out. Sheriff Tucker's face was set in stone. I knew he was just as worried, if not more than I was. Trent scowled while Sage looked as if she were going to be sick. Still, she stood next to her father, ready to do what needed to be done.

I let the fury I felt override any fear that had coiled in my gut. I wouldn't be able to think if I let fear rule over good sense. There was a part of me that wanted to go running, screaming her name like a mad man, but that would only help her captor.

"He doesn't know the land that well, Sheriff. Even if someone told him what to look for, he'd still make mistakes. Sure, he's been out here in the woods for a while, but … he doesn't know this town the way Willow does," I said.

"What'cha getting at, son?" Sheriff Tucker asked.

"He's not from here, so he will be looking for a place to lay low for the night, mainly since it's almost dark. That could work in our favor, especially if Willow can talk him into laying low someplace she knows we will look. And I'm speaking as someone who didn't grow up here."

"He's going to want to go somewhere a bit far, somewhere he doesn't think we'll look because he will assume he's out of Sojourner Falls," Sage said.

I nodded.

Trent asked, "You think Willow will pick up on that and leave some kind of trail or breadcrumbs?"

Sage said, "It's what I would do. And we tend to think alike sometimes." She sighed. "And I can still feel her. She's anxious and scared, but she's alive."

Her brother nodded. "The twin thing?".

Sage wiped at her eyes. "Yes ... the twin thing."

"Hey, Doctor Brookhaven, where'd you get that?"

Turning, I looked down to see Hawk gazing up at me. I wasn't surprised he had heard his friend was missing. I also wasn't surprised to see him out with his father and uncles. He was pointing to the figurine in my hand. I had forgotten I had it.

"Oh, this? Ah, I found this when I was searching Willow's center," I said.

Hawk's eyes were watery, but he was trying to hold the tears back. His lips trembled as he reached for the figurine. I handed it to him.

"That's … this is Tessa's. Sh-She holds on t-to it when she's afraid. She would ne-never leave it unless … something bad happened to her," he said, then whipped around to look at his father. "Something happened or she wouldn't have left it."

"Where'd you find that?" Trent asked. "I know you said in the center, but where exactly?"

"Right by the basement door before I searched it."

"The tunnel," Sage yelled, then took off running toward the center.

"No, Sage, if they in that tunnel, they a longways down by now."

Sage stopped and turned worried eyes to her father.

"We need'ta head to the dugouts and old cabins in Shady Grove," the sheriff said. "Marcus, Blade, Hunter, Vincent, y'all head to tunnels in the center and wait for a signal from us," the sheriff said. "If ya see or hear anything, do what'cha have'ta do to bring my Willowshine and Tessa home."

Sage and Sheriff Tucker mounted their horses and took off toward Shady Grove. Trent followed, hopping on his horse and pushing her full speed. I was on my steed and right behind him.

Chapter 19: Willow

At the beginning of June, there is a Sojourner Falls tradition to start the ushering in the approaching celebration of Juneteenth. Truly, this starts on Memorial Day, then carries on to the first of every June. The tradition says that to honor the ancestors who have passed, the ancestors ready to go, the new generation of elders to come and town soldiers/vets, we paint the large root oak tree in the center of town square. Swirls of haint blue and white adorn the trunk of the tree, and its rising, thick roots that peek out of the emerald, green grass. On Memorial Day we add cloth white streamers that are embroidered with town families and founders' names. Each one is bordered in vibrate colors.

A second set of streamers were set out in a marble box that sat at the base of the tree. That box was used for various things in the year. However, for Memorial Day, it was used for writing prayers, dreams, wishes, and blessings. At the founding of the town, it was used to leave markers to find loved ones who didn't stay in the town but left to find a more secure freedom out of the South through the Underground Railroad route. In June, we tied bells and other wind chimes to the tree and streams, so that during the month, clinquant music could be heard on the wind in honor of the towns spirit and ancestors.

Like with the Christmas leaves tradition, of leaving wishes for the holidays, we carried that on for the spring and later summer months. It was this history and a streamer I shared with Tessa to put her own wishes on, that I was showing when we were both ambushed.

The moment happened before any reaction could occur. A blow plowed against the side of my head. Tessa's high scream was immediately covered by the large palm of our attacker. The fear in her big, brown eyes was the last thing I saw.

When I finally woke up, it was due to a euphonious, susurrus trickle of water. I was covered in a curtain of inky darkness and lethargic. I smelled an earthy, wet scent. There were notes of oak as well. Shaking, I stopped myself from groaning aloud.

The throbbing of my head made me recall that I had been hit. When I heard a scratching noise, I turned my head to where it came from. A fleeting glint of light told me I was huddled on a dirt and wooden planked floor. On my lap was Tessa's little head; she lay on her side, huddled close, eyes closed and where the light was disappearing a towering man dressed in black S.W.A.T attire pushed a brick and wood moss covered wall closed. I gasped.

On the other side, I could see it was a way to the basement of the center.

It was then that I began to struggle. The rule if ever taken was to never let your abductor take you to another location. My father had taught us that as kids. Sage, when she returned from active duty, reiterated it. I knew that I needed to think for Tessa and me, so I had to be quick.

"Tessa-Belle?" I whispered.

"M-Miss Willowshine? You sound funny. I'm scared. That man hurt you. He told me he'd kill you if I yelled, so I didn't. I'm sorry. I'm sorry, Miss Willow. He dragged us downstairs of the center. I was so scared. I dropped my doll." The twilight of light snuffed out, leaving us in a sea of bleakness.

My unbound hands searched in the darkness to feel out the light weight of her head on my lap. "You did good. Like Hansel and Gretel, you helped leave a crumb."

"Sheriff Tucker told us a story about them last year," Tessa whispered. "He told us to remember that story and use it if ever bad people came around us and we needed help." Tessa's quiescent voice paused, then she said, "I-I don't like this ... it's too tight in here."

Pulling her close to me, I held a hand over her shoulder to touch the wall. There were names etched in the wall. I wanted to cry for the strong will of my ancestors, and because we were in danger, but I refused to let a tear shed. Our captor coughed, then cursed. I heard him struggling with something until a match lit and an old gas lamp shone a halo almost our way. It was enough to allow us vision but still shadowed us.

"Breathe slow and hold my hand, sweetheart. The room isn't spinning for me now, I can get my bearings." My palm went flat against a surface. I felt mud, moss, and bricks. Moving it around, I gauged that it was a wall. My ancestors must have enclosed a lot of the tunnel in bricks to secure it, but I wasn't sure.

"I want you to keep your voice very quiet as he comes our way and trust me. Stay near me. If I behave funny, I want you to keep a distance. Understand?" I said quickly.

"Yes, ma'am," Tessa's hand squeezed mine as she looked past me.

Wrapping my arm around her, I whispered, "Good. I hear him coming, so we have to follow his lead so that I can figure out a plan out of here."

She sniffled. "I'm scared."

"I am, too," I reassured. "But listen, remember my favorite song you sang at Tammy's?"

Tessa gently hugged me and nodded against my chest. "Uh huh, High Five's song!"

"Good, I want you to sing that song in your head and count our footsteps. When it feels like we are in the middle of the tunnel I want you to scream as loud as you can. I'll signal you."

"Are you sure, Miss Willow? How are you going to get us out of here?"

A smile spread across my face as the watch on my arm began to glow. I took her hand and placed it on the raised surface of a brick. I guided her fingers to feel what had felt like a horseshoe before the light of the lamp approached.

"Wh-What is that?" she quietly asked.

"It's a mark way used by those traveling the Underground Railroad," I explained, noticing old shoes of the past, packed backs, canteens, and water barrels. "A guide. It means this spot is the old stable saloon. That's what the center long ago was when the town was founded. Keep an eye out for any more signs, and if I get knocked down, don't panic. Now, shhh."

Staring at the man before me, my gaze counted the guns on his person. He didn't wear a vest, but he had military boots, gloves, pants, and more. I was confused as to why this man was here.

"Who are you?" I asked, using the wall to help me stand. It was difficult, but I managed. "Why are you after me?"

The auburn-haired, pale man adjusted a pack with a sleeping roll attached, on his shoulder. He reminded me of Ramsey Bolton from that show with white walkers and dragons. This man was all hallowed, sinister eyes, harsh expression, and athletically built. I remembered seeing him before. His free hand reached out at my arm, gripping so tightly, I winced. He whipped me in front of him, then pushed what felt like a gun against my back.

"Walk forward or I'll kill the child and you," the man ordered.

My gaze dropped to Tessa. Light washed over the little girl. My heart fluttered in worry for her. Tessa's face was marked with dirt. Her pink clothes were covered in moss stains and muck.

Her large ponytail puff was frizzy at the edges, but I made note of the beads on the two braids framing her hair. *We might need those for crumbs*, I thought.

Tessa's little hands slid up to my arm to hold it by my side. I gave her a nod. "Let's do as the man said, angel heart."

We walked forward carefully into the dark tunnel. I stumbled to the side of the tunnel on purpose to run my hand against it and feel the surface.

"Keep moving, and don't try anything," the man barked out.

"You hit me hard, and this … this tunnel is getting narrow. How did you even find it?" I asked, trying to glean any information.

"Hmm … make do, or I'll hurt you more," he barked. "And I had my ways."

We continued walking in silence until he grumbled, "You never should have made the enemies you did, otherwise you and your little girl wouldn't be in this situation," the man said, looking ahead. "Stop here."

We did as he instructed. He held his lamp out against a socket in the wall, slammed a fist against a bronze button twice, and the flame in the lamp flickered then split. I watched on in amazement. Lines of glass lamps lit up in a buzz. If one didn't know a thing about the tunnel, a person would not have found the little compartment. But this man did, which meant he had been down here for some time now.

As my eyes focused, I gasped. The tunnel was nothing but glossy, red stone bricks forming a line tube around us. There was moss, and gnarled roots poking from the walls. I noticed raised markers and some painted numbers, but I'd have missed it if I didn't know what to look for. The floor was once smooth lined brinks as well, but now they buckled with roots, wood beams, and trickles of water that disappeared into tiny iron drains. My ancestors had thought of everything.

We stood in a large atrium with a crossroad compass with markers pointing to the cardinal direction of the stars labeled in old spiritual songs. Above us was a skylight and my mind worked on overload. We were at the Ancestor's Grove well near the old town central! This was amazing. It was gorgeous and well-preserved. I dropped down to touch the slick marble and stone.

The man looked around in a circle as if trying to remember his way. I wasn't sure why. We were walled in, there was nowhere to go but straight, or so I thought. From the right of me, Tessa pulled my arm. She was humming the song still. I could see the fear in her eyes because the tunnel had become dangerously narrow until we made it to the atrium.

"Just breathe a little calmer, Tessa-Belle. The tunnel gets better ahead it seems," I whispered.

"Yes, ma'am …" Her hand slid down my hand and guided it behind me to where I felt a rise. It was shaped like a bridge. That made me think. I knew there was a bridge coming into town. We had walked that long to be out of town?

Before I could ask a thing, the man kicked a wall to the left of us. "Come on," he roared. "Tobias said this was the way out!"

I stepped back, thinking. My father told me the other man who had been questioning about me was named Tobias Pine. That made me wonder again about the name of this man who pushed me to the wall. I saw painted bear mounds on an archway to the south of us and another archway to the west of us had a series of painted trees laying on their sides with a creek. I realized that was Shady Grove. Something in my spirit decided to steer him that way. I then glanced at Tessa with a quick nod her way.

"Push it, now," the man yelled.

Without hesitation, I did as he instructed and pushed. "There's something here."

"That wall looks like it had been moved," I said, and stumbled by it, pushing the brick with the mound.

"Wait …" he said, then stopped with narrowed eyes and shut his mouth. "You people built this crap, and you know nothing?" The man shook his head in frustration. "Tobias said you all were blind about what was in this town when he scoped it out."

So, it was Tobias who found the tunnels. As I pushed, I felt the smooth brick and saw in faded paint two swivel lines, one under each other. I assumed that meant the river out near the grove. When I let my hands cover it as if I were just pushing at the wall, the panel shook and groaned, then bowed forward. Dirt and dust plumed around us, making us all cough.

My eyes watered and I looked at the man. "There's no way you and your friend could have known about all of this."

"No, but it helps being nosy and lucking out on finding a map in an old house in those woods surrounding this little town. Also helps to have a talkative toad who talks in his sleep locked up in a jail besides my partner."

I blinked in thought and knew that he was talking about Stacy. "There's no way you two could have talked to each other about it though."

"There isn't? It's not hard to hide a phone in our case. Now walk forward!" The man grabbed Tessa and yanked her by her arm.

She screamed so loud, it made me react and push at the man who let Tessa go. "Don't you touch a damn thing on her!"

Tears of anger spilled down my face as he hit the wall, dropping the lamp to the floor. My spirit shook at the audacity of the man. A tingle at the nape of my neck let me know that we were being looked for and my twin was one of the searchers. A whish of air surrounded us while I stared the man down. His hand went to his gun as I stood my ground. "Back off, we'll go!"

The doorway we had passed through closed tight behind us, and Tessa's whimpers softened as she appeared by my side.

"Keep close to me, Tessa-Belle," I whispered in concern. "It's clear that he needs us alive."

Tessa gripped my hand, and I looked down. I saw a plastic card with the name Jessie Dalton on it. Brilliant little heart. A smile flashed across my face as I took a quick look. The identification was fake, I could tell from how the man in front of us handled himself, but still. I had a name, even it was possibly false.

Jessie brushed himself off and glared at us. "You two are too much trouble than I have the patience for, but the bounty on your head is good, so I'm seeing this through. Give the card back to me. Now."

"Bounty?" I exclaimed. "For what? And no. You shouldn't have been so careless to have something like this on you, let alone in a spot a child could get to."

"You ticked off a lot of good men in Chicago for your antics." The man pushed us forward. "You lied on good men and women who were only doing their jobs. You lied. You made good citizens lose their jobs and brought on too many eyes on us, for what?"

It then dawned on me what this about. Renewed anger flared in my heart. "For what? For unethical practices in the conducting of a domestic violence family case, one with a man you all noted as being dangerous. A man who was noted to be physically abusive toward others."

Heat burned in my lungs with rage. Ragged breath came from my lips at the reality that this was all my fault. Tessa was in danger because of me. I was only doing my job to protect my case and the family. But because the family was Black, and because the lies and politics put into place to cause a multiple family death was ignored, there was a bounty on my head and Tessa was in danger.

"How can you justify that family's murder? Because he was part of your precious guild of uniforms, you all turned your back on a wife and children who needed your upmost protection! The ingrained systemic sociopathic insanity and racism is a damn cancer in you all! There is no justice for us people, for my people. Even if they wear the uniform like you do. That is a problem. That is unethical. That deserved to be called out!"

The man before me reached out and slapped me. The world almost began to spin but I did my best to swallow the pain. I cradled my face, stared at the furious, red-faced man in front of me, then rushed forward to close the space between us. Hitting with an open hand against his chest, I made sure the force was strong enough to hurt him and not my hand. My fist swung up and under his chin to knock him back. I kept close enough to find his eye and dig my fingers into them.

"Run forward, Tessa! Now, and don't stop. Listen for the water, listen for the wind!"

"Yes, ma'am! Please don't die, Miss Willow, please!"

I heard the cries of the little girl I prayed I could call daughter soon enough, disappearing into the dark tunnel. I covered her in prayer, as I swiftly turned to the side to use my elbow to jab into the man's chest. It let me get close enough to snatch the gun he had holstered on his body.

The man rubbed his eyes, then swung out at me again, knocking me to the rotting, wooden beam and dirt floor. This meant that we must be at an older part of the tunnels. If I made it out of this, I planned upon talking to Miss Sara about everything I saw.

"Get back here, girl," the man yelled after Tessa.

I couldn't let him get to her. I rolled on my stomach, reached out, and grabbed him by his leg. Pulling with the strength of the women in my family and our ancestors, I gritted my teeth until I heard a loud thump. My heart was in my throat by this point. I pushed myself up and went at the man on the floor. We rolled in the narrow tunnel until we both stood back up. My knee went up into a strike to the groin. When he bowed forward, I fisted my hands together to drop them down on the back of his neck. Once he fell down again, I picked up the gun from the floor and turned on him when he tried to rush me.

A stream of light lit up the side of the tunnel to allow me to see clearly. I squeezed the trigger, hitting the man in his shoulder, then leg. "This is a citizen's arrest. Stay down. Stop resisting."

"You bi—" My fist slamming in his face, in the same manner he did me, stopped the expletives spilling out of his nasty mouth.

I exhaled slowly, put the safety back on the gun, and placed it against the small of my back. I then stepped over the man, kneeling to remove his weapons. I patted him down and found a zip tie.

"More will come for you, especially for the gold, once Tobias gets out," Jessie groaned as I heard feet coming my way.

"There's no gold here. However, if the people come, then that's their problem and the winds and this town will deal with them. Until then, you will be handled, as will the people who sent you my way. This town has old, deep friends, as old as your good ol' boy union, trust that."

He stared up at me with red, bloody eyes, then spat out, "Who the hell trained you?"

Pointing the gun at the man before me, I calmly stated while looking down at him, "Sheriff Trent

Tucker, formally Sargent Major of the U.S. Marines, Lieutenant Sage Tucker of the U.S. Navy, and the Sojourner Falls Buffalo Soldiers self-defense squad!"

Chapter 20: Kamal

"Wait," I yelled as we all circled the dugouts again. "You hear that?" I dismounted.

The area where Sojourner Falls was first settled looked the same as it did the day I brought Willow on our second date. The fire pit I made to cook for us was still visible. The grass was tall, and the smell of wild onion rent the air. Hare stuck their heads up from hiding places, then skittered off after seeing humans in their domicile. The sun was setting, casting an orange glare over the whole field. I didn't want darkness to fall before we found Willow and Tessa. I couldn't fathom the danger they were in and what the man would do to them once he had them a safe distance away from Sojourner.

The dugouts were in a circle with about twenty feet between each one. It was hard to know exactly where the sounds were coming from. I felt as if I were in a vacuum. My head swam and ears pounded like I was rising in elevation. I'd been questioning whether or not it was possible for me to love someone within a few weeks of knowing them. I didn't know if I was infatuated or if what I was feeling was truly love. However, the way my gut knotted and coiled at the thought of something happening to Willow, told me what I felt was the real thing.

"I hear it," Sage said as she dismounted her horse.

"Is someone screaming?" Trent asked.

The sheriff frowned. "Sounds like a child.".

"Where is it coming from?" I asked.

I walked a hole in the earth as I circled each dugout, trying to pinpoint the screams.

"They're closer now," Sage said.

"Help! Help me, please! Please help … me …"

"That's Tessa!" I rushed toward the dugout north of the circle. "It's coming from here."

"That thing could cave in, and they could get trapped down there," Trent said.

Sheriff Tucker nodded. "It's unstable. They all are."

I didn't give a damn. I'd risk it just to get Willow and Tessa out. I kicked down the rickety, wooden door that was held up by mud and bricks.

"Y'all be real careful in yonder, ya hear me?" the sheriff barked.

"Help me," Tessa cried again.

Apparently, Sage didn't give a damn the dugout could cave in either as she crawled into the space with me. Once inside of the earthy, musky space, it was hard to get my bearings. Because some of the ceiling had fallen, there was no way Sage or I could stand fully.

"Tessa," I yelled.

"Yes," she squealed immediately, then started crying harder. "Please help!" Her voice echoed and made it hard to get an exact location.

"We are, sweetie. We're going to get you out of here," Sage assured her.

"I can't see anything and it's little in here," Tessa whined. "There was light when I left Miss Willow, then it got dark again."

"Is Willow with you, Tessa?" Sage asked.

"No. She was fighting with the bad man and told me to run."

My heart dropped.

"Tessa, it's Doctor Brookhaven. Can you help us find you? Tap on a wall for me."

A few seconds later, Sage and I heard a faint tapping.

Sage frowned. "These dugouts are made entirely of sod, mud, and bricks. That's about as good as it's going to get."

"I know, but there has to be a way. I'm having a hard time breathing in here. I know Tessa has to be struggling."

"I can't breathe," Tessa cried as soon as the words left my mouth. Her voice sounded faint.

"Take slow and easy breaths, Tessa," Sage told her.

"I … I'm … trying … hard."

"We've got to get her out of there," I said.

Three loud thumps sounded to the right of us. First in slow pounding, then in three rapid successions. Those were the only cues we needed. Sage and I started kicking in the wall in. Once we got through the first layer of caked-on sod and mud, the second and third layer crumbled like plaster.

Sage gasped. "There she is.".

There, Tessa lay on the ground with an old coat under her head. She lay there as if someone had placed her there. The area was as small as Tessa had said it was, but there was an old stool, a, broken oil lantern, wanted posters with a …white woman? It was hard to tell because of the weathered look of the posters. I frowned, confused, but didn't have time to dwell on how Tessa had been cognizant enough to place a coat under her head before passing out. I reached in and grabbed her through the hole.

Sage looked alarmed as she took Tessa from my arms. "She's barely breathing."

"She needs to get to the hospital. She needs oxygen."

"I got her," Sage said.

"You can ride with her on horseback all the way back to town?"

"Don't really have a choice, but yes, I can."

Sage and I crawled out of the dugout with Tessa. A few seconds later, she and the girl were mounted with Tessa's legs wrapped around her waist and the girl's head on her chest, and they rode off.

A gunshot erupted through the air. The rickety door to one of the cabins flew open. Out stumbled … Jessie Dalton.

"Crazy bitch," he yelled as he fell backwards, then tried to scramble to his feet.

He was bleeding from gunshot wounds to his shoulder and leg. A few seconds later, out came an armed, battered, and bruised Willow.

"You shot me," Dalton yelled, eyes wide.

"You deserved it," she said coolly.

Dalton's face balled into an angry scowl. "I should have killed you when I had the chance."

Willow stormed forward and kicked him in his bleeding leg. Dalton howled in pain as he went down to the ground. The expletives that left his mouth were unfit to be heard in any company.

"That's for kidnapping a child, you dirty bastard. I should shoot you again."

"Willow," Sheriff Tucker called out.

Willow turned to us.Her eyes widened. She had been so focused on Jessie that she hadn't even noticed us. Once she did, she ran toward us.

The closer she got, the more I saw the bruises and cuts to her face. When Tessa had said Willow and the "bad man" were fighting, it had been an understatement. Willow's bottom lip was busted and swollen. Her left eye looked as if she had been punched or slapped, and her right cheek was bruised and split.

I thought she would run to her father first, but to my relief, she ran into my arms. I held her that way while her father and brother walked over to a cussing Dalton.

Gently cupping her chin, I studied her face. "He did this to you?"

She gazed up at me with watery and tired eyes. I saw she was exhausted by her labored breaths. Tears trickled down her cheeks.

She nodded. "You should see *his* face,'' she said, trying to joke away the pain and fear. "Tessa?"

"Sage left with her to the hospital." I eased the gun from her hand ... well, I tried to. She had it in a death grip. "It's okay. You're safe now, I got you."

After a few seconds of prodding her fingers from the butt of the gun, I took it from her. When her father and brother walked back over with a limping Dalton, I passed the gun off to Trent. Willow hadn't been lying about his face. She'd given it to him good. Scratches ran up and down his face and neck. The corner of his mouth bled, and his face was red with bruises.

"You should have that gal locked up. Crazy wench shot me," Dalton fussed.

I felt the muscles in my jaw twitch. My fists ached with the need to knock the man out.

"Cut him loose, Junior, so I can cuff him," Sheriff Tucker said to Trent, then to Dalton, "I'm half hoping you run. That way my son and I can chase you down and show you just how honest Willow got her crazy."

Dalton snarled at the sheriff, then turned wild, crazy eyes to Willow. He spit in her direction. I moved her out of the way, but I wasn't quick enough. The man's saliva landed on her shoulder. Before I could catch myself, I raised a booted foot and kicked him square in the chest. He went down hard, dust kicking up after him. For good measure, I stomped on the leg Willow had shot him in. When he screeched and grabbed for his knee, I stomped on his knee. Thinking about the criminal assaulting Willow caused all rational sense to cease. He was lucky I didn't cave his skull in with the heel of my boot.

"That's enough, son," Sheriff Tucker said, placing a hand on my chest, urging me to back away.

"No, Daddy, I think a little more of what Kamal gave him would most definitely help him to remember to never step foot in Sojourner Falls again," Willow said as she moved next to me.

The sheriff chuckled. "Just like ya mama, you is. Always raring for a fight when someone brings one to ya door. Ya mama wasn't afeard of much, and neither are you and ya twin." Sheriff Tucker looked at his son who had deadly eyes trained on Dalton.

I didn't know what to make of the calm, cool, and collected way Trent eyed the man, but if I were Dalton, I'd pray I wasn't left alone with Trent for too long.

Sheriff Tucker said to Trent, "Go on cut them ties so I can cuff him."

As soon as Trent cut the zip tie, Dalton took a swing at the sheriff. The older man pivoted left smoothly, then sent a hard elbow right into Dalton's face. The moment Sheriff Tucker's elbow caught him the eye, I knew he regretted it. He let out a long, strangled yelp. One smooth leg sweep from Trent took Dalton to the ground.

Trent grabbed the man up by the collar of his shirt. "You're really trying my patience. I'll have you know my father deputized me when we were looking for you after arresting your scoundrel friend. We make our own laws here. I can walk into that jail anytime I want … do anything I want to you, and no one would bat a lash."

"If you hadn't noticed, you're the minority here. You kidnapped my woman and a child … You're lucky I don't tie your sorry carcass to a tree, slice your chest and arms open, and let the bears and bobcats have a go at you," I snapped.

Dalton's eyes went wide. "Y-You can't do that."

"We can do what we want. We've been deputized, remember? Lots of things can happen from here to the jail," Trent snarled.

Dalton looked at Sheriff Tucker. "You going to let them do this to a fellow white man? Aint you got no balls left?" he yelled.

The sheriff laughed, then slapped the cuffs on the man. "You the only white man here. I'm mixed-race. My loyalty is to my family and to the town of Sojourner Falls."

The horseback ride back to town was an eventful one. Dalton refused to saddle with the sheriff or Trent, so Trent tied his hand with a length of rope and made him walk behind his horse. By the time we got halfway to town, Dalton had passed out from the pain and exhaustion. Trent and I hoisted the man up, then tossed his limp body side saddle the back of the sheriff's horse. Willow sat behind me, hands around my waist and cheek pressed against my back. She didn't say much. Just held me close. That was good enough for me.

As soon as we got into the town, the Freemans were there to take care of the horses and I got Willow to the hospital. After helping her to get cleaned up and changed into a hospital gown, I got her hooked to an IV for pain meds and hydration. I was sure Sage wanted to help clean her sister up, but not even a wild herd of elephants could make me leave Willow's side.

"Are you hungry?" I asked once she was resting comfortably.

"No, not right now. Where's Tessa?" she asked.

"In the pediatric ward with Sage. Doctor Jones will be in shortly to let you know how she's fairing."

"As long as she's okay ..."

"I think she is. She's a brave, little girl."

"Think I can see her later?"

"We'll see. First, let's finished getting you patched up and healed."

While I doctored her cuts and bruises, I listened as she told me about what happened.

"So the coward snuck up on you and hit you from behind?" I said coolly. "He better hope the jail keeps him safe."

"Speaking of jail, he says his partner has a phone and that Stacy talks in his sleep … but that didn't make a whole lot of sense to me. If his partner has a phone, wouldn't he have called in reinforcements or something? Also, it was if he knew things he shouldn't have about this place. He says he found a map and heard about some gold, but … I don't know. I still feel like someone told him these things."

"I'll tell you the same things I told your father and brother—"

She weakly waved her arm. "No, no, I didn't mean you! When he mentioned the gold, I thought back to a conversation Hollis and I once had. When I thought he loved me, when I thought we would be married, I would tell him stories about this place. He visited with me only twice. My gut tells me he was in cahoots with these men and their handlers in some way …"

"We'll figure it all out once you're home." I took her hand in mine. "I thought I was going to lose you and it made me realize that I never wanted to. I don't want to go back to knowing what life was like before you, and I most definitely don't want to know life after you. I love you, Willow, and the thought of never being able to tell you doesn't sit right with my spirit."

She squeezed my hand. "Oh, Kamal … I love you, too. So very much."

"I'm not sure when my aunt will make her appearance in Sojourner again, but when she does, I'd like you to meet her. That way I can—"

"Willowshine!" I heard squealed from the hall.

Willow's eye lit up, and I knew we would have to finish our conversation later. Sage rolled Tessa into the room. Doctor Jones had had nurses switch her dirty clothes for a kid's sized, kente cloth gown and robe.

"You're alive! I knew it! I knew you wouldn't leave me," Tessa cried as she hopped from her chair and wrapped her arms around Willow.

Willow groaned and grunted in pain but held Tessa just as tightly.

"I'm sorry." Tessa eased away. "I didn't mean to hurt you."

"It's fine. I'm glad you hugged me. I needed to feel you in my arms to make sure you were really here." Willow cupped the girl's face in her hands, looking her over.

Tessa had a few minor scrapes and bruises, but she looked in good health otherwise.

"She was so brave," Sage said.

Tessa nodded. "I did exactly what you said, Willowshine! I ran and I started screaming, but then it kept getting smaller and smaller. I was so scared and tired. Then I felt like I couldn't breathe … then I got sleepy."

"But she stayed awake long enough to bang on the wall to help us find her," I said.

Frowning, Tessa looked up at me. "I didn't knock on no wall, Doctor Brookhaven."

Sage quirked a brow when I made eye contact with her. "You're probably still tired and don't remember, but you made six loud knocks …"

Tessa was shaking her head. "No, Miss Sage. I couldn't have. The lady put me on her lap and told me to go to sleep. She said it was okay and she would keep me safe. She looked kinda like you and Willowhine, but … she was lighter, almost like Sheriff Tucker. She even gave me her marshal star." Tessa anxiously reached into her robe pocket and pulled it out. "See?" she said, holding it up.

Sage and Willow's hands slapped over their mouths.

"She was the one who told me it was okay to sleep. She must have knocked, too. I asked Misss Kenya if the woman was also here. She said she didn't know." Tessa gazed from Sage to Willow, then back again. "Why are you crying? Did I do something wrong? If so, I'm so sorry," she said to Willow, then hugged her again. "The lady said you told your mom in ancestor heaven that you wanted to be my mom. Please don't change your mind about being my mom! I didn't mean to do anything bad, I swear," she cried. "I'll even give the marshal star back …"

"Oh, sweetie, you didn't do a thing wrong," Willow whispered as tears rolled down her cheeks.

Sage walked to the other side of her twin's bed and wrapped her arms around the both of them. "Not a thing wrong," she whispered, tears spilling from her eyes, too.

I felt as if I were intruding. For as much as I wanted to sit and stay with Willow, I knew this was a moment that should be shared only between the three of them.

Chapter 21: Willow

A huge smile warmed my face while I looked on at the gifts that were now in my life. The loud, clacking of drums in sync to the drumline section of Big Boi's "Morris Brown" transitioned into the town's anthem for Sojourner Falls. I heard the blows of several whistles going in tune to the song being played by the band. I looked up at the little girl with two plump, two-twisted ponytails bopping on top of a magnificent dancing chestnut stallion who was painted in haint blue and white stripes and had a saddle with a Sojourner Falls, Muscogee-Seminole blanket on its back.

A child's Stetson sat on her head. Her two ropes of plump braids had precious cowrie beads, haint blue African grass printed beads and tiny red, and white feathers with gold braid clips entwined in the beads. The adornments matched the ones in my hair.

"I told you, Tessa, Coffey would love you and take care of you as you make her dance," I said in pride.

"She's awesome, Mama Willowshine." Tessa's squeals of delight made my heart swell.

"Coffey was my mother's horse. Mama named her after my great-great-grandmother, the lady Marshal Cathay 'Coffey' Tucker," I explained as I watched Tessa's eyes brighten with the knowledge.

"I want to learn how to be a marshal, too … and a ballerina," Tessa exclaimed, then blew a pink whistle marking her a lead drum major.

Tessa, Hawk, and Chadwick would lead the children's drumline. They would also ride with several other children in my father's rodeo strut through town as new youth members of the SoJo Buffalo Riders Society. Every child would ride with elders of the town representing the town's founding families and elder families: Elder Sara Lee, as lead rider in honor of Black John, my father, Sheriff Trent Tucker, as second lead in honor of Cathay Tucker, Chief Pathwalker as third lead in honor of the Muscogee-Seminole and his family.

Fellow riders were going to be: Mr. Vincent in honor of the Martyns, my love, Kamal, in honor of Fields, Marcus Legend in honor of the Legends, Elder Sheila in honor of the Freemans, Chadwick with help by Deputy Henderson in honor of the Davenports, Elder Walter in honor of the Bellamy's, Elder James in honor of the Percy's, Elder Nita in honor of the Clarks, Jonathan Garraway in honor of Ms. Wilma Garraway. My twin, Sage, volunteered to ride for Banker

McHaven, while Ms. Gladys chose one of the Kwanzaa kids to ride for her.

I was excited about my father bringing back the rodeo and the cowboy struts. They were iconic for us children during Juneteenth. I was sure that tradition of jubilee would continue.

"You know, those are the same words Sage told our mother. Except hers was being a Marshal and a mermaid." I laughed and gave Tessa a wink. "I know without a doubt that you will make the Tucker family proud when you become a ballet marshal, Tessa-Belle."

Tessa stopped Coffey's juke to the music, then asked, "What was your wish, Mama Willowshine?"

"My wish?" I thought back to that day having a picnic with Sage and our mother and riding our horses in Ancestor Grove. A smile spread across my face at the sweet love. I lay a hand on Tessa's calf, then looked up at her. "To grow up and be a wonderful mother like her and help children like she did."

It had been almost a week and two days since the traumatic event in the tunnels. Tessa and I had become closer because of it all and she began calling me 'mama' on her own, ignoring my protests. The fact that my great-great and so forth grandmother had cloistered Tessa and protected her, telling her my heart's secret, only pushed my plan into fruition. Thanks to some networking and strings being pulled by me and the elders of the town, after setting up the perfect room for a little Black ballerina in my apartment loft over the center, I was able to double check the living codes, and be approved to foster Tessa. After everything was cleared with my practicing license and final move were done, the paperwork to begin the process for adoption would go underway.

"I think you're doing a great job at that then! And Grandma Monica would be proud," Tessa declared in the wise way she sometimes exhibited.

Juneteenth was coming up and everyone was downtown doing final preparations. I smelled cooked meats being barbecued. I saw turnips, beets, radishes, and other vegetables being washed for the big day. Kids stood with elders by big barrel barbecue grills learning the trade or helping grill and wash vegetables. Children who were preparing for the band were at the center.

"Keep practicing that whistle routine and horse prancing with Coffey, Tessa-Belle. You've got it down, we just have to see if your persnickety Uncle Trent thinks the same," I said, chuckling while holding the guiding reins attached to Coffey.

Pristine sunshine warmed my skin while a sweet breeze caressed my jaw. The bruises I had were fading away. With Cari's help, the concealer she used to hide any standout marks made my walnut dark brown skin flawless. The front of my sandy brown hair was parted in a weave basket pattern with matching beads, most of my fluffy, long mane fell down my back.

I stood in brown beaded military boots, shorts, and crop top that kept my plump curves looking cute. I also wore a jacket made by the Kwanza Kids to represent their contributions to the town. It was adorable and had the faces and names of the founders and year the town was founded. There was a cameo painting of my mother and father on the back of it.

Tessa's jacket had a cameo painting of my great-great-grandmother's gorgeous picture in her marshal's attire, gun included. Pinned on the front of her jacket was the famous outlaw's marshal star, polished and glinting like new. My father had tears in his eyes when he first saw that old badge. The day after we were found, he laid a marker out in her honor at the old dug out.

Me and Tessa were behind the center in the new section added to the back parking lot for the horses in honor of the old town stables. To the right of us was the colorful mural of the town, framed by the new art garden, black-eyed Susans, indigo, wisteria, and plum trees. It was glorious and I was proud to have developed it. Tessa and I were out with the Kwanzaa Kids and other town members who would be part of the parade, doing our final drills and practice for the Juneteenth event.

"You're a great teacher, my hurricane, but a horrible patient," I heard whispered against the curve of my ear. "But your little girl is taking to the horse like a pro. I respect your loving hand."

An adorning warmth against my back made my spirit smile and dance in joy. "I'm following your rules, my handsome doctor. I just wanted to keep an eye on Tessa-Belle."

The scent of light, smoky cologne and fresh soap made me almost melt. The brush of lips against the sensitive spot behind my ear and neck made me twirl around and throw my arms around the man of my heart. I winced, ignoring the tenderness still in my body. His touch was all the healing balm I needed, along with Tessa's love.

"Kamal ... I missed you," I said against his waiting lips. Our kiss made me levitate. Truly it was his height and hands on my waist that had me floating, but either way, I was so high like John Legend once sung.

"I missed you more, and you should sit and let me watch over Miss Tessa as she practices on the horse," Kamal said against my mouth, kissing me again.

"Ewwww! No more kisses," Tessa squeaked.

We laughed and stepped back from each other with me taking a seat in the chair that I was sure the good doctor had brought over with him.

"Yes, ma'am." Pouting, Kamal stood near the horse, picking up the guiding reins. "No more kisses, but I owe you a hug after we finish practicing and Miss Willow takes a seat. Doctor's orders."

"Okay, thank you," Tessa said with happiness in her voice. She gave us a quick look to make sure that we weren't kissing again, then went back to practicing, only to stop when she saw Hawk running her way.

"I'll help you down, Miss Tessa." Kamal carefully plucked her up with ease, then stood her by Coffey.

Tessa gave him a happy hug, and looked up at him to say, "You have to see my room. Mama Willowshine painted it my favorite color. She said once I'm adopted, we get to find a house. I told her that I hope it's a big one so she can have a garden like her Grandma Monica had with the indigo, wisteria, and plum trees, and a spot so she can paint. What do you think about that?"

"Hmm? I think …" Kamal peered my way, then back to Tessa while playfully wiggling his eyebrow at her. "I think that we all should have dinner so that I can see the room then talk to Miss Willow about some ideas."

"I like that thought," Tessa said. "Okay, I have to practice the dance with Hawk now, watch us please? Mama Willowshine, will you watch? Maybe you two can kiss again if that helps."

A cold filter water bottle was rising to my lips when I paused at my daughter's remark. "Tessa-Belle!" I laughed as she giggled. "Get to practicing the dance routine, I'm watching."

Hawk was watching us both in interest and a slight yuck expression on his face. "I think they're going to get married and make you a big sister. Yuck!"

"Great, great, great! Grandma said so, too." Tessa rubbed Coffey, before she began her routine with Hawk. Both blew their whistles in song, then leapt in the air. Tessa landed in a split while Hawk leaned back as if he were in *The Matrix*.

I let out a whooping praise of pride, then smiled up at Kamal who stood by my side. I could tell from how he watched me that the kids' comments were settling in his mind and the same was happening for me.

My hand reached up to hold his while I drank my water. I set it down and softly said, "I'm in love with you, Doctor Brookhaven."

"I guess we are in a love story, sweet hurricane." Kamal sat by my side in the grass. His hands found their way to me so that he could pull me down in the grass with him and cradle me between his legs. The care he took me love him more. When he rested his head on my shoulder, I blushed like a teenager in love all over again. I prayed this wasn't infatuation. I prayed that it was a true committed and loyal love because it felt that way for me.

"We have a lot to talk about, such as this love between us, our future, Tessa, but I want you to know that I'm a man who knows his heart, and mind. I'm a committed kind of man. I wanted you the day I saw you fussing on the side of the road. It was kismet when I came across you. I don't plan on swaying on the path laid before us. I enjoy our whirlwind too much, Willow. I enjoy being in your proximity too much."

"Kamal," I whispered, trying not to get too sappy, "so much life has happened in the short few weeks I've been back and I'm grateful for it all. I never thought any of this would happen the way it did. I was just coming home to check on my father, then *poof!* I'm in love with one of the town's doctors and now I'm adopting an adorable, little girl with a free spirit and wise heart."

I glanced back to a dancing Hawk and Tessa. They slowed down their moves to practice their Matrix lean. The trick took a little bit of maneuvering for them, but eventually after falling a few times and stumbling, they worked out the move in tandem.

"Our ancestors are smiling on us, I'm forever thankful." Kamal said as he held me against his chest. "I'll always fight for you, my hurricane, my love."

Four days later ...

Juneteenth was here and a jubilee was going down!

Funk music was blasting through the main street to the beat of Chaka Khan with Rufus. Hibiscus flowers, lilies, and other red flowers lined the streets. Mr. Walt worked one of the big barrel barbecue pits, while tasting his thin sliced order of snoots and rib tips. Blade stayed near him handing him whatever he needed if Mr. Percy wasn't already handling it. There was an energetic shine of joy in Mr. Walt's eyes while he did a little shimmy in the middle of wood coal smoke, and it made me smile. The town was flooded with familiar faces and a lot of new ones.

As I stood in the front of my center in my haint blue maxi sundress, hoop earrings, and SoJo riders vest, I smiled to the left of me at the woman sitting at an umbrella table enjoying the A/C from my center and nibbling on some greens with ham hocks and fried corn on the cobb. Townies dressed in white played African drums and shared folk tales and stories while people danced in joy near the Elder Tree.

"Everything came together, albeit quickly and hectically, but it really came together, Grace. You really directed a good thing here, sis," I said while setting a few of my sculptures out on pillars near the outside windows.

One was a colorful bottle tree. In those windows were various paintings done by the kids in the town and three special antique oil paintings. One was from the Martyns, which they found in their home, another was from Daddy, painted by my mother, and a third was from Mrs. Sara, an original that hung in townhall of the original town. Patrons moved in and out of the center and galley section placing orders to buy artwork.

"I might have directed but you came in and saved us all. Look ... I can't believe it! You convinced the Legends to bring back the classic car stroll!" Grace waved as Elder Meredith "Pamela" Legend drove by with a line of cars and bikers playing "Low Rider" and waving at us.

Trailing her were a few fraternity and sorority steppers representing the Sojourner Stepper Squad. The men stepped with sledgehammer in honor of John Henry's legend and in commemoration of the Underground Railroad.

"That was all Sage, as you see there."

Sure enough, my twin rode by on her precious Harley. She also wore a SoJo Buffalo Riders' jacket and had a huge smile on her face.

Grace laughed with me while we watched on.

"Look who's finally here!" Cari came from inside of the center with Hunter.

Her hair was adorned with flowers. She had two red drinks, one each for me and Grace, and smelled like honeysuckle and vanilla, a scent she made from her perfume line, while Doctor Martyn held her waist. Both Martyn brothers were tall glasses of fine. We looked to where she nodded and saw Blade tiptoe behind Grace with Kamal. I smiled as Blade leaned behind her to kiss her and lay a loving hand against her belly.

"Miss Willow," Kamal said, walking toward me with the swagger he's always had since the day I met him.

He wore his Stetson low, boots on his feet, dark jeans with an embroidered vest and camel-colored, button-down shirt; his sleeves were rolled up. On his narrow waist was a fancy brass buckle that held a monogram and house crest representing his Brookhaven and Fields. His long locs were basket-weaved braided in two ponytails, but his hat obscured the craftmanship of the style. Nothing took away from how jaw-dropping the man was. He was my summer knight.

"Doctor Brookhaven." I smiled into his eyes and held his hand. "You ready to ride some horses and show off for the town?"

"I sure am, but one quick kiss before your father shows up," he drawled low for me to hear.

He removed his hat to hide our faces while we shared in our intimacy.

Honey warm passion spread through me at his words. Our lips touched, hands entwined, and my world tilted upside down and around for the man who had stolen my heart.

"A'ight you two, unless you plan to officially announce to the town that you want my baby gal's hand, then you catch you some air and move them there lips away. Five seconds is good enough," my father's teasing voice sounded.

He strolled up with Monae, Trent—who was decked out in his band leader suit—and …

Dropping my arms, I pulled Kamal with me. "Kamal, meet my grandparents … my mother's parents! I never thought they would come back to Sojourner after my mother's passing."

A statuesque, gorgeous woman with snow white hair, who carried my mother's cheeky smile, rushed me and pulled me into her hold. "We had to. We couldn't live in our grief and bad behavior anymore, sweetheart."

I looked over her shoulder at the tall, regal elder with salt and pepper beard who looked my way. His eyes carried the sweet bear crinkles of love in the corners. His big, brown hand dropped from around Trent's shoulders, then he come my way to swoop me up.

"We heard about what happened, sunshine. We came as fast as we could get here. This old civil rights activist and investment banker had to clear up some lagging things in regard to that. My son over there …"

My grandfather gave a respectful nod my father's way. A genuine smile of acceptance was on my father's face as he watched us from under his Stetson.

"He and I spoke for hours about my family ties to high places, and we took care of that little … vermin issue, as you say down here," my grandfather's molasses deep voice ebbed against me as he embraced me. "Besides, we wanted to meet the man who should have been in your heart long ago. Good to meet you, Doctor Brookhaven."

Kamal took my grandfather's outstretched hand and shook it. "I told her the same thing, but we were miles apart, never met, but our souls must have been connecting to join us together."

They laughed, and I said, "As the ancestors and my father planned."

"I sure did plan it and it's not over, got these two other chilren to work on," Daddy said in pride.

We laughed some more, then my smile became even bigger as my grandfather's voice deepened with emotion. "And we've been waiting to meet the little angel I was told resembled my Mo. And by the Lord, she does ..."

"Mama Willowshine! I'm here! Hawk told me that you wanted me." Willow came rushing up with her fellow musketeers to wrap her arms around my waist. She wore a billowing skirt, with her SoJo marching band uniform.

"My Tessa-Belle, I want you to meet your other set of grandparents from Chicago."

"Happy Juneteenth, Grandpa and Grandma Emory," Tessa said as she hugged them. "This is my best friend, Hawk, and my ..." She cleared her throat and shot an eyeroll at Chadwick. "I guess ... friend, Chadwick."

We all chuckled when Chadwick's chin rose in the air with an air of uppishness. After introductions were made and tears of joy fell, we all eventually headed down the block to meet up with the parade crew to start the big show. While we were doing so, I noticed a gorgeous stallion of a women, shapely with thick, plump crinkled long locs with swoop bangs in a peach, curve-hugging dress and heels heading our way with another person. The woman and her friend wore press vests. She respectfully greeted my father, asking him for a quick interview about the parade.

"Hello, I'm Lacy St. Julian and this is my friend, Naija Mackie. We're with Alexander Press, a small, Black female owned news outlet that celebrates Black culture and news in the Black Diaspora. I was hoping to quickly talk with you as an elder and sheriff of this precious history Black township. If that was at all poss—"

I chuckled to myself, because the woman speaking into her cellphone as a recorder with her friend who had a camera, stopped midsentence. Lacey's mouth dropped open, and the recorder in her hand hung low in her hold as her cute, cat eye lined glasses zoomed past my father and fell flat on my big brother. Trent was clueless to the matter because Tessa had drawn his attention away about something. He did briefly look her way when he heard her voice and flashed a smile, but that was it. I made note to look up the gorgeous, bourbon brown sista for future reference. My father shooed us on so we wouldn't be late to prepare for the start of the march. As my brother passed by and gave a nod, Miss Lacy and her friend both gawked and followed him with their eyes.

People walked by taking their historic tour bike rides or getting down in a two-step boogie and line dance with red drinks: strawberry lemonade or soda, hibiscus tea, fresh pressed juice, or flavored water with red fruit pieces. Others walked around with samples of the different foods in town by our elders, restaurant, farm vendors, and other SoJo residents. A lot of plates had strawberry butter pound cake, 7-Up cake, or red velvet cake, cookies, peach cobbler, vanilla, or other desserts. We had our own ice cream and popsicle vendor who handed out various ice cream, especially butter vanilla, and fruit ice pops or slushies. I saw people roller skating while gnawing on smoked turkey legs, lamb chops, ribs, red hot links, catfish, grilled oysters, crawdaddies, crab legs, and shrimp, or other goodies.

Mrs. Nita and Mr. Raymond, with Sage overseeing it, had even used their store, The Green Pantry, as a food vendor to team up with various farms and the local hospital for Afro-vegan Juneteenth based soul and diaspora foods, that spotlighted the vegetable-based foods our ancestors were known to make without any meat. Their area also specialized in special diet foods for those looking to have an alkaline and gluten free diet. Everything cooked in the town was organic and hormone-free.

"I can't believe I'm riding a horse with you, Kamal," I said, staring my beautiful stallion in synch with his. "This is major."

"The ancestors are here! We are their freedom and their wildest dreams," someone yelled in excitement.

Kamal and I looked around the town iridescent in sunshine.

"This is our history, and this is love, my hurricane," Kamal said by my side. He had a shot gun strapped to his back. "We're stepping into renewed and new traditions all because of the power of this town."

My hand reached up to cup his jaw. He turned his face to kiss my palm as I said, "And generational love. Happy Juneteenth, my doctor in shining armor. You look dang good as a Buffalo Rider if I say so myself."

Kamal chuckled, tilted his hat at the parade viewers, and smiled that dimpled grin. "So do you, my hurricane and heart, so do you."

The sharp sound of three whistles chimed, then the joyous thumping of a drumline began. Leading on her horse while blowing her whistle was my baby girl, Tessa, shining bright in her uniform. At the right and left of her were a dancing Hawk and Chadwick in their matching major uniforms following the adult 'So Truth' band. Up ahead, my big brother directed from my father's horse in haint blue dress shirt, white gloves, and a sash across his chest in the Juneteenth colors of blue, white, and red with a star centered on it. Majorettes led by Sage danced to the marching band's rendition of "Before I Let Go" while holding paintings of the town founders and historic facts.

Our Buffalo Rider Elders rode proudly on their horses guiding buffalo and cattle with calves down the road. Elder Sara waved in pride, making her horse dance for the kids. A few of Pathwalker's Muscogee-Seminole family and relatives danced in ceremonial dance regalia in tandem of the majorettes, beautifully representing Sojourner Falls and our joined community with the marching band. Elders and parade-goers needing accessibility who weren't in the parade, sat in their A/C tented booth, watching on in pride and dancing in their seats.

Doves flew in the air. Town people boogied, waving flags in the air while flower petals rained down us all. Other parade-goers yelped in joy as the parade filled everyone with vibrance and jubilee as the chimes from the majestic elder tree swayed in the wind in honor of Juneteenth.

Chapter 22: Kamal

Epilogue

The celebration was winding down. As I looked out over the crowd, I couldn't help but wish my aunt—

I stopped my train of thought. My mother. She was my mother. I couldn't help but wish Felisha Fields was in attendance. She deserved to be, but she hadn't responded to my texts or answered my calls when I asked her if she was still coming back.

A man's raucous laughter caught my attention.

I turned to see Mr. Walt talking with his spouses and remembered how relieved he was when informed he didn't have cancer or anything life threatening. From time to time, Mr. Clark and Ms. Nita would turn to look for him in the crowd, just be sure he was still doing okay, I was sure. I thought back to the day before, when Doctor Martyn asked me to come to his office so he could break the news of Mr. Walt's results to him …

"So, I'm good? This here means that lump was just a regular ole risen?" Mr. Walt asked Doctor Martyn.

Older folk in the south tended to call a boil or a cyst a risen.

Doctor Martyn nodded. "Not quite. It's a cyst, Mr. Walt. Good thing it's not a boil though. Boils can be contagious and can be spread as they are staph infections. So you dodged a bullet all the way around."

"I done had a boil before, but this cyst thang ain't even start out sore," he said, confusion on his face.

"Not all of them start sore," I said. "Cysts are different from boils that way. And the reason it got sore is because it burst under your skin and became inflamed."

"I'll prescribe you some antibiotics and then drain the cyst. All should be well after that, minus a little soreness," Doctor Martyn added.

Mr. Walt nodded as he hung his head while wringing his hands. "I had got all my insurance papers and thangs together," he said, tears welling In his eyes. "Thought I was gonna be leaving them and my Grace. Didn't want to hurt none of 'em that way. Thought it was cancer ..."

Doctor Martyn and I walked over to the elder and laid supportive hands on each of his shoulders.

"It's all right, Mr. Walt," I said. "You're all right ..."

"You okay?" brought me out of my thoughts.

I turned to see Willow gazing up with me. I'd told her about my mother's message about coming back.

I nodded. "Yeah. I'm fine. Just happy and excited to see all of this Black love and see that love in all facets. Just kind of wish *she* was here," I said.

"Your mom?"

I nodded.

"Maybe she's yet coming, but just needs more time. I'm sure she's still hurt behind everything that happened …"

I smiled down at her, loving how soothing her voice was. "I know … I just wanted her to be here for our big day."

She quirked a brow. "Our big day?"

I nodded, then took my Stetson off. By now her father, brother, grandparents, and sister were watching us. And Tessa, who had a big smile on her face. She ran over to Willow, then tugged on her arm.

Willow turned around to look down. "Yes, baby?"

"Doctor Brookhaven will be my dad if you say yes."

"Huh? Wait. What? Yes to what?"

"You gotta turn around so he can ask, silly." Tessa giggled.

Willow whipped around to find me on one knee with a yellow ring box opened. Inside was a three-carat, blue diamond. Willow gasped, then her eyes went wide.

"I plan to get you another one, but it's what the jewelry store in Helen had to offer on such short notice. Willow Tucker, will you marry me?"

She rushed into hug me, and we fell backwards. I laughed. The crowd clapped.

"I love you. I love you. I love you," she gushed over and over as she kissed my lips and face.

"Yes, I love you, too, but you have to answer." I laughed, gazing up at her.

"Oh! Yes, yes, I'll marry you," she squealed.

I pulled the ring from the box before I slid it on her left ring finger as she laid on me. It made me think back to the day we'd met and how she landed on me in that ditch. She stood, then I did. A rousing round of applause, hoots, hollers, and screams rent the air. Trent, Sheriff Tucker, and Willow's grandfather walked over to shake my hand.

"All of you knew about this?" she asked them. They nodded.

"He asked me for ya hand in marriage the night he told me who he really was," Sheriff Tucker said. "I told your grandfather about it when I spoke with him."

Sage said, "Those winds of change sure didn't lie. Some ugly, some bad, and a whole lot of good sure did breeze through here this season."

Tessa took off running. "I'll be back," she yelled.

We stood there for a while, shaking hands and thanking everyone who congratulated us. It went on like that for fifteen minutes until someone called for the crowd's attention.

"May I have everyone's attention," a voice called from the stage. Chief Pathwalker stood there, a warm smile on his wisdom-ridden features.

The crowd gathered and came to attention.

"Way back when we had this jubilee, a tradition was to always ask any engaged couples if they wanted to be joined in sacred union. Marriage was always special and important to our enslaved ancestors, even during slavery. Only in 1866 was marriage between slaves legalized, a year after Juneteenth came to be. Quite a few of your grands and great-grands were married on this day. So, the floor is open. My sons and I are prepared to here and now to wed any who wish to …"

When Blade stood and took Grace's hand, Ms. Nita let out a squeal at a pitch I'd never heard before and so did Mrs. Percy.

When they both screamed, "Yes!" even Chief Pathwalker laughed.

Mrs. Percy and Ms. Nita stood and ran to a long basket and pulled out a ready-made bouquet and a long, straw brook.

Willow squeezed my hand. "This is so beautiful."

"It truly is.".

"Baby, we was hoping, wishing, and praying Chief Pathwalker did this here," Ms. Nita quipped when more howls of laughter went up.

"We was ready," Mrs. Percy yelled.

"Oh my word." Grace placed a hand on her heart.

Blade smiled over at his pregnant and crying fiancé with adoration. I knew exactly how he felt …

Mrs. Percy did a happy dance when Hunter pulled Cari up.

"About damn time," Mr. Percy yelled in rumbling baritone.

Cari's brows furrowed. "But …you haven't even asked me to marry you yet. What are you doing?"

Hunter reached into his pocket and out came a little black box. "I'd planned to …"

Cari screamed! She really screamed before doing a version of a popular African dance called the Gwara Gwara. I knew that because the Sojo kids had been doing it. The crowd roared.

Hawk ran up to his mama with a smile a mile wide. He tapped her arm and handed her a bouquet of flowers. Hunter dropped to one knee.

"Mama, will you marry Daddy?" he asked her.

She took the flowers, kissed her son's cheek then turned to Hunter. "Well, will you?" he asked.

She nodded. "You bet I will!"

It was when Vincent Martyn escorted his fiancé, Doctor Jones, to the front of the stage while she nursed their daughter that all of the elders let out a cacophony of hollers and yells.

"Not Vincent," Ms. Sara yelled.

"The town's Lothario done been pecked by the right hen," Mr. Clark called out.

Vincent chuckled. "And I've got no problems with it."

The elders applauded.

Just then, Tessa showed back up, dressed in a haint-blue sundress with a bouquet of black-eyed Susans in her hand. Sage smiled as she tapped her sister to get her attention.

Willow turned to see Tessa holding the flowers, in a new outfit, and then turned to me with watery eyes. "Are you serious?" she asked me.

"More serious than breathing, my love. Marry me. Today. Right now."

***

Twenty minutes later, I was a married man.

"By the power given to me by the Great Spirit and all my ancestors before me, I now bless these three unions. You are now husband and wife, life partners, and everything in between … Remember, you can do all things through your ancestors who strengthen you. You may now jump the broom, and men, you may kiss your brides."

I didn't know what Blade, Vincent, and Hunter were feeling, but I knew Willow felt how nervous I was by the way my hands shook while holding hers. She was just as nervous, and she shivered with excitement and nervousness. I took her hand, and we jumped the broom.

I scooped my wife up around my waist, then kissed her like nobody was watching.

Somewhere next to us I heard Tessa scream, "I'm finally gonna have my own mama and daddy!"

***

"Juneteenth, known as Freedom Day, Jubilee Day, and a few other names is a day, a holiday celebration the emancipation of Black people who had been enslaved in the United States," Grace said as she stood on stage, microphone in hand, her husband and the mayor, Blade Martyn, at her side.

She was dressed in a yellow, flowing skirt, a green blouse that fanned out over her pregnant belly, and black ballet slippers that I'd heard her husband fussing at her to wear as opposed to the tall heels she'd had on.

"This day originated in Galveston, Texas in 1865. Two years after the Emancipation Proclamation, Black people who were enslaved in Galveston found out that they had been freed-ish." Those of us in crowd laughed. So did she and Blade. "Since then, Juneteenth hadn't been widely recognized. Over the past few years, Black people all over the United States have started to celebrate this day as opposed to the 4th of July." A raucous round of applause lit the air. "Sojourner Falls has always celebrated this day," she said as it quieted down, "but when hard times fell upon, the joy and celebrations that used to keep this place alive took a hit. However, with the ancestors on our side and with us young people coming together, coming back home, and remembering what it means to have pride in who and what we are as Black people and as residents of Sojourner Falls, our annual Juneteenth celebration has once again truly shown us what it means to find our way back home." Grace was crying. Blade wiped at her eyes. "Y'all forgive me. I'm so emotional."

"It's alright, sweetheart," Ms. Nita yelled.

"Take ya time," Mr. Percy hollered.

"Blame it on that baby," Mr. Walt said.

320

We all laughed again and so did Grace, but she started sobbing harder. Blade wrapped her in his arms. He signaled Willow who had tears in her eyes as well.

"Better not be no baby in there to blame," Sheriff Tucker yelled, then shot me a death glare.

I held my hands up while shaking my head. "I ain't touched a hair on her head."

"They just kiss," Tessa yelled, and the crowd roared with laughter.

I knew Tessa had no idea what the sheriff was hinting at, but it was funny all the same. By the time Willow got up on stage, she was so red in the face, I thought she would pass out.

"I'm going to give the mic to Willow who helped Grace pull everything together in a matter of four weeks," Blade said, then handed her the mic.

Willow chuckled. "Some kind of way, Grace always manages to get me in the limelight. Since she has already said all that needed to be said, I won't take up too much time, but I want to speak to the young people, the young adults, the teenagers, and our smaller children. You may get the urge to leave this place one day, and that's your right, but whatever you do, however you do it, it's important that you find your way back. Always, always … find your way back."

Three months later ...

"Kamal, Hunter is on the phone," roused me out of a slumber I didn't know I'd been in.

I had sat down to look over the blueprints for the remodeling of the Fields' ancestral home. Instead of getting a new house built, I'd decided to have the old Fields family home remodeled with a couple new things added on.

I sat up in my desk chair and smiled, at least I thought I smiled, at my wife. "Damn. I'm sorry, baby. Didn't know I was sleeping."

"It's okay," she said, handing me my cell. She was dressed in a black jogging set. The September cool weather called for it. "I have to get Tessa to the inn to meet Hawk. I'll be right back."

I yawned and nodded.

"I told you not to overwork yourself trying to put all the baby stuff together, love, but you won't listen. This baby will be in here for another six or so months," she said, rubbing the small pudge in her stomach.

I grinned wide. "My baby is having a baby." I stood to ease behind her. I also rubbed her stomach. "And the baby stuff isn't what keeps me up. It's my beautiful wife who always seduces me once we're in bed together. Last night you—"

Willow's eyes widened. "Oh, my Loa, Kamal, stop it. I put the phone on speaker when I was talking to Hunter downstairs!"

Just then I heard Hunter and men in the background laughing. Hunter said, "Don't mind us, we're all married or otherwise taken men who're married to beautiful women. We get it."

"Give me a minute," I yelled at the phone, chuckled, then dropped my head. "I'm sorry, my hurricane. Didn't mean to make you blush. Hunter probably wants to know what I decided to do with the underground bank vault."

Willow nodded. "Yes, and he wanted to make sure I still wanted haint-blue steps."

Tessa yelled up the stairs, "Mama, you have to hurry so Hawk and I can leave before Chadwick finds out. He's a toad face and always messing with me. Me and Hawk just wanna fish without him picking at me!"

"I'm coming right now, Tessa-Belle," Willow yelled. "I have to go. You get yourself in the bed and rest. You haven't since Juneteenth. Been busy ever since."

Juneteenth had been a special day all around. Four weddings and a newborn baby. Grace's water broke at the celebration five minutes after she and Blade jumped the broom. She'd given birth to a beautiful baby girl who was born healthy at five pounds and five ounces. She may have come early, but she came full of life.

In the three months since the Juneteenth celebration, Willow and I decided to share the apartment above her center and art gallery until the house was finished. I also filed paperwork to become Tessa's adoptive father. The town still hadn't decided what to do about Stacy Davenport. He was yet locked away in the town's jail, complaining every chance he got.

Jessie Dalton and Tobias Pine were escorted out of Sojourner Falls by Navy friends of Sage. Word had it, Dalton tried to make a run for it and had to be doggedly pursued before being captured again. It was rumored they strung him up by his legs and laughed while bobcats tried to have him for dinner.

They also told us Tobias Pine was afraid of his own shadow after saying a white woman came into his cell and threatened to harm him if he touched her family again. Then he claimed a Black woman flew through his window, threw his cup and plate at him, and then told him to remember the name Monica Tucker the next time he thought about coming after her family. As far as Hollis and the rest of the people who sent bounty hunters after Willow? Well, Willow's grandfather really did have friends in high places.

All involved had been arrested. Willow's money from her 401k suddenly reappeared and previous employer offered her her job back. She turned them down. Her home was in Sojourner Falls she told them.

Downstairs, we heard Tessa singing "Find Your Way Back" by Beyonce.

"I'll sleep later," I told Willow as I kissed her more. I searched for her tongue and feasted on her mouth like I was famished. "Go take our daughter to her playdate and then you find your way back to me."

"Keep seducing me and this baby gonna be doing more flipping and flopping than he is now."

I smacked her backside as she walked away. Squealing, she picked up her purse and headed downstairs.

"It's a big, big, big world … *laaaa, laaaa,*" Tessa sang.

The song reminded me of Willow's speech from the Juneteenth parade. Those simple words had the elders in tears. While the young kids didn't get why it made them cry, those in my generation did. One day, we would be the Elders of Sojourner Falls, and I for damn sure hoped the young folk would always, no matter what, find their way back.

www.ingramcontent.com/pod-product-compliance
Lightning Source LLC
Chambersburg PA
CBHW051218190726
48288CB00006B/2025